THE NORTHWEST PASSAGE

Published in Canada by Engen Books, St. John's, NL.

CIP information is available on Library and Archives Canada Cataloguing in Publication website.

ISBN-13: 978-1-77478-080-0

Distributed by:
Engen Books
www.engenbooks.com
submissions@engenbooks.com

First mass market paperback printing: January 2022
Cover Design: Ariel Marsh
Slipstreamers Committee:
Amanda Labonté
Ali House
AJ Ryan
Ellen Curtis
Erin Vance
Lauralana Dunne
Matthew LeDrew

THE SNOWS OF AETALUS

SHANNON K. GREEN & JD RYOT

CHAPTER ONE

"Okay class, hope you all have a great break." Cassidy Cane watched her students file out of the classroom. Pulling her hair into a ponytail, she took all evidence of herself from the room and walked into the hall. Checking the notifications on her phone turned up the same old things: an email from the university, probably announcing the instructors for the next semester, including the fact that she wouldn't be one; messages from the bank, probably about late payments or the new credit card she wouldn't qualify for; and, just for something new, a missed call from her dentist. At least the last one might just be an appointment and not a bill reminder.

As she entered her office, she slipped her phone into her purse without turning the ringer back on, then sat at her desk to begin grading the first of the term papers. She took the opportunity to bask in the air conditioning as much as she could, and drank as much iced tea as she could handle in the break room before stepping into the humid June air and walking the short distance to her apartment. Once there, she plugged in her phone, setting an alarm for early the next day.

As she shrugged out of her blazer, she remembered that classes had ended for the semester but decided that going back in to grade the papers was a preferable choice to sitting in her sultry apartment alone. True, she could call somebody to hang out, but that would cost money, and money would be getting tight with no lecture position next semester and no digs scheduled for the summer. Instead, she fixed herself a light supper from what was left in the refrigerator, making herself a note reminding her that she needed to do the grocery shopping tomorrow. Then she curled up on the couch with the latest Verdant Church novel between fitful naps.

As she read, her mind began retracing her route from classroom to office, from office to her building, constructing a web of her daily movements. Everyday repeating the same paths, more or less, and soon that would be coming to an end to be replaced by something else. Something new to build a new pattern while she struggled with the same problems of being underpaid when she had work and just plain broke when she didn't. On that cheery note she decided to actually read the messages that had come through on her phone while she had been ignoring it. She saw three missed texts and two missed calls from Doctor Gamgee. Rather than checking the messages she called him.

The phone rang once before the doctor picked up. "Cassidy, how soon can you be ready to travel?" he said by way of hello. "Is tomorrow good?"

Still not used to the focused manner in which he always communicated, it took Cassidy a moment to reply. "Yes, late tomorrow should be fine, I should be able to clear up the end of semester work by then and be ready to go wherever you need."

"Good, I'll email the details to you shortly," was all he said before cutting the connection.

Once the details came through—a world which seemed temperate setting off the tech-alarms in a big way; portal just on the outskirts of town—she gathered together the small bag she usually travelled with and turned in for the night. The next morning, she went into the office and graded the remaining papers as quickly as she could.

One of the benefits of teaching a first-year class was that she could more or less scan the papers to see if they got the gist of the major concepts and only seldom had to dig deeper into the papers than her own knowledge. Occasionally, she would have to muddle through an awkward sentence and correct some small details, but she was pleasantly surprised to find that she had finished grading and was entering her final comments shortly after noon. With her teaching officially concluded for the year, scant pay and all, she made her way to the co-ordinates the doctor had sent her.

Two bus rides and a short hike later, she found herself on a hillside overlooking the main highway out of town. The straight line of the roadway extending to the south, towards the larger population centres, was nearly deserted at the now late hour. The co-ordinates she had been given said she was in the right place, but given the terrain and normal errors within GPS systems she knew she'd have a bit of a hunt ahead of her. She took the portal detection device which the professor had given her when she returned from her last outing and turned it on.

Making slow sweeping circles about, she listened for the pinging noise that would tell her which direction she needed to head. After a moment she realized it was indicating an up-hill trek. As the pinging grew more consistent, she quickened her pace over the icy ground, not caring that her feet slipped with every other step. An adventure waited and that was just what she needed right now, something to help her forget the current mess of her life on this planet. She had just entered a small cave shimmering with light from deep within, when the pinging became a constant drone. A smile plastering itself across her face, she made her way in and through into her next new world.

CHAPTER TWO

Cassidy stepped through the portal into the swirling snow. 'Not the temperate climate I was expecting,' she thought and gathered her field coat more tightly around her. She looked behind her and scratched a series of quick symbols into the stone next to the rapidly fading door. She knew it would be there, invisible, when she returned and would need the guide to return to her world.

She debated stepping back through the doorway to get some warmer gear, but decided that pressing on would be quicker. She'd warm up as she went and hopefully this would be an easy in and out job like Gamgee had predicted. She did pull a hat and gloves out of her bag and put them on. She scanned the horizon through the blowing snow and faintly made out the shapes of buildings in the near distance, and began to head that way, hoping that whatever she needed would be in one of those buildings.

The trek was more difficult than she had expected. Although much of the journey was over heavily packed snow on what must have been a well-built road, more was through freshly fallen or newly drifted snow that often sucked at her upper thighs if she paused at all. She could not reconcile the briefing Doctor Gamgee had given her to the arctic conditions around her. The initial scans had shown moderate temperatures, daily rains, everything you'd expect for a climate-controlled region. Who would voluntarily subject themselves to mountains of snow and sub-zero temperatures?

Out of the corner of her eye she thought she saw a dark shape moving against the shifting whiteness of falling snow. Pressing onward to the buildings ahead, she turned to look in that direction and saw only the snow swirling. Again, that shape at the edge of her vision drew her attention. This time she saw a vaguely human shape towering towards her in through the drifting snow. She quickened her pace, moving as fast as she dared over the snowpack.

With the buildings now coming into clear sight, she glanced over her shoulder to see the large shape gaining on her. Though it was still obscured by the falling snow, it glided its shaggy body over the snow, more like skating than walking. With the cold settling into her joints, Cassidy found another burst of speed, sprinting over the snowpack faster than she thought wise, toward the nearest of the buildings.

When it came fully into view, it looked like a shopping mall. She scrambled through the snow alongside the building, searching for a door that might open and frantically looking behind her as the shaggy giant came closer. Finally, after running the length of two sides of the building she came to a downward slope. Following it down to a bank of doors she tried them one after the other until she felt one swing towards her. Jumping through it, she pulled it tight behind her, scrabbling for something to bar the door to keep whatever had been following her outside.

"Um, child, are you quite alright?" a voice from inside the building asked with clear concern. "You're acting like one of the family's guards are chasing you."

Cassidy spun around to see a group of people, very tall people, gathered behind her. Each held something which could be used as a weapon, ranging from spear-like objects to shovels and one or two guns in evidence. Without exception, each had the shaggy furred appearance of her recent pursuer, though she could now see they were outer garments the group wore.

"I was being chased by something," she began and cut herself off with a shriek as the door thundered behind her. The creature which had been following her was now at the door, knocking excitedly.

"Grant me entry!" it said loudly. "There's some half-dressed fool out here we need to get into the warm."

Realizing he must have meant her, Cassidy released her grip on the door and stepped away with a nervous chuckle. "I thought you were a yeti or sasquatch or something," she said as the door opened and a man in furs stepped through.

"I do not know what a yetil or squamsuch are, but I know you must be near frozen," he spoke with a musical accent. "Come, we must get you warm."

The group herded her towards a fire in the centre of the room, somebody handing her a porcelain bowl of a thin soup. "You need to get some heat back into you. What in the thirteen names were you doing out dressed like that?" the first voice asked.

"I was expecting this to be clothing enough for where I planned to go," Cassidy said simply. "What has happened to the weather here?"

"You must have come a long way to not know that the weather towers are no longer functioning as we intended but are instead doing exactly what their masters want them to. The families decided some time ago that they would freeze those of us who could not or would not pay the exorbitant rates they demand to keep the machines running. Everybody they didn't need to keep the towers operational, that is. Now the towers are nothing more than havens for the families and those in their immediate employ. It's a terrible way to run things. How long ago did you set out, child?"

Cassidy considered what she had just heard. "You mean people are doing this to you on purpose?"

"Not just us," a voice spoke from somewhere in the crowd, "everybody has been forced to take refuge wherever they can, in shopping centres, old schools, all the old emergency shelters that had been set up before the weather control devices were brought online. At least it's gotten us all together so we can try to keep each other going."

She looked about the room: nearly forty people were gathered about a fire surrounded by hanging blankets and a mixture of faux and real furs, huddled for warmth within the small circle so constructed.

"We've formed our little groups against the cold and pooled all the available resources we could, but with the snow falling nearly constant and all our means of production frozen out, we've nearly hit the end of our ropes.

We've been plundering nearby homes and stores, plus hunting whatever we can find. Luckily the cold snap they created has driven a lot of animals into the more settled areas they'd normally avoid."

"Somebody did this to you on purpose?" Cassidy repeated. "I can't believe that with the power to maintain perfect growing conditions that anybody would force you into living in another ice age. It just seems too hard to believe."

"When the device was brought online first, it had been funded through a mixture of private contributors and public grants. People just wanted an end to the harsh winters and scorching summers, so they all paid the extra taxes, looking forward to the day when we could finally bring our climate into something manageable. We had nightly rains, and pleasant days, and plentiful crops which grew in their time. It was a perpetual golden summer. Then the governments lost their control and all rights reverted to the thirteen families who had been the primary private investors. They decided that if they were to keep everything running then the populace would have to pay for the privilege of having the weather guaranteed. At first those of us who could afford to pay did, but not everybody could afford to pay the rates they wanted, so the governments decided to start taxing people to make up the shortfalls. When people and the government weren't making the fees the families wanted, the governments tried to buy back their shares of the devices and enforce regulations that would force the families to maintain the climate within acceptable levels. In response, the families barred their towers, with only those workers they deemed vital to the maintenance of their way of life in the complexes. Loyal employees and necessary workers for the rowers to function were brought in to live out the self-imposed siege of cold the families brought down on us. That was somewhere around four cycles ago. Now all of us on the outside are running low on fuel and food, huddling in masses like this to stay warm but not letting our groups expand too much in fear of using up our stockpile too quickly. How do you not know this? Where have you been all this time that you didn't know all of this, child?"

Cassidy sipped her soup thoughtfully while considering her options on how to respond. "Would it make sense to you if I said I was outside the range of the towers? And that despite all appearances I'm not actually a child? Where I come from, I'm considered about average for a fully grown adult."

"Then you must not be from anywhere on this planet," the man replied.

"I'm not, I'm from an alternate dimension where we have no control over the weather but we can skip through dimensions," Cassidy said.

There was a brief moment of silence then everybody laughed. "Oh, child," a man said. "There will be no punishment here, we simply wish to send word to your shelter that you are safe." This statement was followed by nods all around.

Cassidy finished her soup and said, "I really am an adult, and not from this world. I've got credentials which should be ample proof of what I say," she added, reaching into her shoulder bag. "I know I'm shorter than you all are but trust me, fully grown adult."

"Then why do you speak our language so well," a voice from the crowd asked with skepticism. "You expect us to believe that you just randomly popped in from a different universe speaking our language?"

A murmur ran through those assembled as Cassidy responded, "To be honest, I'm having trouble with that one myself. I've run into language barriers in the past but I've also been in places where there isn't one. I just travel, looking for useful things to take home."

"Okay, we'll accept that you are who and what you say," the man from outside said. "But we're going to have to discuss what to do with you. You're free to roam within this shopping compound, but you can't go outside dressed like that. And nobody is leaving here until morning anyway. We'll find you somewhere to sleep and then figure out how best for us all to proceed tomorrow. Ursula, can you find some extra bedding for our 'off-worlder' please?"

"Sure," a young woman said. "Domina, please come with me. We'll try to find some better garb while we're about it." As Ursula ushered Cassidy away, the gathered crowd resumed discussions.

CHAPTER THREE

Ursula led Cassidy deeper into the building. "This was a shopping compound, before the government turned it into a weather shelter. At first, we respected the locked doors and used only what was given. Then we started using items in the found lost bins; eventually we decided to simply use whatever was in the building as a whole. The thirteen took everything they valued into their compounds and most of what was left would have expired anyway. As it is, we had to throw much of the food stuffs into the oubliettes," the woman explained.

Cassidy looked about what she thought of as a mall before she said, "In cases of disaster I think it's more than fair to use whatever resources are at hand. Besides the system here sounds much like the one at home: all the resources in the hands of a few with everybody else having to pay extortionate rates for a very small piece of the pie. Not even really a piece of the pie, just a sliver of the crust that we think is a piece."

Ursula looked at her, confused. "What is peye?"

Cassidy, unsure how to respond, simply stared back at the young woman. "You don't have pie here?"

Ursula looked uncertain how to respond.

"It's like fruit baked between crusts," Cassidy began. "You know what? It isn't important. The point is that there should be enough to go around, with everybody getting a portion that isn't just crap. Sorry, I'm not having the best day. I left a bit of mess behind at home, and I feel more than a little out of my element coming here to find something completely different than I was led to expect."

Ursula directed her into what at home Cassidy would have called a department store. "In here we can find bed clothing and appropriate garbing for you," she said. "What were you led to believe you'd find here? A perfect land of flutter-bys and sunshine, where the only work people did was to better their fellows, like in creche tales?" As she spoke, she guided Cassidy towards a rack of what looked like sleeping bags. "Surely none of these so-called dimensions you've seen has presented anything like that. People need to trade something they value to get other things they value, that's a basic drive among people-kind. That or they need to seize what they desire from others. To think otherwise shows a clear lack of understanding basic psychology. The only thing that prevents people from behaving so all the time is fear of repercussion. This bedding should be sufficient, we tend to cluster near the heat source at night to maintain our relative heat."

Cassidy was dumbstruck. To receive a lesson in the bleakest form of capitalism from a willowy young woman in an alternate dimension which so nearly reflected her own dismal thoughts from earlier in the week was beyond shocking. "I always hope for better. I want people to be better to each other," she responded in a subdued voice.

"I always believe that there is goodness at the core of all people. But I'm always disappointed, I guess. Something about me just doesn't want to admit the reality of it all: that greed is more commonplace than virtue. Let's find me a cool jacket like your people all wear, maybe some chocolate too."

Ursula only gestured to a different portion of the store in response. As the pair made their slow way through the store Cassidy noticed that many of the shelves and racks were empty. What remained were items that seemed to have little use in the frozen wastelands she had made her way through on her way to this shelter. Swimming suits, light outer wear that made her own gear seem more than adequate for the cold, and a variety of items which she didn't recognize. "Most of what's left here, you can't use it, now can you?" she asked.

"We could use much of it, if we wanted to expire from the conditions," Ursula replied. "Much of it simply has no use in the conditions the thirteen allow us to live in, and much of what we could use has been taken back to their towers for the use of the families and their selected. We make use of what is available and of value to us. The rest we allow to sit here until we can find some use for it. Unfortunately, that means much that was available is spoken for. Meanwhile, other items like that bathing garb has no practical application."

The pair continued on until they reached an outerwear section. "Much of what remains will have been too small for most of us, perhaps something will fit your slighter frame. If not, we will seek out the younglings' section to select from their larger pieces," Ursula said. "Perhaps it is a good thing you are slighter than the average Tellan."

Cassidy quickly chose a hooded black jacket in a material which reminded her of the serge favoured for military dress uniforms on Earth. Then she quickly donned a pair of charcoal coloured trousers over her own outfit. Tall brown boots and gloves of a matching animal hide completed the ensemble. She gave herself a quick lookover in a nearby mirror, which Ursula called a "self-viewer", and decided she looked not just stylishly ready for the cold but also like the type of professional who had often come to dig sites for photo ops and handshakes during public relations campaigns. Most importantly, she felt warm for the first time since she had stepped through the gate. "This should keep me warm enough and allow me to function," she said. "Will it pass muster among the local fashionistas?"

"It does look rather elegant and sufficiently warm, unless the thirteen decide to make conditions completely unlivable rather than simply unbearable," the slight Tellan replied. "What is a fash-on-ista?"

"Just me being silly," Cassidy giggled. "It isn't something that really matters, but aside from the height do I look enough like a local to blend in?"

Ursula stared at Cassidy blankly. "Do you mean will anybody assume you are not of this dimension?" When Cassidy nodded, Ursula replied, "Nobody will think you could be from another dimension so no matter what you wear it will be assumed you are from somewhere on Tellas."

The pair were interrupted by a commotion near the courtyard where everybody had been gathered.

CHAPTER FOUR

The two ran to the indoor courtyard to see portions of the glass-like ceiling crashing to the floor. The gathered crowd was already in action, some clearing the debris, while others hastily constructed supports to block the newly formed hole in the roof of their shelter.

"Just another fracture in the structure," a male voice called. "We'll have this sorted in short order. Will you two younglings lend a hand with the detritus while the usual crew places the patch on the canopy?"

"Earliest graduate in my seating, five years as a constructor of buildings, and all they let me do is tend stray younglings and empty oubliettes," Ursula muttered, ushering Cassidy toward the others cleaning the mess beneath the work area. "I have told them countless times that as the portions shatter it weakens the whole and we should simply reinforce the entirety of the canopy. Yes, it will darken the room considerably to do so with the materials we have on hand but it will allow us to retain the heat rather than allow it to escape and endanger more lives with each collapse."

Cassidy looked to her companion, "That seems a pretty specific complaint to have of your living mates. Can I ask why they treat you this way?"

"Because I am female and too old to be a youngling, but not old enough to be an adult in their minds," Ursula responded. "No woman younger than forty years can be considered competent in her field. No male younger than forty-five can either for that matter." The pair began to sweep away snow, watching the debris carefully for broken glass. The snow was collected in bins to melt, for use as wash water Ursula told her. That which might contain glass or other contaminants was taken outside and placed in the oubliettes. Once the mess was cleared, the small settlement gathered around the fire and began preparing for sleep.

The group placed a collection of sleeping mats in a circle around the fire. All the sleeping bags were placed within arm's reach of each other, maximizing the sharing of body heat. Cassidy marvelled at the space the group would share.

Ivan said, "We tried sleeping separately in the earlier times of the coldness, but found that even with fire-minders we would awaken in the night shivering. Many of us began to cluster without thought, preserving our heat by sharing it much as we do with our food. Now we bundle together when the night begins. Those who take the watch are given separate clusters to let the others sleep, but nobody is given watch for more than two nights running, and is never given duty the day after. We have even found light and sound protectors for those who have difficulty with being part of the evening huddles," he concluded, offering Cassidy a sleep mask and ear plugs.

She accepted the offered items with a hearty thank you but selected a place in the sleeping circle between Ursula and an elderly woman Cassidy guessed was an aunt; the woman had been introduced as mother-sister. Excepting the six designated watchers, and four fire-watch, the company settled in to sleep. Perhaps fifty people, huddled together in a circle around a fire burning in the central concourse of a shopping centre in an entirely different dimension than her own, Cassidy Cane felt more relaxed and at home than she had since she shared an apartment with multiple roommates during her undergraduate programme. She was lulled into a peaceful slumber by the breathing of the other sleepers, the pacing of the sentries, and the regular actions of the fire-minders.

The next morning, she awoke chilled and stiff, but well rested despite that, and was fed from the dwindling supplies available to the small group of survivors. Ivan and Ursula were arguing quietly in a corner of the atrium when Cassidy approached them.

"Will you please tell this addle-headed male that we need to reinforce the roof before more damage is done by snow accumulation," Ursula snapped.

"And will you please tell my daughter that more mature people than her have had their say in the matter and we shouldn't involve a stranger, especially not a stranger who claims to be from another dimension," Ivan snapped vehemently.

Cassidy held up her hands. "Leave me out of any arguments, but let me into a debate," she said. "The ceiling will continue to break if more snow falls. It happens on Earth every winter, that's part of why I came here to get the plans for the weather control device. As for my claims of being from a different dimension; I've shown you my identification, what more do you want?"

"You've seen a natural progression of weather cycles?" Ivan asked, disbelief clear in his voice. "Since the weather control devices were set to working nobody has seen that and it is not possible that you are old enough for that."

Cassidy fumbled through her bag to show him the identification she had mentioned. "If you look at this, you'll see the proof of at least some of what I say: it shows that I'm in my twenties and that—" She cut herself off as her cellphone hit the floor. She picked it up, quickly checked the screen for cracks and tested that it still worked, then slid it back into her bag.

The pair looked at her in shock. "You've never seen a smartphone before? You can build these amazing buildings and contraptions to control your planet but you don't have phones?" she asked incredulously.

"We have computers, but nothing that small," Ivan replied. "Every home has a wing set aside for the controlling computer, and they can't do what you just did with that tiny thing. How have you miniaturized the vacuum tubes to such an extent? How does the screen-only interface function?"

"And how do you make the images so clear? The text so clear I could read it some of it from here?" Ursula asked.

It was now Cassidy's turn to be shocked. "You still use vacuum tube transistors here? We haven't used those for any practical applications in decades. I don't know when they were abandoned for computing purposes but these days, they're only used for entertainment purposes. Everything is done on microchips with integrated circuits. I don't know all the science behind it, that wasn't my field of study, but this uses a more durable solid-state type of chip." She trailed off at the confused looks on their faces. "These are common in my dimension, common enough that most people always have one on them, even when they know they're going somewhere that they'll lose the network they function on. I carry this the same way I carry a pen or a pocket knife, it's just something I have when I leave the house."

"Truly you are not from this world," Ivan responded. "Though you are still barely bigger than a child."

"I told you she doesn't behave like children do, father," Ursula said. "Listen to the wisdom she speaks, even if you refuse to listen to it from me. We need to take steps to keep the roof overhead, then perhaps we should assist her in her mission."

Ivan looked from Cassidy to Ursula, and then to the ceiling. After a long silence he said, "Very well, I shall designate a team to work with you to make our people safe. I will take a small hunting party and guide Cassidy to the archives. There we might find that which she seeks."

About half an hour later, by the watch on Cassidy's wrist, Ursula had a small crew of workers collecting materials. Ivan had a team of three outfitted in heavy duty outdoor gear, each armed with a rifle and something which looked like a cross between a sling and a bow, similar to an atlatl but larger in scale than she was used to seeing. 'An unsurprising development given the stature of the locals,' Cassidy thought. 'I guess it would be similar to the sizing of clothes and scaling of other implements; you make it to fit the user.'

Cassidy, Ivan, and their team donned snow shoes, and left their shelter shortly after the work began on the shelter.

CHAPTER FIVE

"The snow should be less vigorous today," Ivan said. "The families have stopped short of trying to murder all of us who live outside the towers. They seem intent to simply torture us with the cold and precipitation. The public archives are little more than a furlong along the roadway so we should reach it in short order, the hunters were all law enforcement in the past and will both protect us as we travel and seek food for our return."

Cassidy simply nodded and followed the group in the direction indicated. Feeling more protected in the group than she had while fleeing the unknown the day before, she took better notice of her surroundings. The buildings, what was visible beneath the snow at least, were similar in many aspects to those on Earth, but were of a different scale entirely. Clearly built to accommodate the natives of this world. They were constructed of wood, stone, or some material which she did not recognize. 'A local stone, or concrete-like material,' she filed the thought away for later consideration.

The streets ran in straight lines, meeting at nearly perfect right angles. She wondered if they aligned to any strict directional markers, as the North to South or East to West tendency in some cities on Earth. Instead of questioning this, she focused on the names on the buildings and the turnings they took in case she was separated from her guides and needed to find her way back to their base. Ivan led them in a straight line, without deviation from their desired destination, the others of the group seemed to split their attentions to search the streets they did not take.

"What are they watching for?" Cassidy asked, indicating their companions.

Ivan looked back. "They watch for predators and prey. They will defend us if they must. Or feed my people if they can. We have learned that if we must journey then we should collect what food we can. While we explore the archives for what you seek, they will search for sustenance, textbooks for the younglings, and anything else that was requested before we left. They have lists of things missed by those who dwell within our shelter."

"You've been sequestered long enough that you have a dedicated scouting party?" Cassidy asked in surprise.

"They were all employed to deliver different things before the snows came. Sulva delivered packages from city to city. Flavius brought foods from restaurants to private dwellings. Claud delivered and installed computers. They are familiar with the layout of the community and were often called upon to defend themselves against the creatures who lurk within and without the community."

"I'm headed to the library with delivery drivers as an honour guard," Cassidy muttered. "It's like a tale from the wild west and some goof in a white hat will appear around the next corner to save the day."

Ivan chuckled softly. "I admit it does sound like a work of cheap fiction designed to entertain, at least that's how I interpret your words. This is the world we live in; people do their best in the circumstance."

A low growl from the crossing street ahead silenced them. Two of the guards, Cassidy thought it was the ones named Claud and Sulva, edged forward, each facing opposing directions along the cross street. Atlatl raised, Flavius walked behind them, scanning the upper floors of the buildings around them. A large creature resembling a koala in shape but coloured like a panda lumbered into view and all three hunters backed away.

"Keep back," Sulva called. "They usually wander off when they see people. So, we'll give this one the chance to survive."

Cassidy watched the creature waddle ponderously to a nearby building, then marvelled as it gracefully scaled the ornate work on the façade of the building. "Are they dangerous?" she asked in a hushed voice.

"Not at all, there were few cineleucia left before the weather was altered and we seek to protect those that remain," Ivan responded, then added with a small grin, "Besides, I hear they taste horrible."

The cineleucia had stopped on a ledge of the building it was climbing and seemed to be settling down for a nap when Sulva waved them on. Cassidy was sure she could hear the creature snoring as they passed. "They mostly sleep wherever they can, move to find food, and then sleep again. Most of them escaped from the custody we had them in, others like them were drawn by the calls of those who had freed themselves," Sulva said in quiet tones, her eyes searching their surroundings the whole time

"Custody?" Cassidy asked.

"Yes, we had some in protective enclosures, along with other animals. Younglings would take learning trips to see the creatures being cared for in such parks, we called them menageries. Many of the creatures who wander the city now were released or escaped their custody in menageries. Those we know are plentiful and edible we eat. The ones who cannot survive in such conditions as we have now are mercied. The others we let make their own survival," the delivery driver shook her head sadly. "It is not the ideal situation, for them or us, but life must be preserved."

The rest of the journey was passed in silence and with no larger incident than the occasional slide on the slippery road surface.

The Archives turned out to be a large, plain building made of the same concrete-like material as many of the other buildings. 'They may be great engineers here but their art and expression leave a lot to be desired, at least down among the groundlings,' Cassidy thought. 'I guess that doesn't vary much with the basically human species, no matter what particular dimension they happen to live in.'

The window opened easily for them and the five entered what might well have been the largest indoor space Cassidy had ever seen. Ivan pointed in what looked like a random direction, "Most of the technological works will be in that portion of the archives on the third floor. I will guide Cassidy there and assist her search. The rest of you should seek the requested items, retrieve any medic supplies and food you discover unless challenged. The Archives have been unvisited since the trouble began, but some determined soul may have decided to change their residence since our last visit. We will meet back here in one klukkutima. We dare risk no longer for fear of a change in the atmospheric conditions." The group all agreed and quickly set about their errands.

The building was silent save for the passage of the small group, their footfalls quietly echoing before being swallowed by the neatly shelved and stacked books. Ivan pulled a small electric light from his pocket and turned it on, casting a small circle of light about himself and Cassidy. They made their way to the side of the building and entered a stairway. As they climbed, he spoke, "These are places of study, material is borrowed as needed and returned afterwards. Speech here is discouraged so as not to interfere with the work of others. Even if it appears that we are the only ones present I prefer to maintain that rule."

Cassidy simply nodded her agreement as they exited the stairway. She followed Ivan to what she would have called a card catalogue in a library on Earth only to discover that it was exactly that. The filing system seemed to be different, using symbols rather than numbers, and the writing seemed to be a mixture of scripts closely resembling Cyrillic and Greek alphabets but not being strictly either. "I can't read your language," she whispered to her guide.

"These are just the symbols employed in libraries to

indicate where certain topics might be found," he answered. "Perhaps you will understand our written words as well as you do our speech." Cassidy was hopeful but unconvinced. After all she didn't need to be able to read the plans herself, as long as she found the right ones.

Ivan made a quick note on a small slip of something that looked like paper and gestured for her to follow. Part of Cassidy felt like a fugitive, hiding from some crazed pursuer. Another part of her felt the calm inherent in all libraries. The mass of the books quieting the footsteps of all who passed among the ordered rank and file of shelves and bookcases, the mingled scents trapped within the pages from those who had used the books previously, the predictable layout of the shelves, and the knowing that almost anything you could desire to know could be found on hand, provided that somebody had researched and written on the topic. Libraries were a comfort to almost every academic and nerdy kid she knew, and she was more at home than she had been anywhere in a very long time.

At random she drew out a book and flipped through it. The writing employed an alphabet much like Latin but different enough that she could only read one word in ten. A quick glance at the illustrations led her to believe the volume to be a user manual for some sort of food preserver, one meant to dehydrate massive amounts of grain. The next book she took down appeared to describe the machinery employed to make pickles in an industrial setting. "Are all the books in this library dedicated to industrial food preparation?" she inquired.

"No, just those in this specific section. The third floor

is dedicated to all industry, we just happen to be in the nutrition preparation section," the burly guide responded. "Do you not have similar repositories on your world? How would you separate them?"

Embarrassed slightly, Cassidy responded, "We do, in many cases we dedicate those repositories to specific topics. We call them libraries or archives too, though. I was just surprised to see these many manuals together."

"Just ahead we should find information on the machines used for travel; after that the weather towers, if I am remembering correctly. Most of my time here was spent on the other floors, pursuing other topics," Ivan said. "The information guide pointed us this way at any rate."

"I am sorry, it's been a long day. I was hoping I'd be able to walk in, find what I wanted, and return easily. I didn't expect all of," she gestured to the half-lit building and the view through the windows. "Well, just this; I didn't expect this. I expected warm days with optimal growing conditions and..."

"You describe a perfect world where all things are available for free to those who need them. Drink is available in streams and food grows on trees and nobody charges for them?" Ivan asked.

"Yeah, big rock candy mountain," she muttered.

"We have a song about the place you speak of, a fairy tale told to lazy children," he replied.

"We have it in my world too," she said. "We also have an expression that claims that nothing is free."

"Such is the dream of many, though there will always be one to tell you that what you pay for is better than what is given," Ivan commented thoughtfully. "Surely the survival of the individual and the desire to better one's state can coexist without causing harm to one another. Ah, now is not the time for such thoughts, let us see if the volumes you desire are here and we can pursue such thought exercises as we fill our bellies around a warm fire."

Cassidy nodded, waiting for her guide to indicate when they reached the shelf they sought. The quiet of the archive, relaxing at first, now left more room in her head for her anxieties to echo. She wondered if she would be forced to live in the library when she went back to Earth, like the urban legend she had heard from students at nearly every university she had visited. She was relieved when Ivan said, "This unit."

CHAPTER SIX

The pair checked the shelves. "The records indicate that the documents you desire should be here," Ivan said as he scanned the spines of the volumes shelved there. "In this empty slot."

"Maybe they were just shelved wrong," Cassidy said and began browsing the shelves at random, hoping she would recognize what she was looking for if she saw it.

After individually checking each volume on the shelf Cassidy asked, "Is there a sorting area, where the plans might have been laid after somebody had them out for study?"

Ivan nodded and guided her to a rolling cart full of books awaiting their return to the shelves. As he inspected the few titles on the cart he said, "There are two of these for each floor."

"One for the floor it's on and one for other floors," Cassidy replied, some things being universal to libraries and archives no matter what dimension they were in. "Will we have time to check them all?"

"If we hurry, we may," the stoic man replied. "The others will await our return regardless."

The pair made their way swiftly through the building, finding no sign of the desired documents. When Cassidy and Ivan met the others at the main entrance, they were greeted with a collection of what looked to Cassidy like first aid kits, snack foods, and books. Sulva and Claud were separating the items into convenient carry packages while Flavius kept watch.

"The weather seems to be worsening," Flavius said. "I hope everybody has found what they sought because we'll have to make our way back to the shelter swiftly."

Cassidy swiftly explained what she was looking for and what had happened as the goods were divided amongst the quintet. Claud said, "The families ordered those documents pulled from all public archives before the troubles began. Had I known that was what we were looking for I could have saved us this trip."

Flavius looked to their packs, "We have plenty to show for the trip at any rate, so it was not wasted. Let's get back before travelling becomes harder. I never thought I'd say that about travel within a community before all this started."

They started back towards the shelter, Cassidy and Ivan walking sullenly while the others chatted about the items they had found and marvelling that nobody had more thoroughly explored the archives before. The winds were gusting higher than before, kicking dervishes of snow into the air and making the passage more difficult.

"We'll stay closer to the buildings on this side of the roadway," Sulva shouted to the group as the wind tried to snatch her breath away. "We'll take the extra shelter from the wind where we can, besides everything should be bedded down out of the storm at this time of day."

The group trudged forward. Cassidy, while thankful for the fact that it would be a straight line to their destination, trusted the Tellans to ensure they didn't miss their destination. 'Why did I think this would be such an easy mission for a change? Just stroll into a library and check out a book, easier than falling off a bike.' Her thoughts were rudely interrupted by the roars of the cineleucia. The creature stood before them, forepaws raised, claws extended.

Sulva, who had been leading the expedition party, raised both hands and started backing away from the five-meter-tall bear-like specimen. She waved for the team to circle around the bear, swinging wide into the street. The bear roared its defiance as they started around, going silent when the group stopped and began to back away again. Sulva decided to try again, this time leading the group to the other side of the roadway before attempting to resume their forward progress. The cineleucia renewed its roaring, this time lumbering a few steps toward them and slashing the air with its razor-sharp forepaws.

The terrified group stopped. Sulva shouted something but the wind carried her voice away unheard. Instead she gestured again, and ran for the door of the closest building. Using the carrysac full of books, she smashed a window and waved to the others as they sprinted inside. Then she closed the door firmly behind her, or tried to at least around the now trapped forepaw of the cineleucia. Cassidy, having seen similar situations, grabbed Sulva in a bear hug, first leaning to open the door, then throwing her weight fully backwards. On her third try Sulva joined her in repeating the motion, repeatedly slamming the door on the cineleucia's paw until the beast withdrew its paw and fled with a roar that rattled the door.

As the two caught their breath Flavius looked out through the nearest windows. "I don't think it's gone far. What could cause a cineleucia to behave in such a manner?"

Claud shrugged. "A bunch of things, like a mate or offspring. Both of which would be great news it would just mean avoiding this stretch of the roadway for however long the bear decides to call this patch its home. Guess we need to find another way back home though. Any ideas?"

Ivan looked around the building, "Maybe there is another entrance we can use on next parkway, and then we might return to the roadway we were using?" Cassidy and Sulva, still slightly winded from their encounter with the cineleucia, waved the group into motion, following them deeper into the building.

CHAPTER SEVEN

The group made their way deeper into the building, past open-faced lockers and a trophy case. "Was this a school?" Cassidy asked. "A place for the education of younglings, I mean."

Ivan nodded in response. "It was where they learned the basic skills they would require for chosen career paths, preparatory to higher education."

"Younglings study here to their eighteenth year and then either enter the working forces or pursue more education," Claud clarified. "We would do well to search for further supplies as we search for a way out."

"We stay together and make our way swiftly on," Ivan said. "The day is short and we must return to the shelter before dark, lest we worry the others."

The others readily agreed, making their way deeper into the school as silently as possible, their footsteps echoing in the abandoned hallways and empty classrooms. The dim sunlight through the windows creating eerie shadows all about the small, slow moving group, they ventured onward. Claud and Sulva checked each classroom they passed, sometimes finding small first aid kits or snacks in the desks, occasionally a hat or pairs of gloves, but mostly finding nothing more than dust and abandonment.

They had made it to the end of the corridor when they heard laughter behind them. They froze, looking about them in the dimly lit corridor. "Is somebody else in here?" Cassidy asked. Sulva repeated the question, in a louder voice so that it carried down the corridor. After a span of several heartbeats Cassidy thought she heard the sound of feet running in the distant darkness, and more giggling. "Is there somebody here?" she repeated, louder than Sulva. Again, nothing answered but the sound of scuttling feet and muffled giggles.

"It is crocuta," Ivan whispered in a trembling voice. "If they are the larger ones we must flee, if the smaller ones we will be fine."

"Crocuta?" Cassidy asked.

Flavius answered, "Pray we don't see them; terrifying creatures that will eat anything they can sink their teeth into. We often find them in the unused buildings. Like Ivan said, if it is the more common smaller ones, we'll be fine. Either way there should be an exit up ahead. Keep moving."

The group seemed to move a little faster now, Cassidy needing to speed her steps to keep pace with the longer-limbed Tellans. She hadn't realized that they had been slowing themselves for her sake before she had started to fall behind. As they proceeded, the sounds of giggles and scuttling feet grew louder and closer. In panic, she glanced over her shoulder to see several pairs of glowing red eyes.

The sight leant her feet extra speed and she began to gain ground on the others, soon passing Claud, who had been in the rear position. He sped as she passed him, matching her speed. The giggling grew louder and Cassidy again risked a glance over her shoulder, this time seeing mottled brown and black fur on squashed snouts below the still glowing eyes. One of the creatures let out a call that reminded her of the calls of the infamous laughing hyenas from Earth, but these creatures were little larger than, and strongly resembled, the dock rats she had seen in various seaports.

Some instinctive part of her still recoiled from the creatures, adding an extra shot of adrenaline into her system and extra speed to her step. "There had better be a door at the end of this hallway, or a window," she gasped as the crocuta began lunging around her feet. They didn't attack, playfully running ahead, then circling back to charge her again. She almost laughed at the capering creatures, while also inwardly shrieking in panic at them.

Over the laughter-punctuated pitter-patter of the rodent-like feet she heard the sound of a heavy window sliding open on rusty hinges and looked ahead to see a rectangle of light splitting the darkness before her. From somewhere deep down she found another burst of speed that carried her through the now open window and into the rapidly worsening storm, slamming the window closed behind them as the crocuta hit, first as a few falling pebbles, then as an avalanche.

Sulva edged toward the roadway they had been travelling when they entered the school and took a peek around the corner. Pleased with what she saw, the former delivery driver gestured urgently for the team to continue on their way. They filed out of the alleyway, each of them casting nervous glances either towards the window holding back the crocuta or cineleucia standing sentinel on their backtrail.

CHAPTER EIGHT

They returned to the shopping plaza at the height of the storm winds, battling the doors open between hurricane force gusts that whipped the snow in lashing strands that stung the face and blinded the eyes. Once inside they sat, backs to the door, panting for breath, rubbing hands and arms to return circulation to their extremities.

Ursula ushered them closer to the fire, under the newly reinforced ceiling, and gave them a hot beverage to drink that reminded Cassidy of heavily sweetened Darjeeling tea. Claud took the packs from the others and distributed the items they had retrieved from the archives. Flavius and Sulva reported on the new wildlife situation in equal parts hope, at the potential mating of a pair of cineleucia, and despair, at the detour it would mean for travel in the area.

Cassidy sat glumly before the fire as the snow melted on her clothing, the damp fabric adding to her overall feeling of misery. She ate what she was offered without tasting it, though the sensation of having a full belly brought up her mood somewhat. When Ursula came to take the empty bowl away Cassidy asked, "If the plans were taken from the archives where would they be now?"

"They'd need to keep copies in the towers," Ursula responded. "I assume you mean the plans for the weather towers themselves; they would need to have a copy for maintenance at the towers. That is an issue for tomorrow. The issue for right now is getting you into something dry and properly warmed up to face the night. Come, I have some dry clothing that should fit well enough." Cassidy took the clothing, changed, and hung her wet items to dry. She sat and watched the fire silently until she drifted off to sleep.

In the morning she approached Ursula, "Where is the nearest tower?"

Ursula gave Cassidy a confused look.

"Any tower will do," Cassidy continued. "I just need to know where it is, get a really good look at it, and I can figure out the rest for myself; but some idea of how to begin would be a big help."

"Cassidy, I don't think you've thought this out, you can't just," Ursula began but Cassidy interrupted.

"Of course, I haven't thought it out, that's why I'm asking you questions about the tower. I need to know everything I can about the tower before I make a full plan," the archaeologist said. "I need to research the place, and figure out how best to get in and.... I don't know what else but I know I need to get those plans and make my way home to deal with the mess I currently call my life."

Ursula took a moment to examine the feisty and, to her, diminutive figure. "First, we'll eat, then we will seek out books from the bookseller here in the plaza and make decisions from there. I know there are people here who have been in the nearest tower; we can talk to them as well, after we have eaten. Please, Cassidy, I'll help but right now I'm hungry."

The pair made their way to the line for food and each took a bowl of thin gruel. Cassidy, being too excited to eat, passed her bowl to Ursula, who ate both bowls of the gruel with great satisfaction. Then the pair made their way to a book store within the plaza. The fiction and home maintenance sections were nearly empty, Ursula saying that their contents were probably with the residents near the main shelter area or taken to homes before the group had taken refuge in the shelter. The rest of the shop, including the science, technology, and tourism sections were largely intact. The pair scoured the volumes they could find about the towers, especially those focused on the local tower.

"It turns out that the Steward Tower had a museum before the expulsion," Ursula said. "It may be the easiest way to sneak into the building, although this says that it had no direct access to the rest of the tower."

"Maybe not the best way in then," Cassidy responded. "This book has a map that shows multiple entries on each side of the building, but I still haven't figured out the writing here and can't read how it's labelled."

"Secure entrance, private entrance, office entrance," Ursula responded, pointing to a different set of markings each time. "I know that before the lockouts those entrances required keys or were guarded; I would think that now all would be more heavily guarded than before, if not simply closed forever."

The pair turned back to their books, periodically choosing new ones on the same topic. Eventually they had built towers out of the books about the Steward Tower. Feeling like she had absorbed all the knowledge on the topic which she could from the books in the store, and having gone through all the books about the Steward Tower she could find, Cassidy stood and stretched her back.

"Now let's see if we can find some food and primary sources on the topic," she said. At a questioning look from Ursula she clarified, "Now we look for people who have been in the building, anybody who had family living in the tower or who worked there or might have visited the building; and learn whatever we can from them. But first we need food, scholarship is hungry work."

The two returned to the fire once more, queueing for whatever food might be available. Once again, the thin gruel, this time bolstered with some dried bread that had been retrieved from either the school or the archives. "Have supplies grown so low already?" Ursula asked the man portioning out of the food.

"The parties were sent out yesterday; some haven't returned, some returned with empty carrysacs," he answered. "What was brought back is being distributed as we process it, but I was ordered to tighten rations while a full accounting is done. Truthfully, I feel supplies are not that low yet, but will be soon."

The pair walked a short distance off, Ursula savouring each bite as if it might be her last. Cassidy, eating slowly and thoughtfully, said, "I guess this means that any plan to infiltrate the tower should involve a plan to set the weather to rights as well. Not much point in letting this go on much longer if we'll potentially be in a position to solve both our problems at once."

Ursula finished her small meal and stared into the fire glumly. "This could require more research and planning than we initially anticipated," she said morosely. "I will return to the bookseller to see if I can discover anything else. You should begin your queries to see who may have knowledge of the Steward Tower."

With their easy agreement, Ursula set off into the shopping plaza. Cassidy began doing interviews with those who remained in the shelter that day, only now seeking those who had worked with the machinery as well as those who had simply been to the tower. At first many of those in residence were eager to talk; though Cassidy's notebook made many uneasy, they were simply glad to converse with the new person after so long cooped up with the same people; but it soon grew apparent that few of those here had any useful knowledge on either the tower or the weather device. Gradually Cassidy came to realize that those who did have any practical knowledge of the tower were most likely those who had gone out with the gathering teams.

She put away her notebook and began instead to make herself useful about the shelter: tidying things, playing with the few younglings she hadn't realized were in residence, teaching them how to build slingshots from what was on hand, and just casually chatting about what she had seen during her trip outside on her previous journeys. Though she could offer little in the way of information to those she spoke with, the news of snow accumulations and general state of the buildings she had seen and entered was welcomed by those she spoke to.

She especially enjoyed making skipping ropes from

electrical cords for the younglings and teaching them some of the rhymes she remembered from her youth. Their smiles and laughter spread to all those who remained inside on the cold and blustery day; some of the less staid adults joined in with varying levels of success. It might not have been her most productive day, but Cassidy still felt it was a day well spent and was smiling herself when she went to her small bedroll before the search parties had returned from their expeditions.

CHAPTER NINE

The next morning, she awoke early, crept from her sleeping place quietly, and joined those awake by the fire to sip the always ready strong tea that many of the adults seemed to survive on. Discussion with the small group revealed that while there were sufficient supplies for a few months—provided the protein stores could be supplemented with game animals—it had been decided that everybody would begin rationing now rather than waiting until circumstances made the need truly dire.

"A few months to adjust to being hungry rather than a few days of having nothing," one of the fire-minders said. "We have enough firewood to keep us warm for much longer if we use all the furniture in this building but we need to send our gatherers farther afield to find more food and medicines."

"That seems a little pre-emptive to me, but it does make sense. I hope to make a few expeditions to see the tower in the next few days; hopefully I can assist the gathering teams rather than hinder them," Cassidy said.

"Ursula told me of your desire to speak with those who had been in the tower; a visual inspection was the next step I suspected you would take," Ivan said from behind her. Cassidy turned to see the man holding a tea cup. "I was one of the early fabricators of the weather control device. Design and manufacture, but never an operator. I did assist in the installation process and could possibly serve as a guide once you were inside the tower itself."

Cassidy stared at the man blankly for a moment. "You were on the design team?" she finally spluttered.

"Yes, I assisted in the design," Ivan said calmly. "I was one of fourteen engineers who created the rain distribution component of the device. There were approximately fifty other major components required to take full control of the climate, but the rain distributors were among the earliest developed, to guide precipitation into deserts and away from settlements and regions prone to flood."

"That makes perfect sense really, creating arable lands and reducing flood damage is a priority for my own people," Cassidy responded. "Once I figure out how to get inside you can take me where I need to go? That makes that much of the plan much easier."

Ivan smiled "I will tell the gatherers of the information you seek and we shall plot the proper course of action from there. Now I have responsibilities today, it is my duty to take a turn as gatherer today. Perhaps you can join me? I do intend to journey in that direction."

Cassidy chugged what remained of her tea. "Let me grab my gear and I can meet you by the door."

Moments later the pair met by the entryway to the shopping plaza. Ivan, once again dressed in the clothing he had worn to the archives; Cassidy decked out in a combination of her gear from Earth and her new clothing from Tellan stores. When asked if she had anything to hunt with, she produced a slingshot from the pocket of her Earth-side jacket.

"What is that?" Ursula, who had come to see them off, asked.

"It's called a slingshot," Cassidy said, then gave a brief explanation and demonstration of how to use the simple device. "They're easy to make and transport but best part is that almost anything small can be turned into ammunition for it. It does take some practice to use effectively, but I've been practising a lot lately."

Ivan remained dubious but agreed that it should serve the purpose for their expedition that day. Once outside in the clear morning, he turned them in the direction that Cassidy had come to think of as south for the planet. Her reckoning was based on the layout of the roads and streets in the community, based on the shelter in the shopping plaza being the centre of a Cartesian plane. The portal to Earth was sort of to the west, the archives were east, and that was all her travels had revealed.

"Our main purpose will be to check buildings for anything which might be of use to the people at our shelter," Ivan said. "Many of the closer structures have been harvested already so we will advance appropriately before we begin to search in earnest. We must also watch for edible fauna as we proceed: there may not be much on this course of travel as the confines where animals were held in captivity were nearer the archives and little of the wildlife has dared enter the community this deeply yet."

It was perhaps the longest speech Cassidy had heard the man make and she listened to every word as she looked more closely at the architecture in this portion of the small city. It was much like what she had seen elsewhere, all straight lines and utilitarian dwellings built on a scale for those who lived there, nothing stood out save the numbered roadways they passed. She had grown familiar enough with the script used here to recognize that they had just crossed the intersection of fifteenth roadway and twentieth street. After a short march in silence they crossed twenty-first street and Cassidy could picture the neatly gridded lines she had seen on one of the maps in the bookseller the day before. Seward Tower was on the corner of twentieth and one-hundred-ninety-third, perhaps two days travel from their shelter, based on their current rate of travel.

Ivan had resumed talking while Cassidy had been doing these calculations and something he said caught her attention. "Did you say that we'd return to the shelter tomorrow?"

"That is the plan, yes," he spoke in the same calm tones he seemed to always use. "I have bedding for our use, we will use any empty building we can find. Some of the buildings still have the original residents, or some who moved in after the troubles began, but most are in the emergency shelters established after the families began to punish those outside the towers. Our shelter is the nearest to the Steward's home, so shelter will be easy to find; we may even use one of those established by previous expeditions. Perhaps I should have told you this before we left but I had not thought it important: all our gathering expeditions are two-day affairs now that we have to venture further with each trip."

"No, not a problem at all. I just," Cassidy began. "Okay, yeah maybe I'm a little surprised but I can deal. It'll give me a chance to examine your world as it is. Is all the community built like this, the straight lines and lack of ornamentation?" she asked, hoping to distract herself with stories from her guide and hunting companion.

"Most of Aetalus was built to provide support for the weather tower. The towers had to be built within a specific range to ensure that the entire planet could receive the effects. There was nothing here before the plans for the climate controller were finalized. When work began on the precipitation redirectors there was nothing here beyond a road linking other communities. It was, to quote my daughter, untamed wilderness," Ivan replied. "I believe that is the sole reason we receive as much wild game as we do. The land was improperly cleared and the animals desire to return to their habitat rather than establish new ones."

Cassidy nodded reflexively, then processed what she had heard. "You're saying this is a new city and that it's a company town to boot?" she asked.

Ivan took a moment before responding "If you mean of recent construction only for the commercial purpose of the weather tower, then yes. There are many portions of this community that you would find similar to other communities, but that was a designed aspect of the new community. Some developments were made to make this community a model for others, such as the grid of the streets instead of a random assortment of straight lines and curves."

"It must make learning the navigation of the community easier," Cassidy commented.

"Yes, but it removes some of the art from the streets. The normal vitality of a community can be seen in the curve of the roads, the natural grouping of like-minded people. Here there is an arts centre on one side of the community, an actor's pavilion near the centre, and schools of rhythmic movement in a different portion of the community entirely. None of them near each other," Ivan spoke reproachfully. "It was a plan that put little thought into being an actual community, but yes, numbered roadways and streets that proceed in an orderly manner is good."

They walked for a moment in silence before Cassidy spoke again. "I guess there were some faults in their logic. Like most towns built to support an industry where I come from; the basics like work and accommodation are pretty well thought out. Everything else, all the things that go into living a life outside of work, gets shoved in wherever it'll fit. A cinema here, shopping centre over there, green space on the edge of town."

Ivan looked to her thoughtfully. "Yes, I feel it should all be balanced, like a circuit: the power source is industry; the workers are the current; all other aspects of life are the resistors, capacitors, and transistor which allow current to perform efficiently and perform the designated function. This machine lacked diodes to ensure the proper flow of power, the towers became the only inputs and outputs with all other current being forgotten by the design, this will cause a short circuit somewhere."

Cassidy quickly pored through her limited knowledge of technology. "You're saying that because they've neglected the excess charge they let into the system, something is going to malfunction?"

"Something has to," the former engineer said gravely. "Pressure in a water line causes leaks. Excess charge causes a short circuit. High friction will make two sticks catch fire. These are basic principals of physics. The signs of unhappiness were in the people before the families seized the weather makers, in more urban centres at least. Rural life had taken on idyllic terms of routine, balancing itself. There was never balance to be found here, just work, rest, and repeat; no space for enjoyment. I think the families may have brought the cold precipitates to distract us from these problems as much as to punish us for not paying what they desired. Fearing that the people would topple the rulers as they have in past times." He gestured for her to enter a building that looked no different than any other on their left. Cassidy thought it might be an apartment.

"Well, revolutions do have a way of coming around," Cassidy said as they stepped into a building not much warmer than the outside.

Ivan smiled broadly at her, "That they do. That they do."

CHAPTER TEN

The pair took a moment to look around the corridor of the building they had entered. A hallway, lined with doors, ended with a stairwell reaching into the higher floors. Ivan briefly consulted a series of markings on the wall before saying, "This building has been checked. The third room on this side has a warming station and temporary camp we can use if we wish to. I would like the opportunity to warm for a few moments if we can spare them."

Cassidy nodded and gestured for him to lead the way. She stepped into the room to see the walls had been hung with draperies, the floor had been lined with extra carpets, and a number of lanterns lay about the room with matches nearby. Once the door was closed and a lantern lit, the room began to warm. Cassidy hadn't realized how cold she had grown until the heat began to seep through her clothing.

Ivan, having doffed his hat and gloves, settled on a cushioned chair near the lantern he had lit. "I will show you each of these as we pass. Some will be like this, others more or less elaborate, but you should know how to find those between the shelter and the tower."

She nodded as he passed her a scrap of paper with symbols drawn in a precise hand. "These are the buildings where you will find the easiest shelters. I know you have trouble with our script but I know you can match symbols. Once inside each building you may have to hunt for the warming station but at least you will be inside."

"Thank you, but we won't be separated," Cassidy said. "I won't let you leave me behind or do that to you, at least not on this trip. Hopefully I won't be out alone before I return to my own world." She sat in a chair next to her guide and held her hands near the lantern. "This would not be a terrible place to spend an evening, if there were books here I could read."

He nodded silently, mimicking her hand gesture. "We should not dally over long here. We do have to check other dwellings on our way to the tower and it is not a short distance." Waiting for her to signal her readiness he extinguished the lantern and followed her back to the street.

Ivan stood silently, waiting for Cassidy to select the direction of travel. She led them up streets and roadways with only minor course corrections from the elder man. Occasionally he diverted them to a building, either to show her a shelter or to search for supplies; anything they found would be left for later collection, in a shelter or simply just within the entryway of the building they had found them in. The engineer kept careful notes of where things were, making similar notations on Cassidy's map as they progressed. The wind was beginning to rise when Cassidy first spotted the tower.

It rose above the neighbouring buildings like a tree in

a mossy field. A gleaming monstrosity of mirrored glass amidst the three or four floor concrete boxes. She guessed it must be fourteen floors at least, not a big deal at home but easily the tallest building she had seen in Aetalus. Ivan took them down a series of side streets, so the tower would come into view only to be lost again, eventually leading them into another building.

"If we approach directly then we will draw the attention of the guards," he said. "For now, we must be circumspect in the approach, as other scavenger parties are. The Stewards do not like non-residents coming too close to their home. As well, remember that we are still seeking supplies to return with, we must do our job as well as complete the studies you wish to undertake. I think from the top floor you should be able to see the tower and its surrounding grounds better. Ursula and I dwelt on the other side of the tower, but in a similar region of the community, and I feel this building will provide a similar view."

Cassidy thanked him as they made their way to the fourth floor and found a window that gave a good vantage of the tower grounds and lower floors of the tower itself. Ivan left her at the window while he searched the room.

"I will search the other dwellings in this building while you examine the tower," he told her. "Then we return to the shelter if we desire to return today. We should have time for the return trip if we only take what we find here and go back by the most direct route."

Cassidy only nodded by way of response and resumed her study, pulling a pair of binoculars from her ever-present bag. From this vantage she could see that the tower was fenced with what must have been an exceptionally tall chain link, topped by barbed wire which protruded above the snow level. There was only one gate which she could see; it seemed to be manned by a pair of guards sitting in a small guard shelter. 'Probably glorified parking lot attendants,' she thought. The land between the gate and the building was flat and open, no cover existed on the well cleared grounds, save the odd drifting of snow which she would have to crawl through if she was sneaking in. There were doors on both sides of the building which she could see. The guards inside one doorway were plain for her to see so she assumed the other entries would be guarded as well.

As she scanned the grounds again, she caught movement at the gate at the edge of her vision. Focusing on that gate, she saw a pair of figures dressed in a uniform similar to the guards stationed there. The newcomers presented papers to the guards there, then pass through the gates as they opened. She continued watching as the figures proceeded through the grounds repeating the process at the doors of the building that she couldn't make out as clearly. This confirmed her suspicion about the guards stationed there while giving her the kernel of an idea.

After a few more moments of watching the building she grew bored and turned her attention to the room she was in. Her quick search turned up a few items that may be of use, including a pair of sunglasses which she thought looked rather stylish and might help cut down the glare from the snow. Then she moved on to the other rooms in the building. Each time the room presented a view of

Steward Tower she took a moment to examine the facility for a moment before continuing with her task. With her bag filled, she returned to the building's entryway to find Ivan waiting.

"Have you completed all that you wished to?" he asked her from the chair he had settled himself on.

"I think I've done what I can, for now," she sighed. "Let's head back and let me process what I've seen." With that the pair headed back into the windy street under the cover of a swirling snowfall.

CHAPTER ELEVEN

Travelling the most direct route to the shelter meant bypassing the small stockpiles they had deposited throughout Aetalus during the day, but their route combined with the fact that they were no longer stopping to search buildings, ensured that their travel was much faster than it had been earlier in the day. Cassidy almost felt as if she were out for a stroll with a friend in the snow back on Earth, when most people would be huddled inside watching television. The scale of the architecture and her companion made her feel like she was a child walking with a parent or grandparent. She knew this world faced upheaval and hardships, but the way the snow shrouded the deserted streets in the fading light of early evening felt like returning home from a day of skiing on winter break when she was still in school.

Remembering one such day in high school when she and her friends, after a day of skiing, had talked their way into a staff retreat at the resort where they'd spent the day.

"Into that building," Ivan shouted, shoving her in the direction of the nearest open window. He whipped his atlatl out and launched his spear at something on the other side of the roadway. Cassidy plunged through the opening and looked behind her to see the man sprinting towards her. She pulled herself to one side of the window, peering behind him to see what was chasing him. On Earth she'd have called the short creature bounding towards them a rabbit, if rabbits had horns in place of floppy ears. Refusing to let such a small creature put them off the straighter line, she took out her slingshot and slipped a marble into the pouch. She rapid fired a few times, knowing that she must have hit the creature as it scampered off.

"What was that?" she gasped, slingshot held at the ready.

"That was a haribou," Ivan responded between breaths. "A common herbivore in the area, very territorial. Farmers have lost eyes to their attacks. They are an excellent source of protein, if you can kill them on the first shot."

She saw blood in the snow when she stepped back into the street. "We can't let the creature go injured like that," she said. "I have to make sure it gets the finishing stroke, edible or not. Unless haribou have doctors of some sort to patch their wounds?"

Ivan retrieved his spear and said, "No, we must make sure it does not suffer due to our clumsy hunting. Keep your shotsling ready, it cannot have gotten far after losing this amount of blood." The pair followed the combined trail of hoof prints and blood into an alley between buildings and found the creature crouched beneath a metal staircase.

Ivan crept along the opposite side of the alley, seeking

a clear shot at the diminutive haribou while Cassidy took up a guard position at the mouth of the alleyway, sling-shot ready to fire at the first sign of movement from the rodent. The former engineer, foregoing the atlatl's launch-er, gripped his spear underhanded as he edged towards the stairwell, then he lunged. Cassidy let loose the shot in the pouch as the creature bolted towards her. The shot flew true, felling the animal instantly, though its forward momentum carried the body forward over the icy ground. Ivan grabbed the creature by one horn, tying the haribou to one of the straps of his carrysac.

"It is good that this detour was not lengthy. We will still have to hurry to reach the shelter in a timely man-ner," Ivan said. "We must be better prepared to defend ourselves while making such speed as we can."

They resumed their journey at a brisker pace than the sauntering stroll they had been travelling at. Soon Cassidy was sweating and breathing shallowly, though the pace was not unbearable, simply taxing. Ivan settled into a lop-ing jog and they made it back to the shelter shortly after dark.

Ivan passed the haribou to one of the fire-minders and the map to Sulva while Cassidy got them both bowls of gruel from the food line. They rushed their meals afoot while the others prepared the communal sleep area for the evening, then fell into the peaceful slumber that fol-lows any hard labour. It was a measure of how exhaust-ed she was that Cassidy slept the night through without awakening.

CHAPTER TWELVE

The morning found Cassidy the last still in her bedding. She shivered her way to the fire and did her best to let the warmth soak into every fibre of her being. She gratefully accepted the cup of tea and bowl of gruel she was offered, savouring each sip and bite as she warmed from the inside as well. She enjoyed the lazy morning, unsure if it was her status as an outsider or the simple fact of having been sent on procurement runs on each of the two previous days which granted her the privilege.

Breakfast eaten, dishes cleaned and returned to the appropriate stations, she ventured further into the shopping plaza, browsing through the open stores idly. In a store that specialized in hunting and hiking paraphernalia she found a knife with a blade made of a metal she had never seen before. She slipped it onto her belt, knowing that an extra knife can always come in handy. In another store she found goods that left her puzzled; she inspected each of the items she found there but could make no sense of them, 'Maybe a toy store,' she thought after finding what was definitely stuffed haribou and cineleucia lined up on a shelf. It was nice to see the reminder that all societies had some form of cuddling toy for their young. Another shop turned out to have a variety of things which were clearly musical instruments; she might not have recognized many of them but a drum was always plainly a drum it seemed. There were also stores which had specialized in jewelry, all of those had been emptied either by looters or to pay off the families in the early days.

Her wandering finally took her through all that the plaza had had to offer before it became a shelter. She found that many of the shops had been converted for varying purposes. The central area had become the dominant focal point for the residents, where the main fire and cook fire were kept burning and where they slept communally. A news agent had been converted into a reading lounge; what she assumed had once been the food court had become a sort of workshop where they exercised skills like sewing and weaving to generate more clothing and bedding. She found that the kitchen area of the largest vendor in the food court had been transformed to process the animals the group caught, and was told that the hides were tanned in a nearby building, to prevent the smell from becoming unbearable for those in residence. The biggest shock to her was to find that despite the lack of electricity they still had running water and shower facilities. Further inquiry let her discover that she could have a long cold shower today or a short warm shower in two days time when the group would build larger fires in the water heaters. The archaeologist in her decided a quick shower was in order now, with a warm shower to follow when permitted.

She managed to rinse the worst of the grime from

her body before the cold became unbearable, then shivered her way reluctantly into grimy clothing. She decided it was time to find herself some clean clothes while she pondered the problem of the tower some more. But first, tea. While she sipped, she attempted to read some of the children's books she found in the book store. The written language seemed close to English but in an odd script, the images of familiar items with the equivalent of "B is for Ball" allowed her to grasp the rudiments of the local lingo. Hopefully she could pick up enough to manage to navigate the community on her own.

As pleasant as it was to spend the day with little to worry about, the problems she would face when she returned home were on her mind. How would she deal with her current work situation, unless she demanded some form of payment from Gamgee to at least help with her rent? The absences from the university could only be explained as research trips for so long before they began to see some portion of the results from those trips. If she couldn't come up with a workable plan to face those problems then there was no reason to return. With those thoughts in her head she drifted into an unsettled sleep, and dreamt of wolves in three-piece suits chasing her.

She awoke from her nap as the scavenger teams were returning for the day and quickly corned Flavius to grill him for information about the tower. "Well, all I ever saw was the delivery docks in the back," he said. "And maybe the washrooms once or twice, but I couldn't swear to that. I remember it was always a big to-do: show your id at the gate on the way in; show it at the loading dock while they unloaded the truck. I didn't like that part so much;

letting them into the truck seemed wrong somehow. Then I'd have to show my id again on the way out with a receipt for the delivery."

"That seems almost paranoia level of security," Cassidy said.

"Well, they were dealing with some sensitive equipment so I guess they'd want to be extra safe with that stuff. I had to get special clearance just to be allowed on the trucks driving the deliveries," he said. "Plus, they probably had all kinds of orders for safety from the government and from the companies building the devices. Wouldn't want just anybody being able to make their own, now would you?"

"What were you delivering anyway?"

"Parts usually. They can't make everything they need at all the towers so a lot of the parts were trucked from one tower to another. One trip they sent me from Stewards to Marshalls Tower—Marshalls Tower is about four hundred ells north of here by the way," he said. "Not a long haul by itself, but knowing they had armed guards in the back of my truck didn't make me feel very comfortable. 'Course they didn't always send armed guards with the parts, that was for the power core or something like that, a really expensive piece."

"Armed guards with a delivery sounds a bit extreme," replied Cassidy. "Even if the cargo is expensive."

The delivery driver thought for a moment. "It was, and there was no street escort to go along with it. I just remember it being something they were determined to get to Marshalls. That was only the one time though, usually it was just making sure I signed in and out properly."

"Who else here might have delivered to the towers?"

"Sulva did. Just about any of the other veteran scouts really; most of us were short range or long-haul delivery and most of the deliveries here were for the tower or from there," he answered.

Cassidy made a point of interviewing all the scouting crews. Everybody who had delivered to the tower reported the same. Sulva did report that when she had delivered an official from one of the other families, that guest was ushered in while she was turned back to the gate.

"He was taken in like he belonged there and I was sent on. I hear he left a few days later by whichever courier happened to be stopping there; was kind of hoping to get the job myself because it was easier than the normal milk runs with multiple deliveries. He was just straight from tower to tower," the driver told Cassidy.

While she had been given the day to relax, Cassidy was not given the full day of doing nothing. After the evening meals were served, she was put to work with the cleaning crew. Her task for the day was to carry water to the fires to be heated, then return the water for use in the kitchens in the food court. Not an onerous task, but not light work either. Still she preferred it to actually washing the dishes. 'Who likes washing dishes?' she wondered. 'I guess folks who don't do it that often might like it as a novelty. The kind of folks who live in high towers and get special treatment from courier services.'

CHAPTER THIRTEEN

The next morning, she was sent out with a new party. They made the way to what Cassidy instinctively called north in the community, repeating the process she had gone through with Ivan two days previously. This area of the community had been little checked she learned, it was largely residential and they had been focusing on the more commercial and industrial areas out of respect for their fellow citizens, but now months into the troubles they were beginning to have less hope that anybody would be able to return for their personal possessions.

Her carrysac was bulging when she found the key to the idea which had been in the back of her mind. An older uniform for one of the tower engineers, a little big for her but hopefully somebody at the shelter could resize it to fit her. She crammed the outfit into her own bag and continued the pattern the team had been following, finding a new carrysac to take the remaining supplies she found.

As they began their return journey, she held her slingshot at the ready, as she had at all points when they were in the open; between her own efforts and those of her fellows, they had already felled several small animals to bring back to the shelter. She was unsure if she was hoping for more prey or simply worried about running into another cineleucia. But the only other creatures they saw were birds flying in the far distance.

Shifting the weight of the carrysac on her back, Cassidy looked about the alleyway where the group had paused for a break. In the back of the alley she spotted what looked like table legs emerging from the snow. Closer inspection, and some snow clearing, revealed a small table.

"We've got plenty of firewood back at the shelter," one of the others said when she rejoined the group, dragging the table behind her.

"It's not for wood," she said while tying a piece of rope to two of the now upright table legs. Then, dropping her carrysac and bag onto the flat portion of the table, she signalled her readiness to proceed. Just as she had hoped, the small table slid over the hard-packed snow like a sleigh. Occasionally it would catch in a wind-blown ridge of the snow, but such obstacles were typically easily overcome by simply pulling a little harder.

"You look like a caballa," the one who had insisted they needed no more firewood said. "But it seems to make the journey easier."

"I'm not sure what a caballa is but we used similar things where I come from; when the snow was too deep for wheels, we'd put skis on carts to make them into sleighs," she said. "They make carrying loads much easier than just piling it all your back."

"I don't know what skis are but if it means you can glide over the snow, I'd like to try them," he said.

Her going was much easier after that, despite the additional weight her team mates added to her small sleigh, and soon the entire crew had similarly outfitted themselves with improvised sleighs yoked together with whatever strings they could find in the buildings they passed. They began retrieving items from the small stockpiles they had built on their outward journey and had soon doubled their loads, thrilled to be bringing a much larger quantity of goods back to the shelter than they had initially expected.

They were greeted at the entrance to the shopping plaza with shock and joy. The introduction of the sleds was welcomed with enthusiasm and immediate plans for how to improve the primitive devices for use among the engineers who were still learning how to deal with the snow months after it had begun to fall. She did a quick sketch of a toboggan for them, explaining the practical and recreational uses of the simple device.

Later, cup of tea in hand, Cassidy watched the early results of their experiments. She was still amazed that while they had such advanced technology in some regards, they had large gaps in their knowledge compared to Earth. Of course, it could be a simple case of both this region and those who dwelt here being below the normal snowline. With these thoughts in mind, she dug out the tower uniform she had found earlier and began to inspect it.

Ursula, seeing her with the uniform, came over. "What are you doing with that?"

Cassidy looked up, "I'm not sure yet, but I think it might help me get into the tower. I think if I disguise myself as somebody who works there, I could just walk in at shift change."

"It's a good idea, except everybody who works at Steward Tower lives there," the short Tellan answered. "The same as at all the other towers. That was on one of the last news reels, all the important and necessary staff were being resettled within tower confines to keep them running and protect the weather dominators."

Cassidy, who had been feeling like she had accomplished much that day, looked at the dark-haired girl, crestfallen. "Then I guess this just goes in the bins to clothe whoever it'll fit. I still need to find a way into the tower. I can't leave here without trying to at least get you folks out of this ice age. Besides Doctor Gamgee will be furious if I come back empty-handed."

Ursula laid a hand on the itinerant archaeologist's shoulder, and the pair sat quietly for a moment. "What if we pretended to be from one of the other towers?" she asked. "We'd need another uniform, but two guards travelling with a message for Steward sounds like something that could happen, especially if the towers are having as much trouble with their radios as we are."

Cassidy lit up, "We could even just claim to be looking for parts to fix the radio, or some part of the tower. Just about anything to get through the doors, and then I can deal with whatever is inside. Guess we need to go chat with Ivan, unless you can think of anybody else with inside experience?"

Ursula sighed heavily, "I'm still not ready to face him, but if you must then I hope you will do it on your own. I'll make another of those shot-slings you showed me; those would be handy in any situation."

"I'll hold off on that for a little while, I think we need

to explore a little more to see if we can find another uniform. Hopefully one that will fit either you or me better than this one does," Cassidy said. "At least we now have some idea of how we can proceed."

The trio ate their evening meal while quietly adding to their plans. After the meal Ursula gathered materials from the various shops in the plaza to make more sling shots for the group while Cassidy sought out what she thought of as a phone book but was informed was called a community directory, to find potential dwellings where another uniform could be found.

After her search proved fruitless, Cassidy split her remaining waking hours between helping with the sleighs and building more of the primitive weapons she had introduced to this world—so like her own, yet so different than her home. Then she slept the sleep of the just and very tired, glad that she now had some idea of her next step. The cycle of a day of activity followed by a day of rest now seeming routine.

After a solid night of sleep and a rushed breakfast of full rations, she set out on her own in the morning. Searching all the nearby buildings she failed to find a uniform, never mind one near her size; her undersized stature for this world was more hindrance than simply being thought underaged, it seemed. She was about to give up on the plan entirely when she found what she thought would be a perfect solution in a dress bag in the back of a closet of the penthouse suite of a nearby apartment building. It would be one of the least practical outfits she had seen on this world, with the exception of the swimming attire left untouched in the shopping plaza, but might be the perfect thing for her subterfuge. 'This might even make it more believable,' she said to the empty room before she slipped the clothing into her bag and made her way back to the street just as darkness was falling.

She made her way slowly towards the shelter, nervous about being alone in the gathering darkness. Slingshot at the ready, despite the fact that she could barely see where she was going, she wished her cell phone still had some charge left so that she would have some light available for the return journey. Instead she counted the intersections as she passed them, hoping that she would remember the way and not make a wrong turning somewhere in the dark.

Eventually though she gave up on the journey. She could not read the street signs in the dark, could barely decipher them and their still unfamiliar writing in the daylight if she were honest with herself, and while she could usually manage to match the symbols on the road signs with those on the map she had been provided when she went on salvage mission, she couldn't read that by the light of the half moon in the sky. Ducking into the first building she saw, she made herself a makeshift nest in the first open room she found and prepared for a cold, hungry, sleepless night.

A quick search of the small room she had chosen revealed a small supply of candles and some drinking glasses. Relieved, she used her new knife to cut the base of the candles off so that they would fit into the glasses and made herself a travel lantern. Knowing she would be late to the shelter but determined to get there anyway, she returned to the street. A quick study of the nearest sign with a comparison to her map showed her to be less than three streets away from the shelter. That meant she had been more turned around than she had thought: she'd gone little more than a block that day, thinking that what she wanted would probably not have been taken by anybody out scavenging for the surviving groundlings. Relieved to be back on track, she did not notice the scurrying sounds that grew louder until the first of the crocuta nearly tripped her.

Then she saw the mass running towards her, a convulsing carpet of the roughly-furred forms rippling in the light of her lantern. The grey and black and brown furred forms clawed their way over each other and past her with the force of a river in spring flood as Cassidy did her best to stay upright and let them pass while wondering what could have caused the small creatures to stampede through the roadway. When the tide had slowed to a trickle and she had found her feet she looked ahead to see a flickering orange glow reflected on the low cloud cover.

She broke into a sprint towards the glow, slowing only to confirm her direction at larger street crossings, grateful for the hard-packed surface the frequent traffic had made of the snow as she hurried towards what she hoped was not the disaster she feared. The wind brought the smell of smoke to her nose, at first just enough to be aware of before becoming strong enough to hamper her breathing. Eyes streaming, she pressed onwards into the growing light. Soon she could see flames had engulfed one of the low structures just this side of the shopping plaza. The heat of the blaze made it nearly impossible for her to continue along her current route.

Dashing to a side street, she quickly found herself in a narrow alley littered with refuse from the shelter. Discarded bedding and food scraps making walking treacherous, she slowed somewhat but proceeded as swiftly as she could, the sounds of screaming and shouting reaching her ears from the general direction of the fire. She increased her speed and pushed on until she came to a fence. Refusing to turn back and seek any other way to the shelter, she began climbing the obstacle and had just reached the top when a gate swung open with her on it.

Below her passed three figures dressed in the mottled greys and blacks she thought of as a night camouflage pattern. Cassidy clutched the top of the gate like a shipwrecked sailor might grasp a plank in the sea, staring down at the group. The rearmost of the strangely clad figures dropped something as it reached behind and swung the gate firmly shut with a clang only slightly muffled by the figure atop it. She waited until they were out of sight and then counted slow to thirty, just to be sure they were gone, before dropping back to the ground. Torn between following the strangers and going to the aide of her new friends, she opted to give assistance where she could and, opening the gate, resumed her rush to the shelter.

As she rounded the last corner between her and the shelter, she felt the heat of the fire crash into her like a charging bull, forcing the air from her lungs. She gasped in a mouthful of smoke and began coughing, but pressed on to the first group of people she saw. The blazing building, which seemed to be one of the residences neighbouring the shopping plaza, showed Flavius, Sulva, and Ursula guiding people away from the blaze while others were throwing snow at the flames, trying to smother or drown the conflagration. With only a slight hesitation, she rushed to the line of fleeing refugees, calling to Ursula as she approached.

"We need to get everybody somewhere counter to the wind," the dark-haired woman said. "There's a pre-planned alternate shelter a short distance from here, where we're bringing the elders and younglings, but some of these people will need help to reach it. Can you help them? Take their carrysacs, or just keep them from falling too far behind."

Cassidy nodded and ran to aide a wobbly older man, lending him a shoulder to use for stability and taking his carrysac alongside her own. They followed the progression of other folks to the alternate shelter, a building which reminded her of a bank. Once there Cassidy saw to it that the man got inside, then turned back to help ferry the next likely pilgrim to the new shelter.

She repeated the process several times until, barely able to lift her feet, she returned to the shopping plaza and found that only those actively fighting the blaze remained. She joined Ursula in a line of people passing bucketfuls of snow toward the fire.

"We're keeping it contained but can't put it out without accessing the fire fighting equipment," the young engineer told her. "Father was supposed to be getting that back into working order."

Cassidy nodded in reply, too exhausted to use words. Her arms already tightening from the effort of helping people from the old to the new shelter, were finding the simple effort of passing the buckets up the line harder and heavier with each new load. After what felt like thousands of repetitions, she heard shouts of joy coming from the direction of the fire. Looking up, she noticed three things simultaneously.

The sky was lightening as the sun rose. The fire was beginning to falter under the onslaught of those fighting it. Water was streaming into the blaze.

"Ivan got the hose systems working!" Ursula shouted with joy. The brigade of bucketeers took the opportunity to pause, but soon resumed their work. Seeing the end in sight, they passed the fuller buckets along the line faster than before. They fought the fire for what felt like hours before Cassidy finally stumbled from the line and collapsed into the snow.

CHAPTER FOURTEEN

Cassidy awoke uncertain of where she was. She looked around, seeing that she was rolled in bedding on a smooth stone floor, near a fire. As awareness returned, she remembered the events of the previous evening and recognized the building she had seen in the brief moments while she delivered people to the new shelter.

She rose slowly and walked to the main fire on legs that simultaneously refused to bend or support her. Every muscle in her body aching, she collapsed onto a chair and croaked, "Tea? Water?"

The first gentleman she had escorted to the new shelter gestured for her to stay where she was and soon made his way to her, leaning on a short cane. "Thank you," he said. "You helped so much last night."

"Did we succeed?" Cassidy asked. "Did we manage to save the old shelter?"

The older man sat next to her. "They managed to extinguish the blaze but not before it had spread somewhat. The fire had started on the shelter and wind carried it to a neighbouring building. The shelter was lost before you had returned from your expedition." Seeing the shocked look on her face he hurried on. "Not destroyed, but one wall was burnt too badly for us to stay there and stay warm. The plan right now is to send a group back to re-trieve whatever can be salvaged later today."

"At least there was this building to use," Cassidy said. "How did you manage to get it sorted so quickly?"

"When it became apparent that the shelters might be-come long term dwellings it was decided to prepare alter-nates," the man said. "It was something many of us fought at first—why split our resources when keeping them all together was easier to manage? That was the thought of those who refused to leave their homes at first, too. Then the families cut the electricity and we knew that we'd have to take shelter together, save those few who remembered how to live independently. When even those folks started coming to the shelters warning of the increased blizzards and higher winds coming, some went out and prepared these alternates. This one has better ventilation for the fire, but not as good resources for everything else. But it will do for now. I worked in this counting-house, while such business still mattered, before the families closed all the branches in favour of central houses only. My son always joked that I should just live here because I spent so much time at work," he chuckled.

"I'm just glad we're all someplace warm," Cassidy an-swered, then, thanking him for the warm drink, she went off to find Ursula and Ivan, to see what the plan for re-trieving the things from the old shelter would be.

They all waited until the next day, those most able-bodied making the trip back to the shopping plaza to re-trieve whatever they could. "How did the fire start on the wall furthest from the fire?" Ursula asked as she inspect-ed the damage. "There is simply no way I can imagine that the wind spread the fire to the opposite side of the building, especially not considering where it spread after that."

"The night of the fire I had a near miss with some folks I thought might have been bad news," Cassidy began, then related the events of the alleyway.

"I think I know the place but can you take us there?" Sulva asked. At a nod from Cassidy they trooped out into the cold. Cassidy led them to the gate, pointing out where she had fallen and other landmarks she could recognize in the daylight. There wasn't much to see after the recent snowfalls, but a little digging uncovered a container that the locals recognized as a common fire starter.

As they returned to the shopping plaza to finish collecting what they could, the group discussed the situation. "Somebody set the fire; we won't find the tracks now but this is really all the proof we need," Ivan said. "We shall have to carry this news back to the counting-house. They will most likely institute exterior guards now, in addition to the fire-minders. The retrieval teams will be shorted in numbers due to this."

Ursula looked at the container in her hand. "Yes, it was deliberately set, but who would do it? We haven't seen any other refugees in months and most of them came into our party when we moved in here." She finished piling items onto her makeshift sleigh and tied the stack down.

"There were signs of others in some of our stock houses from time to time," Sulva said. "Used candles, missing goods, little things like that we figured were miscounted or one of the other teams used them while they were out. But never any major changes or damages. Do you really think that the Stewards would send out attackers?"

The group looked at each other wordlessly. Their silence held while they finished tying their respective loads to the sleighs and made their way to the new shelter.

CHAPTER FIFTEEN

Though it had taken all of the capable the full day, most of the supplies made their way to the counting-house shelter. Including Cassidy's guard outfit. With the knowledge that the tower was now attacking the refugees, at least their camp, Cassidy decided that she could no longer delay.

Over the previous days she had been quietly sounding out those who the guard uniform might fit, searching for an accomplice for her planned undercover mission. Cassidy had decided to disguise herself as a ranking, but junior, member of one of the other tower families. She would take with her a scientist and an armed guard to act as chaperones while she went to retrieve some component needed to repair her home tower. Once inside the Steward Tower they would hopefully turn off the machinery, hopefully returning normal weather to this portion of the planet.

She approached Ursula and gave her the outlines of the plan, explaining that she would need somebody who not only understood the technology but could pass as somebody who would be sent on such mission as escort-

ing the brat of the family on an outing. The engineer practically leapt at the opportunity, saying that they would
need to visit her former dwelling to get some supplies.

The pair then approached Sulva, who responded with
a simple, "Yeah, sure. Beats letting them freeze us to death
or burn us out of our shelters. Besides I was known to
carry items between towers anyway; if anybody remem-
bers me, they'd just congratulate me on the promotion."
The trio spent the rest of the evening discussing the plan
while Cassidy adjusted the uniform she had found so that
it would fit the former delivery driver.

The next day the trio made their way to the dwelling Ursula had occupied before the troubles started. "It
was not a great dwelling, but it was all I could afford on a
student's stipend," the engineer said. "I had intended to
move when I was a bit more established in my work, but
the troubles..." she trailed off.

In Cassidy's eyes it could have been any of the more
luxurious studio-style apartments she had occupied on
Earth, both as a student and since graduating. The furniture, while not new, was in better shape than much of
what she had seen in most places during her time as a
scavenger, in better shape than anything she had owned
herself. "This is a really nice apartment," she said.

"Much nicer than most of the places I've lived since I
moved here," Sulva said. "I'd almost like to convert this
into a dwelling for us three. Just take a little vacation and
let them all deal with things for a little while."

Ursula shushed them while she went about collecting
her gear. Cassidy thought that her plan might be more
than a little silly on the costuming side, given that they'd

all have to maintain their scavenged exterior clothing, but insisted that they maintain whatever scant cover they could.

Cassidy looked out the window: they were on the fourth floor of the building and it granted them a wider view than most buildings she had been in. Through the snow, in the direction she considered north, she could see the streets laid out in a mathematically perfect grid, each intersection razor sharp. Most of the blocks she could see were snowclad blocks, peaceful in the white blankets. Some blocks, obviously intended as park spaces for the members of Aetalus, were blankets of snow with skeletal trees protruding from the uniform sheets, lending a quilt-like appearance to the city. The squared geometry echoing street after street, roadway after roadway, a monument to urban planning and development, felt sinister in its lack of organic growth; the blanket of snow amplifying. A city meant to support a machine, the people dwelling there an afterthought, cogs and gears to drive society. Not living members of the group, rather functional blocks to hold things rigid in the now twisted permanent winter that faced those outside the tower she pictured rising like a hissing serpent behind her to the south. A small part of her wondered what kind of people could do this to each other, while another part reflected that this could easily happen on Earth if the technology was realized there.

She didn't have to try very hard to picture the type of people who would fund such a mad science project, and they looked suspiciously like those she saw on the business news every day. The politicos who stumped all the posts for their favourite candidates and slung the mud at their opponents in the name of filling their own pockets. The same as the people she saw on the news everyday denying that climate change was happening on Earth so that the companies they invested in could continue to profit. Earth might not have the families, to the best of her knowledge, but it definitely had clans who attempted to run things in the same way. The conglomerates just hadn't gained a strong enough foothold to stand upon the throats of those they saw as being beneath them yet. 'Maybe I should just leave the device here,' she thought. 'I don't think that there's anybody who would use something like this in any better manner at home.'

It wasn't until the cityscape before her started to blur that she realized she was weeping. Weeping for the world she had come to, and the one she had left behind.

CHAPTER SIXTEEN

The three made their way back to the shelter of the counting-house without event, arriving with plenty of daylight left they began sorting the items they would need for their expedition to the tower. It took a full day of sewing but soon they had their disguises complete and decided to set out at the first opportunity.

The next day dawned under a furious blizzard. The highest windows showing only white, the trio hunkered down near one of the doorways with one of the tourism guides for the tower. Ivan, himself at a loss as to how best spend his time, approached them.

"What has the three of you so intimate today?" he asked in his curiously accented manner.

Ursula looked up from where she sat and said, "We are planning to infiltrate the tower. We're trying to learn the layout of the floors we might have access to."

The aging engineer blinked owlishly. "I had thought you would have been gone by now," he said. "May I add my knowledge to that you have already?"

At a nod from Cassidy he began sketching further diagrams on the building plan the group had been studying, making notations in the margins of how things had been arranged when he had last worked in the tower. "They cannot have changed the architecture of the tower substantially since I worked there; all of the basic machinery must remain in their operational parameters. The structure of the management has probably changed significantly though. When I worked there last it was Madame Steward, but I think she has passed and her son Sage is now the head of the tower: it is the head of the Steward family who will have the absolute authority to allow you to stay or force you to leave. He was little more than a boy when I met him, and friendly in his manner, but to let this go on as it has, he must have grown up to become a very different man."

"Thank you for this," Cassidy said. "Anything else you can tell us that might make this go any easier?"

He scratched his beard before pointing to two places on the map he had added his own notes to. "Here is where you will find the master circuit joiner; if you disable this then no power will flow to the device. This other is the main console; from there you can change the weather between here and the nearest towers. But the towers must be balanced, simply turning off the device here will see the normal weather of this region return but tempered by the others."

"Like standing between two heat sources when neither is close enough to provide adequate warmth?" Ursula enquired in an academic voice.

"Yes, but in our case, it will be between cold source and other cold source," Ivan elaborated. "We will not return to the typically humid weather we had before, instead it will become temperate unless the other towers are adjusted likewise."

The quartet sat in silence for a moment while they let this sink in, then Cassidy spoke, "The best we can do right now is attend to the tower at hand. After that we can think on how to broaden the reach, maybe boost this tower's signal or send a team to another tower. Who knows? But step one is the Steward Tower."

"I will consider on the matter while you three take your action," the older engineer said simply. "I simply wished for you to all know the best possible outcome of your action, and to add what assistance I could. I fear there will be too many who remember me within the tower for me to be of any other assistance."

The rest of the day passed under a cloud of nervous energy. The team packed their bags, then unpacked them, shuffling the items they felt they would need, replacing items at random. Sulva commented that they would know what they needed when the situations arose and the best they could do was guess.

Cassidy decided to keep the equipment she had carried when she came through this slip, plus the clothing she had acquired on planet. She had seen herself through so many situations with similar basic equipment, plus she had added the slingshot, which was good for some fun if nothing else. That decided, she settled herself into the routine of checking her gear, sharpening her blades, and packing the bag as light as she could manage. It would be a lengthy trek and those didn't vary much from planet to planet and always ended with the feeling of walking too far with too much weight. Ursula followed Cassidy's lead, selecting similar items to those the archaeologist would carry, selecting the atlatl over the slingshot. "I'm more skilled with it and it doesn't take much more space," she explained. Sulva's bag was mostly food and clothing, though the tough woman carried both an atlatl and a slingshot.

A few days later, when the weather had cleared enough for travel, they set out for the tower. Working their way through the city, first in a dominantly eastern direction with slight southward tendencies, the group saw no signs of life. In fact, they saw little movements beyond the eddies of snow that formed in some of the intersections on the street; the snow dervishes lashed them with sharp ice particles, sometimes necessitating choosing alternate routes.

"The winds seem more intense than yesterday," Ursula observed.

Cassidy, finally growing tired of her stay in Aetalus pushed them onwards. Further from the shelter and only marginally closer to the tower, as they had agreed. They intended to approach the Steward Tower from the rough direction of the Joplin Tower to lend greater believability to their story of being emissaries of Joplin Tower. They pushed on until the winds rose and more snow started falling, then sought shelter in the first building they could gain access to. They huddled together for warmth in the small room they had chosen, burning what they could find in a small metal garbage can Sulva had found in the building.

The next day was a repeat of the previous one, heading more south than the previous day. Another day without incident, and another night in a random building. This time, unable to build a fire, they gathered what coverings they could and built a nest of all the cushions and mattresses they could find in the rooms of the building they had settled on.

Their third day out from the shelter brought them to the entrance of the tower late in the day, tired, cold, and hungry. Cassidy presented her credentials, which identified her as Cassidy Joplin, daughter of Scott and Janis Joplin of the Joplin Tower family. She and her companions were granted admittance to the Steward Tower as ambassadors of the families.

CHAPTER SEVENTEEN

The security team had taken a look at the documents Ursula had prepared and sent the trio into a private room three floors above the ground. There they had been met by a young lady who asked their names and positions before requesting their credentials and, after separating them from their meagre belongings, sent them a further three floors higher.

On the sixth floor they were met by a Nancy Raigin, who told them that for the duration of their stay in the Steward Tower she would be their guide. "The Lord Steward has had a trying time governing the surrounding regions and is not accepting callers at this moment, but will arrange to see you in future days," the official told them. "In the meantime, we request that you refresh yourselves and enjoy all that we have to offer. Anything you require can be supplied by those who work within this tower, one of the harmonious thirteen as prescribed by the great technocrats who preceded the establishment of this glorious age."

Cassidy and Ursula, as those pretending to be the representatives of the neighbouring tower, voiced their acceptance. Meanwhile Sulva made a show of inspecting the room to which they had been assigned. The small group settled into the luxurious suite they had been provided with, enjoying the stark contrast to the horrible cold they had left behind in comparison to the warmth of the temperate room with which they had been provided.

Their well-heated room featured a bed for each of them, twin beds for the scientist and guard but a full-sized queen for the representative of the tower family. Each bed was in a separate room under its own climate control. Despite the luxury offered them the trio slept together in the queen-sized bed, their combined history of huddling together for warmth making them feel more comfortable if they stayed together in an easily defensible unit. They even took watches throughout the night, Sulva taking first and last watch in their four-watch division.

Despite the undisturbed evening, none of them slept well. The combination of finally having infiltrated their goal and the shock of relative comfort versus the hardships they had faced making it to their destination, left all of them on edge, not allowing their adrenaline to dissipate to the point of letting any of them find true rest. They each luxuriated in the hot shower provided in the en suite bathroom and gorged themselves on the food which a nameless tower employee brought to their room. Cassidy felt like she was in an all-inclusive five-star resort back on Earth, the view making her think they'd all be hitting the slopes on snowboards or skis the next day. After a suitable time had elapsed for a very lazy morning under any circumstances there came a knock at their door.

"I hope all is well with you," Nancy said when Sulva opened the door. "I understand that your travels must have been difficult so it has been decided that today we will conduct you on a tour of the tower, so that any dissimilarities between ours and your own will not become problematic. Unfortunately, the Lord Steward is still unable to accept guests as he manages the current situation with regards to the debtors." After a dramatic pause the tower representative continued, "Let us not focus on negative aspects of our current situations and instead allow you to see the new tower you have chosen to visit."

"Please allow us to dress appropriately for the outside," Cassidy responded before quickly retreating to her chamber. "We have been many days travelling with limited recourses so we beg you to bear with us in our difficult times. The roads between us were practically impassable in places, and we have had to abandon much of what we set out with."

"Indeed," Nancy responded. "It is sad that the law-abiding citizens have been forced to suffer the same punishments as those who choose to ignore those laws, but that is not a matter for us to discuss. Let us proceed when you are ready."

As Cassidy emerged from the chamber which the trio had shared, she saw others gathered near the doorway in the finest attire they had managed to find before setting out on their mission. She felt they all seemed under dressed in comparison to their assigned guide who seemed as if she would be more at home in a swank restaurant while her companions were dressed to eat in a food court at the local shopping centre.

"We understand the hardships which you must have faced in simply making your way here. We can provide everything you will need while you are here," Nancy told them. "Today is simply to make you feel more comfortable in our tower while we arrange for the replacement mechanisms you have been sent to retrieve. When you are ready, we will begin the tour. We do our best to maintain the schedule of events here in the Steward Tower."

The three former refugees quickly grabbed their jackets and followed Nancy into the corridor. "This area of the tower, as you now know, is dedicated to visiting dignitaries. It is seldom used since the camaraderie came to rule, but is maintained regularly to be prepared for such as you who brave the isolation outside. During the construction the portion of the building dedicated to visitors was much larger." Nancy maintained a monologue as they walked through corridor after corridor, most dedicated to private chambers or public spaces.

Cassidy did her best to memorize the route they took and locations of interest, but after seeing a dozen themed sitting rooms on the three floors they were shown she asked, "Where do you house the equipment for which the towers were built?"

"In the standard positions, some on the upper floors, others on lower floors," Nancy responded. "They will not be part of this tour."

"I would very much like the opportunity to see the mechanisms in use here to compare them with those in our home tower," Ursula said. "Compare wear patterns on the frequently used components any variations in."

"They will not be part of this tour," Nancy repeated in an annoyed voice before continuing in a soothing tone. "Here to the left you will see the ballroom where dances are conducted every Saturday evening, attendance is mandatory. Fortunately for you this is one of the weeks featuring live music; perhaps you would like to hear them rehearse?"

The manner in which she asked made it clear that any answer other than yes would not be accepted so Sulva asked, "We have no live music in our tower, may we?"

A nod from Cassidy was echoed by Nancy and the small group entered a lavishly appointed room. A grouping of chairs and small tables were laid out around a large, hardwood dance floor. The walls were papered with a purple velvet-like material which, while making the room feel dark, did little to counteract the large chandeliers which hung from the ceiling. At one end of the room was a small stage, and to one side was a short bar with several bottles behind it. On stage was a four-piece act who started playing as soon as they walked through the door. Cassidy was as amused by their timing as she was to find that she recognized the tune. True the lyrics were different, but if she sped it up slightly it was a song that had once been popular on Earth.

After their, seemingly, impromptu private concert, the group were shown the shopping district and guided back to their rooms with the assurance that the Lord Steward would see them at his earliest convenience and that Nancy would be at their beck and call. "Tomorrow you have been scheduled to see the education facilities that we have in the tower and the food production areas," the guide told them. "Your meals will be brought to you at the appropriate time. Please enjoy your evening."

"We're supposed to just stay in our rooms?" Sulva asked as the door closed behind Nancy. She opened the door, finding Nancy nearby. "Can we see more of the tower, perhaps visit one of the public spaces?"

"You may, with a proper guide to ensure you do not get lost," Nancy said in her calmly professional voice. "It is the end of my work day; I will have somebody sent to escort you."

"There are signs showing the way, I'm certain we could make our way to the viewing gallery we passed when we returned to our rooms," Cassidy began.

"Normally we do not allow visitors to travel without escorts suitable to their station. But, of course, yes you may travel freely within the tower so long as you agree to follow all posted signage concerning who may enter selected areas," Nancy responded. "We do hope you will follow these regulations, and not hesitate to ask assistance from any passer-by should you require it."

Upon their agreement to those terms Nancy led them to the nearest public area where they were allowed to peruse a small selection of books and given access to what looked to Cassidy like one of the radios that would have been common on Earth in the 1940s. Nancy went on her way after explaining that the radionic unfortunately only received the broadcast from the tower, but that there was another one available in the sitting room of their suites should they desire to return to their own rooms. They thanked her; Cassidy turned to the window, while Ursula immediately began browsing the bookshelves, and Sulva turned on the radionic.

"What do we do next?" Cassidy asked.

Ursula held a finger to her lips as the radionic began to make faint crackling noises which slowly resolved into a male voice announcing the social events planned for the next few days. "Listeners can listen both ways," the engineer said in hushed tones as she drew closer to the archaeologist. "It's always best to assume that they are listening to us when the radionic is not being listened to."

Cassidy looked back at her with a confused expression, and Sulva cut in, "They can be made so that those on the other side hear us, like somebody staring in a window. This floor was intended to be for the use of those visiting from other families, so it would probably be best to assume all of the radionics can listen to us as well."

"It's been so long since I've seen a working one that I had forgotten about that trick, until she specified that these only received one broadcast," Ursula said. "Equipping them to listen often requires removing much of their capabilities to receive signals. It was a ploy many of the families had begun using to record what was happening in many places before they decided to freeze us into submission."

"Many governments at home used similar tactics for varying reasons," Cassidy responded. Reflecting that the Steward Tower was heightening her paranoia, she made a note to check her offices and phone when she returned home, not that she had any real reason to suspect she would be on a watch list for anybody. "Let's just enjoy the view and small entertainments they've provided for us; did I see wine on that sideboard?"

Sulva responded while inspecting the tray of drinks, "There seems to be a variety of juices, plus the makings for tea and coffee. I have not had any papple juice in far too long, want some?" A nod from Ursula told Cassidy that she should have glass as well.

The juice was chilled, pulpy like orange juice, but the closest comparison in taste she could make was a mixture of pear and plum; it was deliciously sweet after the days of drinking only the bitter tea or plain water available in the shelter. She felt a sharp stabbing pain in her back teeth, a similar sensation to an ice cream headache despite the location, and recognized it for what it was: sugar shock. She had experienced a similar pain many times on her first sip of sweetened drinks after returning from some of the more isolated digs she had been on.

"Do you not like it?" Sulva asked, seeing the newcomer wince.

"It's delicious, just surprisingly sweet," Cassidy answered with a smile and held out her empty glass. "I haven't had anything with so much sugar in a long time. May I have some more?"

Ursula, refilling their glasses, queried, "How should we proceed?"

"I am almost certain that all exits from this floor will be guarded," Sulva said, slowly sipping her papple juice. "Perhaps the best move right now is to take the opportunity to rest and study and wait to meet with the Lord Steward. It is a tactic I have had to use many times when making personal deliveries," she concluded to their puzzled looks.

"We did come to first plead our case to him. Besides, Sulva and I could use the chance to recover somewhat after the months we have spent on shorten rations and limited mobility," Ursula said quite simply. "Besides, how long could the head of the tower delay meeting representatives from another tower?"

The group looked out over the snow-covered city as the radionic switched from community announcements to a jazzy-sounding music. They remained in the seating area until serving staff summoned them to their chambers for a meal. After the meal they returned to the main bed chamber, and slept.

CHAPTER EIGHTEEN

Morning found Cassidy alone in the luxuriant room. She did some stretches and freshened her clothes from the meagre supply she had and joined the others over a tray of pastries and teas. The group were just finishing the last items on their tray when somebody knocked on their door.

Ursula mouthed "Nancy" to Cassidy as Sulva opened the door. As predicted, their guide was framed in the doorway, looking professional and entirely too perky at this time of day in Cassidy's opinion. "Are we ready to begin the scheduled activities of the day?" Nancy asked chipperly.

Cassidy, growing more used to her assumed role as leader of the delegation, said, "I believe so, but may we request a deviation from the itinerary? I feel that we could all do with some time to launder our clothing."

"But of course. I shall arrange for somebody to wash all of your garments," their host responded in her animated manner. "I will have them mend or replace any items which were damaged in your travels and we will arrange for new garments to be brought to you as well, if that is to your liking?"

A glance at the delighted faces of her companions told Cassidy all she needed to know. "That would be delightful. If we may have a moment to collect the items we desire to have cleaned, it won't take long sadly. Much of what we set out with was lost or destroyed on the journey," she concluded and gestured for her companions to follow her.

As they entered her sleeping chamber Cassidy said softly, "We need to be sure we're presentable when we finally meet the Lord Steward, and hopefully whatever they give us will be in better shape than some of what we've got." They quietly agreed while sorting their belongings to be handed off for washing. When they returned to the private sitting room with their clothing, they found Nancy and a team of serving staff waiting for them.

"I had anticipated such a request and had summoned the appropriate residents to complete these chores as I made my way to your rooms," Nancy explained with a slightly embarrassed look on her face. "Had you not been forward enough to raise the matter yourself, I would have made the offer as a matter of basic hospitality. Please forgive my tardiness in making the offer."

Cassidy did her best to reassure their host that no apology was necessary and that the situation was well sorted now. "Let us put the incident behind us and proceed, knowing that all is as it should be," the archaeologist said. After several more apologies from the guide, Cassidy prompted, "I believe that we were supposed to tour the education facilities."

The guide visibly gathered herself and quickly bustled

them off on their tour. Nancy took them to the residential corridors where she showed them various classrooms and laboratories, a small reference library, and a gymnasium which she informed them did double duty as an exercise for the younglings during school hours and adults after school had closed. "We offer educational programs for adults in neighbouring rooms, using the same facilities where possible as well," Nancy told them. "Specialized training for the operations of the tower are taught in job specific work stations."

"You don't offer simulation training for tower operation?" Ursula asked innocently.

"We offer training courses on the operations, but feel that the best way to learn such tasks is through actually performing the actions," Nancy replied simply. "Under proper supervision of course."

"Simulations are only partially accurate anyway," Sulva chimed in. "Most people learn tasks better by doing the things you're training them for."

The tour ended soon after, with Nancy escorting the group back to the sitting room on the floor where they were being housed. "Leave has been given for you to retain use of the entirety of this floor, should you so require," their guide told them. "This will include all the public areas, including the libraries, gaming areas, and lounges. Anything else you desire may be requested from any serving staff you meet."

"When we will be permitted to meet with Lord Steward?" Cassidy asked.

"Your petition has been entered into the official table of future engagements. As soon as the opportunity presents itself you will be added to the scheduled meetings for the day, regardless of how this affects the activities which have been prepared for you," Nancy said, disapproval creeping into her voice with her last sentence.

They thanked her as she left and, turning on the radionic, settled themselves on the couches nearest the window. Eventually, Cassidy rose and poured them each a measure of papple juice. As the trio listened to the broadcast from the in-tower radionic station and sipped their drinks, Cassidy noticed movement in the darkening window. Reflexively she stood, turning to look behind her, Sulva nearly mirroring her movements, which resulted in the pair ending up facing a tall man who had entered their sitting area from the hallway.

"Ah, just who I was looking for, the visiting dignitaries," the man dressed in luxurious velvety imitation of the Steward Tower livery began. "I am Chapel, the head of security and operations for this tower. I understand you have requested an audience with Lord Steward and a tour of the technical facilities. We are currently doing our best to accommodate your requests. In the meantime, I hope that your assigned guide, Domina Raigin I believe, has been keeping you all...entertained?" Cassidy nodded and the officer continued, "I simply wished to extend my personal welcome and offer my apologies for not doing so sooner. I regret that I have no further time to spare at the moment. Perhaps we will be able to meet in the near future." Here he paused dramatically, clearly waiting for some response.

Cassidy broke the silence by introducing herself and her companions. Then said, "Thank you for the gracious greetings, Chief Chapel. Everyone has been more than welcoming and everything has met our expectations. We would like to meet with the Lord Steward as soon as possible; the business of Joplin Tower depends on this meeting and our return with the items my Lord and Lady have requested."

The head of security narrowed his eyes slightly saying, "Yes, we are aware of the need which must have sent such distinguished members of the house of Joplin into such conditions as these. Unfortunately, the telegraphic communication between our towers has been inoperative for quite some time. Such excursions will no doubt become necessary more frequently in the future, but you must understand that appearing as you have, with no appointment, will require the juggling of Lord Steward's schedule significantly. Perhaps he will be able to attend the weekly festivities; normally he does not but may given the special circumstances involved. Now if you will excuse me, I do have other duties to attend to."

As the tall man strode away Cassidy gave a puzzled look to her companions, they shrugged back at her and the group returned to sipping their papple juice until the staff informed them that their meal was awaiting them in their suite. Tonight, the dish was something vegetarian, with fresh vegetables. A treat Cassidy hadn't seen since stepping through the portal. The others hadn't seen such delicacies since the snows began. They all ate ravenously.

CHAPTER NINETEEN

They were all in the sitting area of their suite drinking tea, wondering why Nancy was late, when the awaited knocking began. Mindful of their cover story, Sulva made a point of answering the door: none of them had stood on such ceremonies up to now but felt that such lax protocols may be noticed after their chat with the imposing Chief of Security Chapel the evening before.

"Hello visitors, I apologize for the lateness of my arrival today," Nancy began. "There was scheduled maintenance on the lift I normally use that I did not know of until I reached the lift itself. This required me to adjust my route. Please do not inform my superiors of my tardiness today."

Chapel spoke firmly from behind her, "There is no need to inform me of the late arrival, Nancy, I already know," he said. "And I am grateful to see it so, for I wished to accompany you for at least part of your day."

"Oh! Chief of Security Chapel," Nancy almost shrieked. "Please forgive me for not seeing you, and for my tardiness on this day. I am humbled by my failings," she concluded in a manner that suggested an often-repeated ritual.

"I am sure there is nothing to forgive," Cassidy spoke in gentle voice. "He snuck up on you and we are basically vacationing until we are granted audience with the Lord Steward."

Chapel spoke calmly in a voice clearly accustomed to shouting orders, "As long as our guests are pleased with your performance all will be well." He paused, looking pointedly at Cassidy, then continued after she gave a sharp nod, "If the House of Joplin is pleased, who am I to argue? Please, Nancy, let us proceed as scheduled."

With that settled they began a tour of the areas of the tower dedicated to food production. Their first stop looked like a large glass greenhouse to Cassidy, perhaps a little more angular than she was accustomed to, but most of her experiences with greenhouses was with the gracefully curving plastics ones which could not have withstood the heavy snowfalls which the tower itself was generating. Inside it was warmer than the simple structure would have led one to believe, even considering the strong sunshine which bathed the structure.

When asked about this, Nancy replied, "There are two systems of water-filled copper piping which radiantly heat the structure. One set of piping is bonded to portions of the power plant for the tower, serving to both heat this building and to cool the machinery which allows for the greater operation of the tower. You can see that piping running along the frames which hold the glass in place, those thin structures attached to the pipes allow for greater distribution of heat within this hothouse. The other set of piping, which does not generate as much heat, is fed by coils sunk in the lower regions of the organic refuse heaps. In this way the refuse also serves a second purpose by providing extra warmth to grow the food it is meant to become fertilizer for."

"You use the waste generated to manufacture more than the primarily desired product?" Ursula asked.

Nancy gave her a puzzled look. Then the guide looked to the chief of security and at his nod continued, "Yes, the excess heat from the steam electricity plant is fed through the entire tower in such heat-radiating devices; in the living quarters they are disguised to resemble décor, but here in a work area, they may be plainly displayed. All food and water waste that may safely be reused is composted and reused to nurture future stocks grown in the hothouses. Portions of the harvested plants grown here are given to the livestock which we are scheduled to see later today. The limits placed on us here necessitate that we use all the portions of what we produce in as many ways as we can. I have been told that this is why those who live outside the towers struggle, they don't harness all they produce and allow too much to be lost as if it were truly something to be discarded."

"Perhaps they simply do not have the means to retain all of the heat generated by an open flame. Consider how much will be held by the structure of a steam plant and what would be lost without such a structure," Ursula replied. "Many of those surviving outside the towers, the expelled, lack access to many modern conveniences."

"Surely you follow similar procedures in the Joplin Tower," Chapel inquired. "These were the guidelines established before we began the expulsion."

"We do, but a midlevel mechanical support technician would not be expected to be familiar with all the details within the tower," Cassidy improvised. "Please, do continue, our actual execution may differ from your own."

"And outside the towers is a different matter," Ursula interjected. "I have been compiling the information brought back by our patrols. Those remaining outside the towers often find themselves without comparable conditions to battle the elements. Surely this was part of the plan when the expulsion was brought into effect."

"It was indeed, and it is most of the reason my position exists within the Steward Tower," the security man said. "Though I am surprised to hear your tower still runs patrols of the surroundings, though I suppose I shouldn't be considering that Joplin Tower is located in the heart of the neighbouring capitol. We dispensed with such patrols as most of the occupants of this community were brought here specifically to work within the tower or it's pre-expulsion support industries."

Nancy interrupted, "To continue the tour, in this hothouse we have a variety of vegetables and fruits nearing the production phase of their cycles. In other houses we have earlier stages of the same plants and some others in more specialized houses. The inhabitants are encouraged to grow their own plants as well, both food crops and those for more aesthetic purposes. Unfortunately, not all the pre-expulsion crops can be grown in the hothouses, but we retain their seeds for renewal when it is decided that the snows shall be lifted."

As the guide spoke the group drifted from house to house through a series of artificially lit tunnels, eventually emerging into a hothouse the size of a baseball field. "Here is the papple orchard," Nancy spoke simply. "Right now, it is harvest time; during the rest of the season this area serves as an alternate public entertainment region, but when the papple pickers are working we only allow those employed in the task to enter. This is to ensure the safety of the workers."

The building was filled with evenly spaced trees; here and there among the trunks were benches and small electric lights. Ladders under many of the trees held workers picking the small purple fruits and placing them in baskets worn around their shoulders. Cassidy was immediately taken by the delicious smell of the fruit, quickly followed by a feeling of elation as the heightened oxygen of the building settled into her bloodstream. Feeling slightly tipsy she softly said, "We have a hothouse at home but none which hold a full orchard like this. This is truly awe-inspiring, and that can't just be the oxygen intoxication talking."

Seeing the same puzzled look on the faces of her companions, Cassidy elaborated, "When there is too much oxygen in the atmosphere it can induce a feeling of euphoria for those consuming it. This effect is often felt by those of smaller stature, those who reside at higher elevations, or those from regions where pollution is high for long periods of time. It's the direct biological opposite of elevation sickness. Surely you knew about this effect?"

"We were aware that people entering the orchard hothouse left it feeling more at peace and relaxed than when they had entered, but our research had not revealed anything of note," Nancy replied. "We assumed it was simply the beauty and stillness of the trees combined with the scent of the flowers and fruits when in season."

Ursula spoke into the silence provided by the guide's thoughtful pause, "When the trees would be at the apex of their oxygen output we should perform a test to determine if the oxygen here is indeed higher than in other places. Perhaps a simple flame test?"

The tour guide and the engineer soon devolved into a conversation so full of jargon and scientific terminology that it began to sound like gibberish to the others in the group.

"I see that the Joplins did their best to see all of their children received wide and varied educations," Chapel said.

"I travelled extensively as part of my studies, before the expulsion that is," Cassidy replied. "And studied with Professors who had not yet published their findings when the families united. It is one of the better points of coming from such notable stock."

"Indeed," the security chief said, guiding her off the path and deeper into the regularly spaced trees. "As is having the resources to build such a structure as this. I was led to believe that most scions of the tower families were raised to be little more than signatures on papers, supported by the lower levels, but this changes my opinion significantly."

Cassidy hid the thought she put into her reply by studying the tree nearest to them. "The eldest, my older siblings I mean, were taught what it was deemed important to know for running the tower. As the youngest, and least likely to ever receive any responsibility within the familiar structure, I was given more leeway in my studies. The benefit of being seen as unimportant."

"So unimportant that you appeared in none of the official portraits or at any of the public appearances?" the chief asked. "There is a Cassidy Joplin listed in the records shared among the towers, but there are no records of her appearance." Cassidy sighed inwardly at this, even knowing that this was part of the reason that Ivan had told them to select the Joplins as their alias tower. "And to arrive now, when the Joplin Tower has been silent for weeks, seeking the parts to repair a communication array. I must admit that I did have doubts originally, but if you are an imposter then you have so thoroughly set the stage for your act as to make it utterly believable."

"Then surely you will make the arrangements for us to meet with Lord Steward to request all the components we have been sent for," Cassidy said.

Chapel grinned broadly, "The more commonplace components are already being assembled and packaged for transport, along with a suitable form of transportation for one of your status. I simply wish to know what has transpired at Joplin Tower to allow it to fall into such disrepair."

"There was unrest among the expelled, a faction attacked the tower's perimeter and managed to damage several of our hothouses before we successfully repelled them," Cassidy improvised using the basic premise of a movie she had watched not long before entering the portal to Tellas. "The resulting food shortage was not welcomed by the workers on the lower levels of the tower. We are not proud of the difficulties we faced, or how we overcame them, but we have kept our tower operating."

"Ah, and your associates, they know of these difficulties?"

"Of course not: they may have suspicions but all they were told was that some equipment failed and we have been sent to obtain replacement parts," Cassidy said, throwing as much scorn into her voice as she could. "The idea of appearing weak to those below us is even more appalling than the idea of requesting aide from our equals. Even telling somebody such as yourself is distasteful, but if such brutish interrogation is the only manner to gain access to the Lord Steward then it is a burden I must bear. Much to the shame of myself and my family."

The chief of security for the Steward Tower bowed formally. "Please forgive my clumsy expression of concern, I assure you that my only concern in the matter is to ensure the safety of the family Steward. Please let us put such unpleasantness behind us and move forward now in our positions as appointed by the council of families and tower staff."

He held the bow until Cassidy said "Very well, I cannot fault you for behaving as I hope our own chief security officers would in similar circumstances."

The chief, seeming to have concluded his investigation to his satisfaction, left the group to finish their tour while he attended to other matters.

CHAPTER TWENTY

After an uneventful afternoon the trio were returned to their rooms. Cassidy settled down with a book about growing papple orchards, a process that seemed to differ very little from growing apples or oranges back on Earth. She noted that Ursula and Sulva were doing a more intense survey of their quarters. Closing the book around her forefinger, she waited for them to finish.

"We do have something very important to discuss," she said once they finished their inspection. "What are we all going to wear to the ball?" The pair stared at her, their faces showing a clear lack of comprehension. "The dance tomorrow night," Cassidy continued. "Surely, we visiting dignitaries cannot appear in this borrowed everyday wear, no matter how comfortable and finely constructed. I didn't think to pack anything suitable for such an event."

Ursula slumped to the floor unceremoniously, a look verging on terror painted on her fine features. "I hadn't given it any thought. I assumed we would wear what they have given us."

"I don't know what the appropriate attire for such an event would be," Sulva apprehensively murmured.

"I usually just wear my uniform to such things, but then again I'm usually only there if I'm working."

The three looked at each other for a minute before rising in unison and rushing off to their respective chambers. Moments later they returned to the main sitting room to compare the garments they had brought with them. Both Ursula and Cassidy had serviceable, if not exactly fashionable dresses which the group agreed could work in anything except the most formal of settings, but Sulva had not thought to bring anything of the sort. As they were sorting through the remaining items, attempting to settle on a choice for the delivery-driver-turned-guard, the serving staff entered with their evening meal.

"Let's ask them," Cassidy said and quickly outlined their current situation.

"We always wear our finest to the gatherings," one of the girls dusting her hands after laying down a tray of bread answered. "I've heard Domina Raigin make arrangements for something to be delivered for your use tomorrow. In your house colours and all, Domina Joplin. And for your staff, not to worry. I'm sure that the hardships of travel must not have been kind to whatever you were carrying with you."

"Well that is both a pleasant surprise and a relief," Cassidy answered.

"Now Winnie, you've gone and ruined Domina Raigin's surprise," the taller server scolded. "Attendance in full regalia is mandatory of course. Lord Steward is scheduled to be there after all."

Before Cassidy could ask how that would affect the dress code, Ursula spoke, "Of course, full respect must be accorded to the high seat of a house. Even from junior members of the other families."

"Well that and the fact that he's almost never seen outside his chambers these days," the first server muttered under her breath, blushing furiously as she realized she had spoken the words aloud. "Oh please, don't tell anybody I said that. It's just he's such a handsome young man and he prefers to spend his time on the upper floors rather than coming down to the lower levels and seeing how things are being run."

"Not that things are run poorly," the older server put in. "It would be nice to see him more than once every three-nine days though. Just to know that the Lord does care how we're all doing."

"The lords are too often busy with other affairs, to monitor all the daily operations," Cassidy said simply. "I'm sure it's just a sign of how hard he's working."

"You kind visitors shouldn't worry yourselves over such matters at any rate. I'm sure your meeting will be arranged in soon," the second server said.

"And I'm sure whatever it is you came here seeking will be dispatched for you to return to the Joplin Tower with. Lord Steward is as generous as he is handsome after all," the first server finished with a blush.

After the pair of servers had left, the group settled down for their meal. They passed the remaining hours of the evening with Sulva and Ursula attempting to teach Cassidy some of the more popular dance steps. Ursula, having spent most of her time in offices and on production floors, only knew one or two of the more common dance routines performed at such gatherings. Sulva, on the other hand, was a veritable treasure trove.

The former delivery driver walked them through a number of styles similar to many Cassidy had seen in movies and plays, including a solo sequence that seemed to blend tap dancing, line dancing, and what she thought of as traditional highland dancing. At the end of the lesson Sulva told them, "Hopefully the dances will be of the easier sort without the pomp of the higher forms, there just isn't enough time to teach them to you properly."

Cassidy, flushed with exertion, grinned sheepishly, "Perhaps I'll sprain an ankle to save you the embarrassment of seeing your student flub the steps."

"That might be for the best," Ursula spoke from a nearby chair where she was rubbing her feet. "It might save the toes of whoever is fool enough to ask you to dance."

With that the group went to bed.

In the morning they awoke to find three packages neatly wrapped in a pulpy-looking off-white paper that reminded Cassidy of newspaper. A note pinned to the top of the packages read simply:

To: Joplin Delegates,

For tonight. Please ensure the fit is correct before our scheduled tour,

Barbara Shrub

"Who's Barbara Shrub?" Sulva asked of nobody in particular as they opened the packages. Each contained elegant fringed dresses in the silver and purple of House Joplin. The smallest dress, clearly meant for Cassidy, was of a silver silk accented with purple sequins, with fringes that alternated a royal purple so deep as to seem black and silver. The other two dresses were plain black with the same silver and black patterning to the fringe-work. The two Tellans seemed scandalized by the low-cut necklines and high hems on the skirts. Cassidy thought them rather conservative but fun enough, something she could wear to pub night at a conference. Each dress was accompanied by a pair of soft slippers—thick silken socks really, that stretched to fit the wearer's foot. "Dancing in those might really sprain my ankle," Cassidy told her friends as she examined the footwear.

"They allow you to pivot and twirl as you dance," Sulva explained. "There's a gripping pattern of tree sap thread woven through them that will provide extra traction while allowing for freedom of movement. They've been the standard footwear for dancing for years."

At Cassidy's dubiousness Ursula told her, "Just try them on, you'll see that they are more than sufficient for interior wear, and should fit comfortably under your normal footwear. Let's try these frocks on and see if the local seamstresses are better than those we're used to."

The trio made their way into their separate rooms. Once alone, Cassidy was relieved to find that she wouldn't need any help to don the dress since it was designed to be fastened by the wearer. As she closed the small buttons, she noted that it was a little loose but was quite comfortable and, upon examining herself in the mirror, looked better on than it had in the box. The colours complemented her hair and her lightly tanned skin in a way that she was more than a little satisfied to see. As she pulled on the dancing slippers, she decided that she quite liked the full effect of the ensemble. She did a quick walking test of the slippers and found the mixture of tractions provided by the gripping pattern—which ranged from a very firm grip to absolutely no grip—an odd combination, but hopefully she would learn how to walk in them at least before the ball that evening.

As she emerged from her chamber, she saw her companions already waiting for her. They simply stood for a moment, staring at each other. Cassidy felt like she had only seen her new friends as caterpillars but the joy on their faces in their borrowed finery revealed them as jewelled butterflies. After a quick study of them she was relieved to see that the looseness seemed to be more a fashion of the world than a failure on the part of their seamstress. They each did quick turns for the others in turn and agreed that the frocks would do for whatever the Steward Tower might hold for them, especially once Cassidy took the time to master her new shoes.

Nancy stopped by, informing them that with the upcoming festivities they would be given the day to themselves in order to better prepare themselves for the evening, and that they should take the available time to rest. When she returned, the trio were ready for the event. The small group made their way through the corridors in excited silence, the faint echoes of music drawing them in the lavishly decorated hallways that led them to ball.

The room was filled to capacity with only those performing essential tasks in absentia. Each attendee was announced via the public address system as they entered while the musicians played a piece that reminded Cassidy of slow summer days spent in the sun. All heads turned when the Joplin party was announced, everybody curious to see the visitors from out of tower.

They made their way into the room, sipping drinks handed to them by a server in the tower colours, exchanging pleasantries with any who approached them, as Nancy took them to their assigned table. They were seated within sight of the Lord Steward's table, well out of conversational range, yet still in a position of prominence. It did not matter since the Lord's seat sat empty. A meal, noticeably smaller than that which they typically received in their rooms was served as they sat, with Nancy urging them all to eat before the dancing began in earnest.

The trio watched as the band moved effortlessly from one song to the next. The Steward Tower residents moved through dance routines that involved both rounds and single partners, Sulva rising to join after the third dance, with Ursula joining the steps at the start of the next song. Cassidy sipped a glass of papple juice, the only thing being served at the tables, and watched the intricate steps as the dancers circled the floor counter-clockwise.

"I would have thought that a daughter from the Joplin Tower would know the steps to all the popular dances," a man in simple green and red plaid said to her.

"Sadly no," she responded. "My education covered many topics, but formal dancing was left for my more agile siblings. I can manage simple steps but very little else."

The figure gestured at a chair, seating himself at Cassidy's nod. "So, a solitary observer from one of the larger towers comes to my tower and doesn't recognize the man she has been sent to meet?" he asked. "Or should I say a solitary observer and her carefully selected team of escorts?"

Cassidy blushed and nearly rose to bow to Lord Steward before she caught herself. Gripping the seat of her chair with the hand not holding her glass she responded, "Forgive me, Lord Steward, between the lighting in here and the fact that we have been here for nearly a week and you have not found time to meet with me, I simply didn't realize it was you."

The surprise on his face was too plain to be an act. "You've been here how long? I was told you arrived yesterday and requested the evening to recover from the hardships of your journey," he stammered.

She sipped her drink, taking a moment to study how he sat like she would a student who had come to her asking for an extension on a paper. "We came seeking parts for some malfunctioning equipment in the Joplin Tower and have been here for more than seven days and have requested meetings with you each day since our arrival," she told him flatly. "Each day we were told you were busy but could possibly see us the next day."

He lounged back in his seat with a long sigh and reached for one of the glasses at the table. "You are the youngest Joplin, are you not?" At her nod he continued. "I too was the youngest and never meant to take control of the tower. Like you, my family would send me on errands to fetch and carry and deliver messages, missions just like this, until my brothers fell ill. Now the staff keeps me in the dark and makes proclamations in my name. Which is fine, everything is functioning just as it should. I'm surprised I managed to sneak away from them tonight but I guess the extra scrutiny placed on your companions made them relax their vigilance on me."

Cassidy choked on her drink a little at this.

"Oh, you didn't know, I'm little more than a prisoner here," he sipped his papple juice and made a face. "True I'm kept in all the luxury we can manage here but I'm only trotted out at formal occasions and have little say in anything that happens here at all. If you want your parts, or whatever it is you were sent here for, you'll have to get it yourself and make your way out of here. If you could bring me out too, I'd be ever so pleased."

"You want me to take you out into the frozen wastelands your parents have made this region?" she blurted.

"Ah but your family has done it too Domina Joplin. Your hands are every bit as filthy as mine, despite us both being the expendable children," he sighed as he emptied his glass. "I wish they were serving some sort of brandy at this event, perhaps later. But I digress, I do see the things being done in my name and despise them. If I had the freedom, I'd shut the tower down. It might only affect the nearby region, but surely with the loss of a thirteenth of the influence the other towers might struggle to maintain the mess we've managed to create. Ah, I believe I see some of my security team approaching."

With a nod over her shoulder to confirm his words, he leaned across the table, as if attempting to better hear her words. He managed to lay a hand on her upper thigh as Chapel placed a hand on the Lord's shoulder. "Lord Steward, there you are," the security chief said. "I see you have made the acquaintance of Domina Joplin. Unfortunately, its time for you to address the tower. I've your speech right here. I'm sure the Joplin emissary will excuse us."

As the pair made their way towards the stage Cassidy noted the rough way in which the chief handled the young Lord Steward, though the security officer made it look like assisting a drunk on his way. As the pair reached the stage the crowd paused wherever they were and turned to face the dais. Cassidy shifted her weight and felt something slide along the smooth fabric of her skirt. Looking down, she found an envelope which she quickly slid into the top of her socklet, disguising the motion as simply adjusting the garment.

The speech the Lord gave was full of the expected pleasantries: production was up, the weather was behaving properly, the people outside the tower were starting to see reason and would soon perform their part in the great planetary order of families. Through it all Chapel stood beside Lord Steward, a reptilian smile on his face and satisfaction in his eyes. The Lord concluded by formally welcoming the Joplin delegation to the tower and asking everybody to enjoy the rest of their evening.

As the Lord left the dais to rousing applause Chapel gestured to the band, who struck up a lively rock-a-billy-esque tune that set Cassidy's toes to tapping. It was with a certain relief that she saw that the formalized sequence dances were concluded for the evening, to be replaced with a free flowing form of movement that reminded her of the common steps seen in bars and at house parties, wherever people felt the rhythm of a good beat.

Ursula returned to the table with a pair of glasses in her hand. "That was the Lord Steward I saw you speaking with, wasn't it?" she asked.

Cassidy took the glass from the engineer, sipped it, then replied, "Yes, and it is not a conversation for us to have here."

"Really?" Ursula asked archly.

"Yes," Cassidy replied, annoyance plain in her voice. "Is it too early for visiting dignitaries to duck out yet?"

She was cut off by a tap on her shoulder. Turning, she saw a trio of the garden guards with sheepish smiles, "Would you ladies like to dance?"

And Cassidy danced with the guard, with an engineer, with a chef, with servers. She danced until the band started to pack their instruments away and Nancy ushered her and her friends back to their rooms. As they began to settle in for the evening Cassidy told them of her brief meeting with the entrapped Lord before climbing into her bed fully clothed and promptly falling into a deep slumber.

CHAPTER TWENTY ONE

Cassidy was surprised to awaken in the early hours of the morning feeling so well rested, almost as surprised as she was to find herself still dressed from the night before. She made her way to the wash chamber where she indulged herself in a hot shower, luxuriating in the steamy stream of water in a way she hadn't for months back on Earth. She felt like she was at the end of a field season and taking advantage of the facilities before she'd return home and have to take responsibility for the bills again.

Feeling as relaxed and clean as she had after her first shower in the tower, she wrapped herself in towels, collected her dirty clothing, and made her way back to the bed chamber. As she sorted the dirty clothing, she rediscovered the note from Lord Steward tucked into the socklet. Amazed that she could have forgotten something that must have been important for the prisoner Lord to take such a risk to deliver to her. Opening the envelope, she was surprised and a little disappointed to discover that the message consisted of a string of numbers and a crudely sketched map.

She quickly dressed and made a quick search of their

shared suite for Ursula and Sulva. She found the pair in the sitting area down the hall from their suite proper.

"You're finally awake," Ursula exclaimed as Cassidy seated herself at the table.

"Thank you for letting me sleep, I needed it," Cassidy said with a smile, pouring herself a cup from the teapot on the table. "I found this and I'm not sure I can make any sense of it."

Sulva took the document and quickly looked it over. "It's a duty schedule. I hope whoever lost it won't miss their shift start," she said quietly and reached to turn on the radionic. "Specifically, it's the duty schedule for the tower control centre and a map through the air ducts to get into it."

Ursula took the missive with the inquiry, "Where did you get this?"

Cassidy placed her tea aside and said, "It fell into my lap, literally. Lord Steward dropped it there as they took him away. He seemed to be fully aware that his staff were giving us the runaround but wanted to help. He thinks the whole permanent winter thing is wrong and wants it to end. At least that's the impression I got from him when we spoke."

Sulva grunted, "From what you've said he's little more than a prisoner. Kept on so the residents don't realize that Chapel is actually in charge. You said he actually asked you to shut down the network?"

Cassidy took a deep breath before saying, "Yes, he asked it as one fourth child to another."

Ursula smacked her forehead with her right hand, "Of course he did, I forgot all about the accident just before the towers were vitalized. Three of the four Steward children were killed when a portion of the tower collapsed on them during a tour of the construction. There was a huge investigation made by the guardians but they determined that there was no wrong-doing, simply a fault in one of the beams that had not been seen during the construction. Although that didn't stop the rumour mongers from repeating all sorts of imprecations against the Lady Steward."

"I remember that," Sulva cut in. "It wasn't until after a few similar incidents had occurred at other buildsites here in the Aetalus that those rumours died down. Though among some of the guardians and private security forces people claimed that the other accidents might have been the Lady's doing as well. She had expressed doubts about if it was wise to tamper with the weather to such an extreme and some thought she'd committed the sabotage but accidentally killed both of her daughters and one of her sons."

"That must be why she disappeared from the social circuits in the time before they vitalized the towers," Ursula concluded for the trio with the tones of a detective in a television melodrama. "Not just the loss of the majority of her family, but also the guilt of having killed them with her actions."

Cassidy shook her head at the deluge of Steward family history, which seemed to have played out in the local news like some kind of radio drama for the residents. "Will any of that help us get into the control room? Beyond it maybe explaining why the Lord Steward is willing to throw us this huge assist?"

"By all accounts, any of the families with a fourth child just let that child grow more or less wild, at least by their normal structures. That's why we chose for you to impersonate a fourth. They're known to be eccentric," Ursula said. "The Steward fourth was little known before the accident, though it was said he favoured his mother's politics. I think everybody just assumed that with the death of his siblings he'd taken on the mantle of head of the family willingly."

"You mean people thought that his stance was posturing, designed to get attention?" Cassidy asked. "Like everybody seemed to assume that Cassidy Joplin's studies were an effort to stay out of the papers?"

Sulva sipped at her tea for a moment before she replied, "Yes, exactly like that. A face not meant to draw attention with no regard of what might be behind it."

"I guess we do whatever it is they have planned for us and try to get in on the next day the plan says we can," Cassidy said. "When is the next time that the roster should be right?"

Ursula folded the document into her pocket and said, "Two days from now. It feels as though we've wasted so much of our time here already."

The others nodded in agreement.

"I'll make sure I'm ready," Cassidy began as she stood.

"Us too," Ursula chirped excitedly.

Sulva shook her head, "It might be best if only one of us go. And I think we all know who it has to be."

"Me, of course," both Cassidy and Ursula spoke, then looked at the flat disapproval on the face of the former delivery driver.

"If the Joplin emissary disappears for a time it will cause concern. Likewise, for the engineer," Sulva began adopting a tone that brooked no argument. "The only one of us who won't be missed is the transport officer, the glorified guard, and that means I have to do it. I'll take whatever advice you can give me, but we all know it's an operation for one."

"Adopting the role you were thrust into, is that it?" Ursula asked.

"No, she's just thinking further ahead than we are," Cassidy replied. "And she's right. The Steward staff will take note if you or I go missing for any amount of time, but if our guard goes missing, they'll just assume that I gave my servant some time off. Makes no difference that Sulva isn't actually staff as they see it, that's how they see the three of us."

"But neither of you would know how to adjust the tower controls," Ursula said urgently. "You haven't studied the mechanisms and might not be able to follow the procedures properly."

"Then you will make sure to write out the step-by-step procedure for her," Cassidy said with a sigh. "I don't like having to sit back and do nothing, but it has to be her. We'll arrange for us to have a meal with the security chief or something and say Sulva felt ill or just wanted the evening off. I assume that it works that way here too anyway, people aren't expected to work all the time."

Cassidy drifted about their floor, casually looking at the books they had been provided, checking the doors of the other suites and finding most of them locked. When she found one that was open, she went inside. The suite was almost identical to their own, just as she had expected. The floor was set aside as a guest accommodation for visiting dignitaries of a certain station, after all. With couches and chairs to sit on, tables to work and eat from. Basic structures repeating across the floor, echoing through the levels, with variations to suit the time. Like a game of telephone or rumour played out in the levels of the tower and across the dimensions. She sat in one of the chairs near the window, looking out at the community from this new side of the tower, seeing it from this new angle.

In the street below she saw the snow piled to the second-floor windows of the vacant building across the street. Beyond that first line of buildings she saw smaller structures, visible only as corners poking through the crust of snow. Some of the roadways, now little more than troughs in the snow revealed by nothing more than the shadows caught in the depression caused by the passage of those left outside the tower.

The plan seemed foolish to her: freeze a world to extort money from it. Force them into small groups and deny them all the comforts their society could provide, based on nothing more than the greed of those in power. The human experience echoed and distorted again on the inter-dimensional scale. But what if they could change that here? What if disabling this tower could be the spark that started the fire of societal advancement, freeing at least this small corner of the world from the yoke of oppressors? She was tired and longed for the comfort of her own bed, even with the worries that awaited her at home. The bills piling higher than the snow outside, not knowing if her contract would be renewed next semester, the yearly scramble for grants to continue her excavations. She rested her chin in her hands and watched as the snow began falling, again.

It was dark when she rose from the chair, stiff from having dozed off sitting up. Slowly she made her way to their chambers and found her companions just starting their evening meal. She ate with them silently as they discussed the procedure to disable the weather device. She excused herself from the table and went to her bed. Once she was sure her companions had retired to their own chambers—when had it become their new normal to sleep in their own beds, she wondered—she put her bag over her shoulder and left the suites.

CHAPTER TWENTY TWO

Cassidy made her way through the darkened corridors to the unlocked suite she had found earlier that day. Once inside, she locked the door behind her and pulled the cover from an air duct, took a deep breath, and climbed in.

The ducts were bigger than they would have been on Earth but still a tight fit for her. Slowly she made her way through the hot air in the ductwork, in the light of a flashlight, towards the nearest vertical shaft she could find. Once there she saw somebody had scrawled the words "Gym, Guests, Laundry" on the wall in descending order and, hoping that this would be the case at every floor, she began to climb. Her footfalls echoing on the ladder, she paused on the next floor to remove her shoes in favour of the socklets she wore underneath and shed her outer coat, then resumed her climb. She passed words which read "Office, Accountants, Repair, Residence" before she finally reached a floor labelled "Mech and Con" in the same inky scrawl.

She climbed onto the nearest ledge, extinguishing her flashlight once she was settled. She lay flat with her eyes closed, allowing herself a moment to both catch her breath and let her eyes adjust to the dim light in the ducts. In truth the light did little more than allow her to see which vents opened on lit areas, which were the most likely areas to be occupied. She checked her map, straining to make out some of the detail on the paper and failing, she moved towards the nearest light source as quietly as she could.

She was within a meter of the nearest vent, eyes focused on her goal, when a pair of boots stopped on the other side of the slatted opening. Cassidy held her breath, wishing the boots to move on. She watched as a hand came into view, opening the louvres a little. Making herself as small as possible, she turned her face to the floor; it wasn't until she heard the boots move on that she exhaled and looked up again. She took a further count of thirty before she continued her approach to the now wide-open vent.

All that she could see through the slats was a corridor. Nothing was visible from her floor-level vantage point to indicate where on the level she might be. Quickly she pulled out the map and attempted to puzzle out where she might be on it, an exercise that proved futile. The sketch gave her little information beyond the control room. Sighing, Cassidy pulled the louvres closed and turned back toward the upright shaft. She treated as she had been told to treat mazes as a child, and using the shaft where she had entered as her starting point, she took every right turning where she could see a light. She found many openings on corridors, and some on offices, when she found herself at a broom closet, she took the opportunity to step in and stretch.

As she breathed the cleanser-perfumed air, she reflected that she really had no idea what she was doing;

she was no technician trained to operate anything more complicated than her phone, but given that they relied on transistor tubes here the controls couldn't be much more complicated than her phone anyway. Besides, every piece of equipment will break if you try hard enough—hadn't she seen proof of that on every dig she'd taken part in? Taking a deep breath, she pressed her ear to the closet door; hearing nothing, she opened the door a crack and risked a peek at the hall and was delighted to find she was actually at the starting point indicated on her map. Pulling the door closed behind her, she did a few more quick stretches, then climbed back into the ventilation shafts and followed the path laid out for her.

She peered through the grating at the underside of several desks and saw three booted feet. At least two people in the control room, but there was no noise of human activity. The tubes hummed with their stored charges, the ventilation whispered around her, and a clock ticked in the room before her. Gently she grasped the grating before her and began to ease it free from the wall. With agonizing slowness, she forced it free, millimetre by silent millimetre, until her shoulders throbbed with the strain. When it came free of the housing, unexpectedly quicker than she anticipated, she nearly dropped the piece of metal to the floor. Instead she managed to hold it while debating her next move.

After what felt like hours of watching the boots not move, a high warbling sound rang through the tower. The booted feet sprang up. "Fire alarm," a woman's voice said. "Make sure the auto is on and let's get out of here." The walking of boots followed by the sound of the closing door was the only response.

Cassidy wasted no time and crawled from the cramped vent. Immediately she crossed to the door and locked it. Next, she turned to the control panel. She had expected a large computer but what she saw before her staggered her. The device hulked against the wall like something from a 1940s sci-fi movie, almost as big as a moving van, covered in knobs and dials and flashing lights. Close inspection revealed that everything had been labelled at one point but whatever material they had used to make those labels was worn away with use. Here she could make out a letter, there part of a word, but nowhere was there anything to indicate what the controls did. She tried her best to remember the instructions Ursula had given to Sulva in order to reset the machine and shut it down, but even if she could recall them, she wouldn't have been able to find the controls needed with the incomplete labels. Taking a deep breath, she reached out with her right hand and did the only thing that made sense to her: she simple flipped all the switches. Every knob that was dialed clockwise, she dialed counter-clockwise. If a switch was in the up position, she flipped it down. Where possible, she broke the control as she went, snapping the dials from potentiometers and cracking the levers on switches. Seeing nothing else to tamper with, Cassidy grabbed one of the chairs, raised it above her head and brought it down on the console repeatedly. Feeling that her task was accomplished, Cassidy took a step back to survey her work.

Realizing all had gone still, Cassidy crawled back into the ventilation shafts, pulled the grating in behind her, and scurried into the darkness. She had had almost made her way back to the cleaning closet when she heard a new alarm begin to sound. Adrenaline pumping now, she attempted to retrace her path through the vents. At the first vertical shaft she came to she headed down; checking the legend scrawled on each floor as she descended, she made her way as swiftly and silently as possible.

With each floor she descended the ventilation system grew lighter as the levels were lit. Frantically, she searched for the items she had abandoned on her travels as she drew closer to her destination. Finally, she found her boots and outer wear and stuffed them into her bag as she emerged into the empty suite where she had begun her journey. Taking a moment to tidy up, she let her hair down and entered the chaos of the hallway.

The corridor was in chaos; crowded with security personnel, serving staff, and people in tower uniforms Cassidy didn't recognize, all pushing against one another. All shouting at each other. It was into this tumult she was drawn as the door of the suite closed itself behind her. With no other choice, she tried to ride the flow of the crowd towards the suite she shared with Sulva and Ursula. She had just entered the crowd when she felt herself being grabbed from behind and hands attempting to pull her from the crush of people.

Struggling against the unknown assailant, she lunged into the crowd, straight into the back of one of the security personnel. The guard spun around and reached for her. Cassidy ducked beneath the taller man's grasp, thankful for her shorter stature on this world and began weaving her way deeper into the crowd seeking what she hoped would be the safety of her rooms. She was nearly there

Slipstreamers

when she heard cries of "Get her!" erupt behind her.

A surge of the crowd sent her crashing into a door. Feeling the pressure build behind her, she took a blow to the back of her head as she grabbed the doorknob and twisted, feeling momentary relief as the door opened followed by immediate panic as more hands took hold of her and pulled her deeper into the room while other hands closed and secured the door behind her.

Cassidy lay facedown on the floor where she had been dropped, gasping for air. With what seemed to be the last of her strength, she forced herself to roll onto her back and found herself looking up into the faces of her best friends on this planet before she blacked out.

CHAPTER TWENTY THREE

Cassidy had no idea how much time had passed when she awoke, the sounds of a thunder storm raging outside the window of her darkened room.

"Finally awake?" Ursula's familiar voice came from just outside her door. "I was going to ask where you went, but I think we've figured that out by now."

"I got tired of waiting and might have done something rash," Cassidy gave a rueful smile.

"Well from what we've been able to put together it was a good thing that you did decide to do something rash," Sulva said as she walked into the room with a cup of tea. "You heard the alarms, I take it? Apparently, there was a dispute between a group of engineers and the security team."

Cassidy gasped, "I thought it was a fire alarm."

"It was; one of the engineers pulled it during the ballyhoo from what I've been told," Ursula interjected. "When we heard the alarm and found your bed empty, we were afraid that it might have something to do with you, but on our way down the stairs we ran into one of the ladies who usually brings our meals and she told us."

"Under no circumstances are you to leave your floor tonight," Sulva cut in with a passable imitation of the red-headed server they had chatted with many times. "She had seen the fighting and was on her way up to warn us to stay clear. I think she was hoping that we'd give her shelter too. She's asleep on the couch by the way."

"When she discovered that you weren't actually in our suite, she figured that you'd gone to visit somebody special; I think she was hoping it was the Lord Steward in all honest. For the most part nobody tried our door through all the fighting, they gathered on this floor because it divides the upper and lower castes' residences," Ursula paused. "We kept hoping you'd come by sooner or later."

"When I heard the shouting in the corridor change, I decided to see what had happened," Sulva said. "By the time I worked up the courage to take a look you had made it to the door and fell in when I opened it. If Ursula hadn't acted so quickly then I'd never have gotten the door closed again.

Head spinning, Cassidy pulled herself out of bed. It took her a moment to realize that the thunderous noise was coming from outside the building as well as the noises from the corridor. "Did it work?" she asked, turning toward the nearest window. "Did I shut down the tower?"

Looking at the rain lashing the window and the lightning arcing through the sky was all the answer she needed. "Storms were predicted as a potential side effect of a tower failing," Ursula said smoothly. "If the system can be brought back online then complete control can be resumed. If this one remains incapacitated then the others should fail within days and natural weather patterns resume. It looks like you did it, yes."

The three stood at the window for a moment, watching the play of lightning in the dark sky as the pounding from the corridor grew louder and louder until the door came crashing into the room followed by a quartet of the engineers and labourers.

"Oh, good, you're all in here," the Lord Steward said from the rear of the group. "There's been a bit of bother tonight and, long story short, the security forces have all been locked away. Also, somebody has wreaked absolute havoc on the weather manipulator but that's a by-the-by sort of thing since I was going to shut it down anyway. Now, Cassidy not Joplin, mind telling me what your role in all this was?"

CHAPTER TWENTY FOUR

Lightning flashed behind the trio and thunder rumbled through the night before Cassidy responded with, "You knew? You knew and didn't say anything?"

The Lord of Steward Tower spoke through giggles, "Of course I knew. I met Cassidy Joplin at boarding school years ago. Even carried somewhat of a torch for her, though she never had any interest in dating one of her students. You're at least five years too young and perhaps half a meter too short. I'm impressed that you fooled Chapel; I might have believed you if I didn't know her personally."

"Then why not reveal her?" Sulva asked. "All of us for that matter?"

"Well there was the whole thing about me being a prisoner in my own home," he chirped. "Besides, the whole not wanting to be an evil overlord so much. I was hoping you lot would be my key to freedom. And, if I'm being completely honest with everybody, I was bored."

Those gathered in the room stared at him dumbstruck. "You were bored! With everything that's going on in the world around you. Everything that's happening in Aetalus. Everything that's gone on in your tower. You let a bunch of outsiders do what they pleased because you were bored?" Cassidy took a deep breath and slapped the Lord Steward as hard as she could across the face. "You let yourself be locked away and used as a figurehead: did it not once occur to you that you could have been doing something to help the people who had allowed your family such control?"

Grinning behind the hand currently rubbing his cheek, "I suppose convincing the engineers to help me oust the security forces that held me prisoner might have been a little self-serving, but it was also the easiest way to take back control of the tower. And let's not forget passing information to you as well—that was neither easily arranged or entirely for my own good. But you still haven't answered my question: who are you really and why are you here?"

"I'm a traveller from another world sent here to find whatever any useful technology my home planet could benefit from," she said calmly. "I entered your realm through a portal from my own."

He sat heavily on the floor "Are you truly from beyond the portals? They were only emerging when, well, when my family and the others started to freeze those refusing to pay the scandalous rates the families expected. So at least one does lead somewhere habitable: all those who had entered them had failed to return."

'The portal worlds have portal worlds,' Cassidy thought, then quickly pushed the idea down. "I need a copy of the plans for the weather control centres and then I need to make my way home," she said in the calmest voice she could muster. "I've been away for too long as it is and must get back to where I belong."

Sulva spoke up from nearby, "I'll help you get wherever you need to go, Cassidy, but we'll need to wait for the weather to calm a bit."

"No, I've been here too long as it is," the frustration in Cassidy's voice plain. "I need to go home, I need to tell the professor about the other portals here, I need to sleep in my own bed, I need to get back to my normal life, what's left of it anyway. Get me a copy of the plans and let me go home as quick as I can."

Quickly she went about the room gathering her belongings and stuffing them into her messenger bag. "I've got a rough idea of where I came through in relation to the first shelter we were in and—"

"And you will sit down and have something to eat," Ursula said, thunder punctuating her words. "If the rains cause the snow to melt, we'll all be stuck in this tower for at least a few days. I'll find you a copy of the plans if you're sure you still want them, but nobody will be going anywhere in this mess."

"If only we had some sort of device that could stop the rain, or at least allow us to slow it's falling," the Lord mused quietly. "We'll offer whatever assistance we can, when travel is possible, but given the abrupt shift from controlled weather to being the only pocket of natural climatic activity, that will be at least a few days. Settle in here. We'll monitor the outside and keep you informed of the situation as it develops."

Cassidy shuffled to the window, watching the lightning play across the skyline as the snows melted, revealing the streets beneath.

CHAPTER TWENTY FIVE

Six days passed, by the count of the clock, the sky had begun to lighten. Six days of discussing the places she had seen through other portals. Six days of staring out the window as the snow became water that flooded first the streets and then the buildings. Six days of watching people seek shelter on the higher floors of buildings until their own nearly deserted floor had seen all the rooms filled to capacity. Six days after she had demolished the weather control device, Cassidy saw the sun in the sky once more.

"I've arranged for a dory to take us to the portal," Sulva told her. "Hopefully you'll be able to make your way through and return to your homeland."

Cassidy thanked all those present as she collected her belongings. Anxious to be off, she left a note with Ursula explaining how to contact her or the professor should either ever make their way to Earth, then made her way to the waiting boat with Sulva.

As the pair rowed down the roadways she marvelled at the submerged buildings. Here a roof just broke the surface, there a full floor of a structure could be seen. In most cases structures were only revealed by ripples in the stagnating waters that covered them. Occasionally they saw people waving through windows and from exposed rooftops, but mostly the voyage was little more than stroking the oars.

As the sun began to set, Cassidy fished out her portal locator and began to scan the area where she thought the portal was. As the device began its pinging, they steered towards a mountain on the outskirts of the community; it seemed much shorter in the flood waters than her downward trajectory during the snowstorm had led her to believe. The pair circled, looking for some point of entry. Cassidy couldn't believe her luck when she saw some of the symbols she had marked at the mouth of the cave where she had first entered this world. True the water would be nearly to her hips when she entered the hollow, but finally her home was in sight.

Sulva sat in the small craft outside the cavern until she saw a flash of light, and waited a little longer until she was certain that her strange friend from another reality had gone. The she turned her small craft and headed back to the community they had freed together.

Cassidy stepped through the other side of the portal and pulled her phone from her pocket, only remembering at the last moment that she hadn't charged it in days. Time to make her way back to the office again.

A few days later, back in her own clothes and with a fresh haircut, she entered the office of Professor Gamgee. "I can't keep haring off on whatever new quest you've come up with for me," she began. "Sure, side missions are great in video games, but I've got bills and rent and a main story-line for my life to consider."

The professor looked up from his tablet, keyed the display off and placed it facedown on the table before him.

"When I left, I was looking at a performance review to explain my abscesses from teaching and a pile of bills that I could barely afford even if I hadn't missed any work," she told him. "I love the work you give me, but I need to survive too."

"I was thinking you needed a salary," he told her calmly. "A salary, an expense account, and perhaps a gratuity for items retrieved. To be quite honest, I have been concerned about your divided focus, even without the added pressure you receive from the department to recruit more archaeologists."

She looked at him with stunned silence.

The professor continued, "Very well, you will be compensated for your lodgings as well, but that is all I can manage at this time. My research grants are large but are still limited for all of that. Is that agreeable?"

Cassidy, unable to fully articulate her thoughts gushed "Yes, thank you, oh my goodness that'd be great."

The professor nodded curtly and pointed towards the nearest empty table top, "Now let's see what you found."

THE KEY OF IMPASTO

CAROLYN R PARSONS & JD RYOT

CHAPTER ONE

"Tell me quick. You know I simply *hate* waiting."

It was rare that Professor Herbert Gamgee didn't hear someone approach him, given his lab was in a wide-open space, stark, sanitary, silver and cold that sound echoed through like an early warning alarm. Today, however, he was clueless that Cassidy Cane was behind him until she tapped him on the back and spoke. Professor Gamgee turned, and as he did, he knocked a small glass item over that rolled to the end of the table and off its edge. With the reflexes of a much younger man, he stretched out his hand and caught it before it dashed to bits on the cold hard floor. His heart pounded. *That* was a close call. He peered into the bulbous globe and gulped.

"Are you okay?" he asked.

"I'm fine, thank you. How are you doing?" Cassidy wound her hair into a ponytail and slipped a band over it to hold it in place.

"What?" Professor Gamgee asked.

"I said, I'm fine, how are you—" Cassidy repeated.

"No, not you, *her*," he said pointing to the odd-looking object he'd just saved from being bashed to dust on the floor. He turned back to it, tapped the noise-reducing headphones on his head and asked again.

"You know, Doc, there's a fine line where eccentricity slips over into wackadoodle, and you're close to crossing it. Her *who*?" Cassidy sized him up, finger at her chin. His white headphones and microphone oddly balanced with his thick glasses. Was he talking to a snow globe? No, he must have somebody on Skype. Yes. Of course.

"It was an accident, I didn't mean to...no, no, she's capable, she isn't clumsy at all. I was wearing the headphones and I didn't...yeah maybe you're right, we can put you in a—"

"I hope you and your *snow globe* will be *very* happy together. I'll leave you two alone." Cassidy lifted a sardonic brow, folded her arms and waited for him to regain his sanity. She had no intention of leaving.

"What?" He yelled, this time to Cassidy and not his imaginary friend.

"Take off the headphones." Cassidy rolled her eyes and pointed to her own ear to indicate what she was saying.

"What?"

"Take *off* the headphones," she repeated louder.

"Oh, yes. Cassidy. Okay, sorry, yes. Just a moment. Corie, I have to talk to Cassidy, I'll be right back," he said, before he pulled off the headphones and set them on the table.

"Who are you Skyping with?" Cassidy glanced around, looking for the computer.

"I'm not Skyping with anyone." He indicated the laptop on a shelf, lid shut.

"Then you're talking to yourself? And what is that anyway?" She pointed to the oddly shaped rock or geode or something on his desk that he'd nearly broken when she'd startled him.

"That is not a what. It is a who. Well, it's a what as well, I guess. It's all quite spectacular really, she I mean. Both, it, and her. She's your next assignment and she's a marvel."

"She?" Cassidy moved in closer, feeling a bit ridiculous. It looked was an inanimate object. She reached out and with her fingernail. *Tap tap tap.*

"No, not that. That's her, um, container. She's inside. Look right there, at the tiny window. I didn't notice at first, either. I found this in a potato field in the Netherlands near the portal at Kleve years ago. It was filthy, I washed it and used it as a paperweight. Can you believe it's been on my desk the whole time? I thought it was an ordinary lump of glass. Forgot all about it. Until yesterday when I finally heard her."

"Okay, back up. Heard who?" Cassidy was getting exasperated at his disjointed explanation.

"Corie. Corie in the jar."

"What?"

"Look. Here. Put these on, and look."

Gamgee held out the headset and Cassidy took it. She put on the headphones, adjusting them to fit over her hair.

"Say hello," Gamgee encouraged.

"Hello," Cassidy said, shooting him a look.

"Hallo," a woman's voice answered.

"Oh, hello," Cassidy repeated. Looking around the

room for the source of the voice. "Where *is* she?"

"Look in *there*," Gamgee said with a triumphant grin. "As I said, look through the tiny window."

Cassidy bent down for a closer look at the globe. There was a tiny electronic device attached to one side with tape, otherwise, it appeared to be a ball of etched glass and not really a globe at all. It was more jar-shaped, kinda fat in the middle, flat on the bottom as if it were carved out of a solid chunk of quartz or some similar crystalline mineral. She touched the top of it again, noting it had diamond-like cuts as well, tiny facets so small that it nearly appeared to be smooth until you looked at it closely.

She picked it up.

"Careful," Gamgee cautioned.

"I'm always careful," she volleyed.

Startled that it was so lightweight, she turned it over. Hollow perhaps? It caught the light as she rotated it and colours refracted off its surface, red, yellow, blue, Primary colours only. How peculiar, she thought. Then she spotted the window Dr. Gamgee had referred to. It was tiny, no bigger than a nano sim card for a smartphone, square and clear, like a little keyhole. She squinted and peered through it.

Then it opened and she didn't need to squint anymore. Without changing at all, in any discernible way, it expanded and suddenly, somehow, there was a full-size window in front of her. An illusion of one anyway as she still held the orb in her hand. It was impossible. The scale wasn't right. She glanced away, everything appeared normal, the globe still the same size in her hand, yet when she looked at the tiny window. Bam! It grew larger so that while she held a palm-sized container, the window to the inside of it allowed her to look as though she looked out one of the windows in Professor Gamgee's lab towards the outside.

"Say hello to Corie!" Gamgee said, his voice high pitched and excited as though he were introducing her to Howard Carter, the famous archaeologist who excavated King Tut's tomb. Except this was even more unlikely than meeting a dead hero.

Cassidy looked again. She'd seen the window but no person. In fact, all she could see was a swirl of red, yellow and blue that glazed the view, like a painted curtain over a *window*. She was about to call him on his practical joke when the colours morphed into a more defined pattern and churned like a smoothie in a blender until it seemed as though all the colours in existence blended together like the molten wax of a Crayola 64 crayon pack.

Then a whorl of light arranged itself in a mesmerizing prism until a tiny dot appeared in its center. The dot, that could only be explained as a point of clarity. It grew so that the window enlarged further before her eyes and she could see into its depths.

Cassidy was held spellbound. "That's incredible," she said as fields of green grass and blue sky unfolded in her line of vision. Then, finally, into the field, walked a young woman, probably around Cassidy's age, in a blue dress with a red blouse and yellow shoes. Her hair was the colour of wheat in sunshine and a smile dented her lovely face.

"I'm Corie Kerkvest and I need you to return the key home," the pretty young girl in the globe said. "Professor

Gamgee says you are the one who can."

"I'm Cassidy Cane," Cassidy replied, breathless at the scene before her.

"Do you see her? Do you?" Professor Gamgee asked, his voice as excited as a child's.

"I do," Cassidy said. She could not tear her eyes away from the world in the palm of her hand. She didn't even want to try. She wanted to look into the depths of the orb forever.

"Oops, Corie, she's stuck, like I was. Perhaps you should—" Professor Gamgee said, noticing Cassidy's trance.

The colours faded and in a moment Corie stood under a pale blue sky as ordinary as the one outside the lab, with bland white clouds that shuffled along.

Released from the hold on her, Cassidy looked away from the globe.

She turned to Gamgee and said in her best Desi Arnaz impression, "you, professor, have some 'splaining to do."

CHAPTER TWO

"I should have thought to connect *two* amplifiers before." The professor fussed with the electronic device attached to the side of the globe next to the first one.

"Can't I just talk to her without you?" Cassidy waved to the woman inside, still reeling from it all. Corie waved back. It was so strange. She should have looked like a miniature, but some trick of the window created the illusion that the inside of this odd globe was as large as the outside world — her world. Corie, inside the strange capsule, looked to even be a few inches taller than Cassidy herself. And those colours. They were just regular colours but — not. Somehow, they enthralled her far more than regular colours ever could. She had no idea why. Perhaps it was the lighting inside that caused that peculiarity. Whatever it was, once captivated, it was impossible to look away and the joy of that beauty, the swelling of pleasure in her chest from it, well, it was inexplicable really. It made her incredibly happy yet after, left her disconcerted.

"Waiting isn't so difficult if you learn to enjoy the view," Corie said, waving her hand so that the clouds over her head turned once more from ordinary white puffs to startling red, blue and yellow swirls blending into an incandescent mix of brilliant hues.

Cassidy jumped at her voice then, once more, became mesmerized by the spectacular effects.

"Cassidy," Gamgee said.

"Leave me alone." Annoyed, she swatted the air with the back of her hand in his general direction.

"Can you both hear me? Test-test. One, two, three..."

Corie jumped and placed her hands over her ears.

"Roger," Cassidy shouted, "but it's too loud though. Turn it down. For fritter's sake, turn it down!" She had been working hard to clean up her language a bit and had taken to substituting food terms when the urge hit. Having her ears blasted by Gamgee was reason enough to break out the baked goods.

"Who is Roger?" Corie yelled, pursing her lips in confusion.

"It's a saying, it means 'yes,'" Professor Gamgee replied. This time the volume was at a normal level. He looked chuffed with himself at his cleverness at having solved their communication issue.

"Alright, now you can tell me what this is about and what the job is," Cassidy said, disappointed that the clouds were back to boring puffy white but able to look away and ask the question of the professor to his face.

"I found Corie—" Professor Gamgee said.

"I was sent outside our—" Corie said at the same moment.

"Please, stop, I can't listen to you both at once. Professor, go first. And you're still a bit loud, lower your volume a bit more please."

"Okay!" Gamgee's voice blasted. Cassidy jumped and pulled the earpieces away from her ears.

"Wrong way!"

"Oops," He adjusted something. "Sorry. Is this better?"

"Yes," Cassidy adjusted her headset as well. "Now that we're all wired and my eardrums have been saved from shattering, go on, Professor." She peered at Corie who still had hands over her ears, just in case.

"I found Corie, the container specifically, in a potato field in Holland when I was scouting the portal there. It was covered in filth and I tossed it in my bag with a few other items. I brought it back with me and shined it up, laid it on my desk and pretty much forgot about it.

"Until I finally attentioned him," Corie said.

"How long has it been here?"

"A year," Gamgee responded. "Just a bit over that really. Anyway, I thought nothing of it. It sat there pretty and useful as a paperweight."

Cassidy had noticed it on his desk; hadn't thought much of it either. He had an assortment of odd artifacts about, some of which she'd acquired for him in her many jaunts through the portals this past while.

"I tried so hard to call him. To wake up him. But little is the sound of me." Corie had an interesting voice pattern but Cassidy could understand her. That would improve as the universal translating kicked in.

"So, you sat here? You could hear him? Us? But couldn't get us to respond?"

"Yes. Sound it is in but not it is out. Certainly, it was not much to listen until arrived you. Professor talks no interesting things. All sciency and boring it is."

"Physics isn't for everyone." Gamgee bristled and looked put out.

Cassidy held back a grin. He was as dry as paper at times though no one dared tell him that.

"I learn the language of you but no you me hear. And I try not until you much understood. Then I hear you, Traveller! That made me harder try."

"You found a way to be loud enough for him to hear you?"

"I found a way for him to see me. By making my, bows of rain."

"She means rainbows."

"I understood her."

Corie had learned the English language very well by listening and while she flipped words around sometimes, she was easy to understand because her pronunciation was nearly perfect. Oddly, Cassidy's translation abilities hadn't kicked in and while translating a new dialect of English into correct English was a bit of a challenge, it didn't matter. She could understand her perfectly well.

"Now we have to get her back home and the key has to be returned," Gamgee said. His spectacles perched on the bridge of his nose, his owlish eyes darting between the globe and Cassidy as he spoke.

"So, this receptacle that you're in, isn't your home?" Cassidy asked.

"Oh, no, this was my pod of escape. Created by my friend to save me. But I can't live here longer. I have to go back home."

"You see, she's the rightful Queen of her people," the

professor explained.

"President, but only *to be*, no *is*." Corie corrected. "We are democratic. I was voted. It was a large majority."

"She's the president-elect," Gamgee corrected. "She was in dire danger it seems and her friend, Eryn, figured out how to save her. By putting her in the pod and throwing her out the portal.

"Why the pod? Why not just come here. Or were you afraid because you are so tiny?"

"Because we know not if my form can live in your world without. But also, I am not tiny. I am the size of you. The pod smallerizes. But in my world, we'd be like-sized."

"What? So you've been shrunk?"

"It is hard. The inside of here is big, the outside of here is small. I am big inside. My container is small outside."

"Like a TARDIS?" Cassidy's eyes grew round.

"Without the time thing," Gamgee said. "At least, I think. Don't know for sure. If there are portals, and *smallerization* perhaps there are temporal possibilities as well." He grabbed a pencil and paper and started jotting down numbers and formulas. "Who's to say if there isn't a difference in time between our world and hers? We cannot know these things without further studies and the mathematics of it all is boggling even to me, and if I start figuring and I—"

"See, he is not exciting with the words," Corie said, rolling her eyes.

"Right, so, anyway, let's get back on topic." Cassidy's grin broke through, at Gamgee's crestfallen expression.

"So, if you're not sure you can survive in my world,

how can you know if I can live in yours?"

"Because travellers have come to our world before. The atmosphere is surviving okay but the militia no."

"So the air won't kill me but your army will. So why won't it work the opposite way?"

"A thousand days ago when it was old times, the old Gaughan-president make it so. I don't know how she did that."

"A thousand days?"

"See! There is a time thing. I think their time is different than ours. First I thought it was a language thing, but it seems their days are very long. Either way, this previous Gaughan made it so their people can't survive out here. Even though we can in their world." Professor Gamgee was still jotting notes down, focused again on the time element.

"That would explain why a year doesn't feel long to her." Cassidy guessed.

"That and because beautiful it is in the small world," Corie replied, waving her hand around and suddenly grass sprung up around her feet in more shades of green than stars in the night sky, waving and dancing about on the ground and into the distance. Cassidy lost herself in the beauty of it until it faded and Corie regained her attention by waving it all away.

"I can't think of anything else when you do that," Cassidy said. "I can't stop looking. Is your entire world like that? Because if it is, I will be absolutely useless. Professor, does it suck you in too? So that you forget everything else?"

"Yes. And you're right, there is no way you could navigate her world with such a distraction. In the globe she can change things but not in her world. Travellers have been there before, as she said, but they never get past the guards. I think that's why the Gaughan easily removed anyone who entered her world. These other travellers didn't know what it was like there and weren't prepared to handle their preoccupation with the colours."

"So if I do this, how do you expect me to not become mesmerized and captured immediately?"

"Because the fix is easy, it turns out. I tried a few things before you got here." He handed Cassidy a pair of aviator-style amber sunglasses. Ordinary, black-framed cheapies, not even Ray Bans. She put them on. The professor put a pair over his bottle-thick specs and then they peered together into the tiny window that somehow drew their vision forward so that they could both see in.

"Do your magic," Professor Gamgee requested.

Corie waved her hands and once more the brilliant green grass grew around her feet and the clouds in the sky burst into myriad colours. The air morphed into a dark blue and across the backdrop, a million stars swirled into being in a glorious yellow and orange pattern. Flowers sprung up from between the blades of verdant grass and waved their haughty yellow heads in an invisible wind. All this happened with all the glorious splendour as it had before, but this time Cassidy could think and look away, smile and respond. She was enamoured but not as literally spellbound as she was previously.

"That's spectacular but now I only see it, I don't feel like it has a hold on me. Much better." She pushed the sunglasses up.

"I wonder if maybe we can use a Bluetooth earpiece instead of these big headphones?" Cassidy asked. "I can hide that, blend in better?"

"Yes, we'll modify this. I had to amplify her voice to hear her well and made do but, certainly, I think we can make a smaller, wireless gadget before you go. To communicate I quickly modified a digital hearing-aid and connected it to the headset. All very simple really, but I was in a rush." Gamgee said. "We'll improve it a great deal before you leave."

"Now. Let's clarify a few things." Cassidy pushed the Ambervision glasses up and looked straight at Corie. "You were elected president of your country but your enemies decided to stop you so a friend threw you out here in a pod to save you but now you want me to go back to a place where others like me normally can't last more than a few moments before being tossed out and my only protection is a pair of cheap Ambervision sunglasses where we communicate via a device made from a hearing aid and a Bluetooth earpiece?"

"Well, yes…" Corie admitted.

"And your excellent navigation skills," Gamgee added.

"And if they catch you with me, they may not simply toss you out, they may imprison you. I am their president-elect who has vanished."

"What are the other obstacles?"

"They will be guarding the portal and the Crystal House of government. The service will not allow constituents into the Crystal House. I'm afraid that is a big challenge."

"Given there was an attempt on your life, why do you think it's safe for you now?"

"I don't. But I was only supposed to be hidden, not exiled. I must go back because people need democratic president, not stolen one."

Cassidy removed the amber glasses, Corie wiped a hand around so that the swirling mesmerizing colours vanished, much to her disappointment.

"I see." Cassidy folded her arms across her chest and pondered.

"Professor, what do you think?"

"I think it's likely a very dangerous trip. That you will need to utilize skills you've never used before and that it might be one from which you never return," Gamgee said.

A ripple of fear zipped down Cassidy's spine. So much could go wrong. This journey to Corie's land sounded rife with danger and was likely a journey of pure folly that could wind up with her imprisonment or worse. Plus, she hated the idea of a companion on an excursion such as this one. She had always been a loner on her adventures and sometimes she'd come close to disaster. Corie would be a distraction. So much of her success depended on instinct. This was a bad idea.

She looked from Corie to Professor Gamgee, all these thoughts swirling in her head like the magic in the domed container Corie inhabited.

"Perfect," she said. "Let's do it!"

CHAPTER THREE

It was not tulip season so Zundert, Holland didn't have the brilliant tulip fields The Netherlands was famous for. Cassidy would have to return in March or April and tour around Lisse a couple of hours south of this municipality if she wanted to enjoy their brilliant display. The famous windmills didn't have a specific season however, and near a potato farm behind the stone house of a local farmer was just such a structure, De Riekermolen, originally built in 1636.

"These are dreamt of in our land too," Corie's voice came through the tiny Bluetooth speaker in Cassidy's ear. They'd placed the orb in an exterior pocket of the backpack strapped to Cassidy with a small clear plastic front so she could see out her window.

"They are? So did you choose not to build them?"

"Of course we built them. If we dream something beautiful, it is built." Corie said as though that should be obvious.

"Ah, yes but here we have a few more steps that we take between thought and getting something built. Some ideas are not so good. These are though. Windmills were very useful. I think we're close to the portal. We're clear on the plan, right? We enter and you guide me past the guards. I'll be faster than most because I won't be distracted by the scenery like all the others and should make it to the Alizaron Hills where we'll solidify our plans before we journey to the presidential residence. Some changes may have occurred since you left that you're unaware of. But does that sound right?"

"Yes," Corie replied. "Where we get Eryn, start a search for the key, if he hasn't found it, and then reclaim my right to be president."

"And the militia?"

"Will follow the one with the key."

"And Eryn? You're sure he'll be willing to help?"

"Yes, he is trustful worth. Do you see a field of potatoes?"

"Potato field right over there, creek running through it past the windmill, so we're close."

"I wish I could guide you more," Corie said, "but being tossed through like a ball in a game is not memory making. And then I couldn't see until Gamgee cleaned my window."

"I hear it!" Cassidy said. A slight whirring sound indicated she should turn. She sniffed the air and veered to the left.

"It is a sound? Wait. Is it a smell too? My memory of it is of something lovely like—"

"Absinthe? I smell absinthe, licorice and spice." Cassidy sniffed again, turning towards where the aroma was stronger.

"Our word is turpenia, and yes, it is a delicious beverage. As your world loves its wine, we adore our turpinia. I recall a strong smell of that now. I had forgotten! Unfortunately, like your wine, a little accentuates the beauty of our lives but too much causes a blur of our colours and erases the light from it. We do not overindulge. For me to smell it so, it is too much." She broke into a sob.

"Okay, pull yourself together. You're a president and we're on a mission. No time for tears. Let's go." Corie sniffed again as Cassidy walked along the creek, following her nose towards the strong odor. She plodded past a wind-row of trees, walking like a tightrope walker between the lines of knee high potatoes, going straight through for acres. The ground became muddier and wetter as she walked and the smell of the heady fragrance grew in its intensity. The stench of the absinthe overpowered her as she closed in. She wrinkled her nose, her stomach rumbled, rejecting what had become a foul odour. As the colours had through Corie's window, the odour of the pungent elixir was entirely overwhelming. Cassidy took the bright red scarf off her neck and tied it over her face.

"This stinks," she grumbled into the Bluetooth.

"It smells like too much," Corie agreed, although for her it was somewhat dulled by the protection of her container.

Cassidy plodded on a few more steps then stopped. The suction of the mud held her fast.

"What the...?" She tried lifting her boots but to no avail.

"Is there a problem?"

"I'm stuck, Corie, I can't move even an inch." She wrenched to one side then the other trying to twist her boots out of the gluey mud. "I don't know what to do—"

Boom! The earth gave way and was drawn down, down, down, further, further, and further into the muck until she was up to her waist. She looked around for something to grab as she sank deeper and deeper into what smelled like pure absinthe, the essence of fennel and wormwood assaulting her nostrils as the ground pulled her in.

And then she saw the portal. Right at that moment that she stopped sinking. Of course, she thought. The mudhole was in the perfect spot to deter anyone from approaching it, if the heady stink didn't send them back first. Invisible a moment prior, now Cassidy could see it clearly.

Like a glazed window, the air swirled a slightly different colour, and someone in a panic, not looking for the opening, would be too distracted to see it or care. They'd haul themselves out of the mud at this point and go home to clean up. She had stopped sinking and could move again.

She used her arms to create purchase and hauled herself towards the portal, the smell of absinthe strong but bearable as she moved forward. Then with a big slurp she was out and only a few feet from the portal.

"I better get sorted first, Corie." She sat on the grass and whipped off her boots, dumping the gooey mud out, grimacing as the smell of the absinthe lingered around in the air. She quickly put her damp boots back on and stood, closing in on the portal that was now like a swirling frosted window as though a stained-glass pane had been caught in a whirlpool, all the colours swirling and glittering against the backdrop of the sky.

"Corie, I see it. Are you ready?" Her heart skipped a little and her stomach did a familiar flip-flop that could have been fear but was equally likely to be excitement. Or like the portal, a blend of all feelings one has when one is about to leap into the unknown.

"I am very ready," Corie said, excited to be going home at last.

Cassidy stood, bright green pants, now splattered with mud, blue top in the latest fashion Corie recalled from her home dimension, and a huge grin on her face. She pushed up the black-framed aviator glasses and steeled herself for the adventure, a rush of adrenaline bringing a smile to her face as she leapt.

"Ouch," Cassidy said, landing faster than she expected, a pain shooting up her leg. A curse word would have followed but before it could escape her lips she was struck from behind and knocked to her knees. She knew a second blow would follow so she ducked, then dodged to the right. The guard missed and she ducked to the left as he yelled for back up. Cassidy righted herself, noted there was no real pain in her wrenched foot and got her bearings fast. She sized up the guard, a portly old fellow with nothing more than a club type weapon. She could outrun him even if her ankle had been injured.

The distraction of the colours didn't require good guards at the portal and Cassidy had not been surprised that she evaded this guy's slow reflexes. Two more guards were running — if you could call it that — both of them, a man and woman, so languid in their movements they could have been a slow-motion film scene.

"Are they *all* this slow?" She yelled into the microphone. Without waiting for a response, she broke into a run.

"Yes, we put older, retired guards here. It's an easy job. Go, keep right, always keep right," Corie's voice in her ear said.

"Right, got it," Cassidy's swift legs darted towards the most brilliant green forest she had ever seen.

"Go, you are faster, I know you are." Corie encouraged. Cassidy didn't answer. But her speed increased at the pep talk in her ear. The distance between her and the guards lengthened.

"You are the fastest runner in my world," Corie said, and Cassidy believed her as even more distance fell between them. A glance back over her shoulder indicated that she was even further ahead, and she marveled how she had run so far, so fast. A handful of other guards had joined the first, but they had all stopped, watching as Cassidy disappeared into the spectacular forest.

Winded from the run, Cassidy found a tree and sat beneath it. She inhaled slowly. She'd run faster than necessary really, but better too fast than too slow.

Cassidy looked around at the spectacular colours. "How is it that things are so much *more* here?" She hoisted the backpack off her shoulder, opened the pouch and lifted Corie out. She peered inside. Like it had in her own dimension, the window gave the impression that the interior of the canister was so much bigger than it could possibly be.

"I suppose we are good at being more when more is good. And the opposite is true as well. We can be less when less is good. It was more of the less that got me inside a small place."

"Uh?" Cassidy rolled her eyes. "I think you're saying that you are able to create a small space that looks like *more* inside." Cassidy swiped at the mud on the lower half of her limbs, the smell of absinthe fading now that they were inside. The *how* of this all was a mystery. She mulled things over in her mind. Corie was president-elect and there was a key somewhere that they had to find and deliver to her ally, Eryn, and somehow this time Corie would be staying and standing up for her presidency instead of hiding in a jar and allowing herself to be tossed into another dimension. How this would happen, Cassidy didn't know. She'd placed a lot of trust in a tiny woman in a snow globe.

The best thing she could do was take stock of where things were right at the moment. She looked around her.

The damp moss huddled against the trees smelled of fragrant greenness while the dark fertile earth perfumed the ground upon which she sat. Ferns waved in a warm breeze that flitted through the spaces between the large evergreens and tall deciduous trees, that bore a remarkable resemblance to a regular forest back home. The woodland sounds were similar as well, and Cassidy identified several familiar chirps. With the glasses on, there were many similarities between their two places. The intensity of colour and light being the only difference and even with her eyes shaded by the amber lensed glasses, it was far brighter here and somehow, *extra*.

"This smells so much like home, like a regular forest," she commented.

"Then a regular forest is as good as smells become,"

Corie said.

"So, do you still want to stay inside? Perhaps we can make our way back together? Or do we stick to the plan?"

"I must stay inside. I need an apparatus to come outside. But even if I could, should somebody see me too soon we may not get inside the presidential house and that is where I need to be. I will have to stay inside, though I long to be free now that I'm home. Plus, I have to be on the pedestal." Corie wiped at a tear and Cassidy glanced away.

"An apparatus? A pedestal? Alright, we'll discuss these details later." Their flight had been booked so quickly and between cab drivers and other passengers they hadn't had a moment alone to discuss the details.

Cassidy unzipped the backpack, pulled out a smaller pack that had been custom made. For jumping through the portal the backpack was more secure. but for regular traversing of this world, Cassidy would transfer her into the front. The pocket they'd created was shaped perfectly for the canister that held Corie. She slipped it in, wriggling it to get it to the bottom. Then she aligned the window through the tiny square at the front of it so Corie could see out. Once that was in place, she slipped the straps over her shoulders, winding them around and buckling the bottom ends like a belt.

"Alright in there?" She knew Corie was, of course. Whoever had designed this weird pod had made it so Corie didn't bounce around in it at all no matter what sort of shaking happened. Cassidy pulled her ponytail tight, stood and threw her backpack over her shoulders again. Corie simply stood at the window and watched nearly completely unaffected by all the movement.

"I am well, and this is better so much." She exclaimed.

"It is for me too. You can give me better direction. So where to now, President Corie?"

"To the mountains! Go straight forward, the path will be there."

"To the mountains!" Cassidy repeated and started her trek forward towards the tall peaks that prodded the clouds in the distance.

CHAPTER FOUR

It took an hour to walk the scenic path into the Mountains of Senremy. Cassidy walked along the path, until they finally came to a plateau. There, a large village, Nommickdamen, sat underneath the foothills of a massive mountain range that stretched far into the lavender clouds and extended beyond their line of vision in either direction.

The town itself sat on an ocean inlet that travelled miles inland and around which wooden houses, brightly painted in all imaginable colours had been built. Like jellybeans they perched bright and joyful at the edge of the bay. The porches and walkways were adorned with brilliant blooms of unfamiliar flowers, their blossoms wafting a heady scent in the temperate air. The architecture of the homes had a European flair similar to Amsterdam but with an almost cartoonish extravagance to them. The sun blazed hot over the village and Cassidy felt a trickle of sweat down her spine. She whipped off her backpack, pulled out a canteen, wiped her brow and took a big swig. The cool water was like nectar and she took a second before replacing the lid.

"This is the land of *Moreisbetter*," she mused to Corie before replacing her backpack. The mud had dried and she could dust it off her legs now and even her boots were dryer as they strolled along the meadow to a wooden boardwalk that skirted the bright blue inlet. Fishmongers held out samples of their catch as other boats made off into the horizon, their vivid red, blue and yellow planking and sails blooming bright against the cornflower blue sky.

Cassidy blended in well. Aside from everybody wearing primary colours exclusively, they could have been home. She strolled through a small marketplace, pretending to browse.

"We need a car, or some other sort of transportation," Cassidy mused.

"There should be some around here somewhere."

"Do you see one?" Cassidy asked after they'd walked for another fifteen minutes.

"Keep walking. There should be a car park near the red house at the end."

"This street is so long I didn't think it had an end," Cassidy said.

"There, see?"

"Those are not cars! Those are electric scooters!"

"Is it? I mix the words up then."

"Maybe you should speak your language, what is it? Danch? Let me just use universal interpretation instead of using English," Cassidy said. She could drive a scooter, these looked similar to regular old earth scooters overall so that wasn't a problem. They'd just be more exposed than they would be in a car. And significantly less comfortable.

"Yes, I could do that. I will speak Danch," she said in her native language. Immediately Cassidy went into interpretation mode, the lilting dialect of English Corie had been speaking vanishing in an instant.

"Wow, that is much better. Who knew?"

"Is my English that bad?"

"No, it's actually quite excellent but the translation is superior it seems. We really don't need miscommunication to cause us problems. Now which one?" Cassidy walked along the rows of scooters so that Corie could see the choices."

The blue scooter with the red seat. That one. It belongs to the fishmonger and he won't miss it until later."

"How do you know it's his?"

"It's on his licence plate," Corie replied. Cassidy autotranslated the licence plate. Sure enough, it said "Purveyor of Sea Catch."

"So, I just steal a scooter?"

"*Borrow* a scooter." Corey corrected. "We shall replace it."

Cassidy glanced around the busy parking area. "So nobody will notice if I take it?"

"Nobody ever takes anything here, so they'll assume you own it."

"So I'm your first thief?"

"No, we borrow here. As I said, nobody steals, they borrow and repay."

"That's a lot of trust. And isn't he going to be inconvenienced when he discovers it missing?

"Why would he be inconvenienced? Somebody will

lend him another. He will know his will be returned or replaced."

"Your people are very trusting."

"My people are mostly very trustworthy."

"But not all or we wouldn't be here."

"Sadly yes. Not all." Corie's voice held despair at her betrayal.

"Well, cheer up, we'll get things all fixed up for you. Hang on, President-elect! Here we go." Cassidy heaved a leg over the seat of the scooter and settled in. She glanced around. Nobody looked their way.

"Hold the brake on the left handle, then push the yellow button."

Cassidy did and the scooter purred to life. She checked out the instrument panel, sized up the handlebars.

"You just push the initiator," Corie said. It's the handle on the right. That will make it go forward, again to go faster and then again to go even faster. I would only do the first and second notches until you have practiced a bit."

"Okay. No helmet?" Cassidy didn't fancy a fractured scull in a strange new world. Or even in the old one.

"Oh, yes, in the pouch beside the seat."

"There is a little pouch here, but that can't be it." Cassidy looked on the other side.

"It will be blue with a helmet symbol on it."

Cassidy bit her lip and narrowed her eyes. This tiny pouch, the size of a coffee mug could not possibly hold a helmet, but she opened it anyway. Inside was a small, flat, silver square. She reached in and pulled it out.

"Unfold it." Corie instructed.

A doubtful expression on her face, Cassidy did as she was told, pulling apart the tiny foil square. It opened into a hat shape that somewhat did resemble a helmet.

"This? This is soft. How does this protect the head from injury?" She slipped it over her hair.

"Fasten it." Corie grinned. She liked surprising Cassidy and anticipated this would be a good one.

Cassidy pulled the band underneath her chin and with a snap connected it to the other side. The moment she did the soft silver material engaged in a metamorphosis whereby it became a solid helmet, perfectly molded and held fast to Cassidy's head.

"This is spectacular," Cassidy said, moving her head from side to side. "How the heck does that happen?" She closed up the case, considered its size, touched the helmet and again shook her head.

"More is less when less is needed," Corie's voice in her ear said.

"And less is more when more is needed. I don't think this is possible. How?"

"How it works is a secret. It uses proprietary technology owned by the government. It must only be used for the betterment of the people."

"And using it to save the president-elect counts for sure, right?"

"Eryn thought it counted. It's the first time it was used to secure a person, however."

"Wasn't that risky?"

"I've never been opposed to some risk. You can't rise to become president without taking chances."

"A girl after my own heart. Well, now we're off to the

castle."

"Presidential residence," Corie corrected.

"Presidential residence. Got it. Hang on."

"I can't really hang on?" Corie's wan voice said.

"I mean, here we go!" Cassidy said and hit the control. The scooter started to move. She felt for her balance, settled into her seat. Slowly they inched forward. Feeling the familiarity of the machine — it was not unlike a scooter back home — feet on the pedals she pulled out, checking each way for traffic before edging out onto the quiet street then around and up over the hill and away from the canal side of the village.

She hit the control again, picking up speed. She tested the brakes. They lurched to a stop. Too much. She moved forward again, this time using a gentle touch on the brake control easing to a stop.

This street was filled with traffic, and more people felt better to Cassidy, less out in the open and noticeable, a preferred state on a stolen vehicle.

"Follow this upwards then you will come to the sign for Senremy Road. That is the mountain road that will take you through to Dream Tams, the capital city of Ashlen Der Tenth where the presidential residence awaits."

CHAPTER FIVE

Senremy Road. Dream Tams. Ashlen Der Tenth. Cassidy repeated the three over and over under her breath so she wouldn't forget. *Senremy Road. Dream Tams. Ashlen Der Tenth.*

Cassidy laid on the speed once she was out of traffic and in the clear on the isolated mountain pass. Without the rumble of a noisy engine and the incredibly smooth handling of the scooter, she found she was enjoying herself immensely. The mountains were unlike any others she had ever seen. The rock formations were an azure colour in some places and then further along the road was tunnelled between cliffs of the brightest emerald green. The trees were taller in the foothills. As she ascended, she found open places where the mountainside shielded her with a rock side on the left and a clear open drop on her right that was filled with trees of amber, gold, red, and green. The sky above was a deep blue and the roadside was edged with blossoms in every possible shade of yellow. There was little black or white visible although there must have been to create the dark purples of the landscape in the distance and ruddy brown of the dirt road. It was highly distracting in its stark bold beauty, even with the sunglasses. So much so that the other scooters were nearly at her taillights before she saw them in the tiny rear-view mirror on her right handlebar.

"Corie, we've got company. Bright fuchsia scooters with white lights flashing. Police?"

"Yes, law keepers. Are you going too fast?"

"What is the speed limit?"

"Second button!"

"I'm on button four, butter on a biscuit!" Cassidy exclaimed, shooting a glance at the mirror.

"Hit button five! If they catch us, they will put us inside the dungeon for this. We can't delay, we must get away."

"Alright, hang on tight!" Cassidy flicked the accelerator to five and the whirring of the scooter's purr got a shade higher. The wind slapped around her face and she saw a distance between her and the law enforcement behind her grow incrementally in the tiny mirror. Revved from the excitement of the chase she leaned into the wind and considered the road before her. It was narrow with a thousand-foot drop on one side, a steep rockface on the other, turns and twists like spaghetti in a bowl, and nowhere to go but up. With the cops of another realm hot on her trail, a tribble of excitement flitted through her. Now *this* was an adventure.

The cops narrowed the gap again and Cassidy considered the button. She felt like she was flying now, and the quietness of this scooter's engine amplified that feeling. This was a new vehicle to her and these were treacherous mountain roads. She wasn't afraid of heights, but she had no desire to die by falling from a great one into a forest, no matter how leafin' pretty it was. She leaned in further, kept going forward but the police were gaining on her.

Then she spotted an approaching scooter. It appeared to have the same markings as those at her tail. Cinnamon Buns, she thought. Still, kept going, the momentum driving her forward, pure adrenaline in her veins now.

They could stop her, but would they? Suddenly the cops ahead of her stopped. They maneuvered their bikes sideways to create a roadblock. They knew she'd have to stop or slam into them. She slowed a little to give herself a second or two to think.

Then bam, the bike accelerated at a push of the button. And they were back up to six.

"Hang on Corie, your cops are playing chicken and I'm not one. We're going through."

"Yes! That is the right thinking! You are the best scooter rider on this mountain, I know you can go through and past them at your top speed. You are so much better than they are."

"I believe you!" Cassidy shouted and with a loud whoop she pushed the final button igniting a flame beneath the bike that shot it upwards and forwards at the same time. It rose only a few feet off the ground, but it was enough to take Cassidy up, up, up, then over, over, over the police scooters and onwards along the mountain trail until they were well past any chance of the police gaining on them, then she pulled her scooter back to six level, applied the brake a touch and they slowed and lowered until the wheels touched down on solid ground. Upon impact Cassidy lost control of the scooter for a moment, bouncing like a rubber ball but she regained it by leaning in the opposite direction, eyes firmly on the road. Once she was on solid ground she decreased further to a far more sensible three speed.

"Woah, these things can fly!" Cassidy said with a loud laugh of delight.

"All the things can fly if you write them so, I knew it." Corie said. "But today it was just this scooter."

"Did you know it could?"

"The first flying thing I saw was in your world. Once I believed it could, as you did, so it could."

"This is a very strange place, Corie. But I like it."

"I do as well, Cassidy Cane. It is good to be home."

CHAPTER SIX

Stars popped out in spiral clusters against a darkened blue sky. Cassidy manoeuvred the scooter up a pathway towards a bright yellow cottage trimmed with yellow. Corie directed her to a doorway on the side and they parked with the scooter facing out the path in case a getaway was required.

"We'll rest here for the night. This is The Lamartine Cottage" Corie said. "It once belonged to our greatest artist. I purchased it after I graduated from Huysmans School of the Arts." Corie knew she could sleep at any time, but Cassidy wasn't in a controlled pod and needed to rest before entering the city tomorrow.

Cassidy looked around the cottage. It was essentially one large room with a kitchen to the left and on the right there was a bed facing a wall of windows. Everything in the room was painted various shades of white giving it a sense of space in the small surroundings. It was a stark contrast to the brilliant colours of the outside world which could still be seen, despite it being dark outside, through the large panes of glass that overlooked the natural environment.

"This view is spectacular." Cassidy walked over to the window. Outside a lake glittered in the light of a fat gibbous moon. Surrounded by forest, she felt calm and relaxed for the first time since entering Corie's world.

"I agree. And you can remove the glasses. The night will protect you from the enthrallment."

Cassidy slipped off the amber visions. The view outside the window transformed from a darkened pretty scene to a swirling canvas of colour against a backdrop of brilliant flaming stars. Cassidy was spellbound. But not literally this time.

"It's like I can see the wind," she said. She pulled off the pouch that carried Corie's container and set it on a table by the bed facing the same view that mesmerized her.

"You can. But you can also look away at night. It's not as magnetic."

"Yes. Perhaps we should have come at night. Just travelled through and I wouldn't have needed the glasses."

"I didn't know the time difference between your space and mine," Corie said. "We got lucky. Our night lasts eight hours only. We will have lots of daylight to finish this journey."

Cassidy rarely knew what she was getting into when she entered a new dimension, and this was the first time she had a guide. It would be highly unfair to expect her to know how to make this one hundred percent easier. But it certainly helped. Almost too much.

"I feel like this is too easy," Cassidy said, pulling out a toothbrush. When had she had time before to enjoy such luxury on a mission?

"That chase by the law enforcers was easy?"

Cassidy grinned. "No, that was, er, somewhat challenging."

"Then what is easy?"

"Perhaps it's this." Cassidy waved her arm around the cottage. "It feels very cozy and safe. It's also beautiful."

"Thank you. I like it too. It's a retreat really. A place to meet my muse."

"And this muse is very important to you?"

"Ah, yes. Inspiration is everything. Imagination is our most glorious gift, and we must allow it free reign to fully develop our society."

Cassidy waved her toothbrush around, "Hold that thought," she said as she went into the bathroom, brushed her teeth, and slipped into the shower, scrubbing off the mud still caked on her from earlier in the day. She returned in a sheath of white that Corie said would be hanging in the bathroom. Everything inside white, everything outside all the colours possible.

"All sorted?" Corie asked.

When Cassidy glanced inside the pod, she saw that Corie was dressed in white nightwear similar to what she'd given Cassidy.

"I have questions. Are you too tired?" Cassidy asked.

"No, it's been an easy day for me. Please ask what you want to know."

"Explain your politics. How you get elected. Who runs?"

"Oh, that is a very interesting thing. Mainly we have a competition as to who can do the most for people's lives. Everybody gets a vote, man, woman, and child and voting is mandatory."

"Children vote too?"

"Of course, even children, though parents may help them understand but who better to have new ideas and great understanding of what can be, the potential out in life, than those at the start of it?"

"I guess. And whoever gets the most votes wins?"

"Yes."

"You won?"

"By what you would call a landslide. My imagination is far superior to my opponent's."

"Your imagination? What about your policies."

"Well, they are built accordingly, after I'm elected."

Cassidy's look of disbelief was not subtle.

"Surely that's not far-fetched. Your world has similar."

"No, we don't."

"Do you think your amazing airplanes exist without somebody imagining flying? Radio? Have you ever seen a radio wave? Still, you have radio, wireless internet, electricity. You had people on your moon?" Corie replied. "We have no flying. We have no birds so we have not thought of it."

"Wow, no flying? Also, those people are not who we elect to run our countries."

"Perhaps they should be. The people with the best imaginations for what could be, the dreamers should lead those who implement the ideas, which in turn leads to better society."

"But there is a reality that to be good at governing you need to be more business-like, more pragmatic."

"We take a different approach. We elevate the creators,

the visionaries and put them in places of leadership. The artists, the poets, music makers. The storytellers imagine and share the world we want to live in. Then the scientists, the businesses, all work to ensure it is realized."

"Is everything you think of eventually created?"

"Of course not. We have many failures. But that isn't a worry. We're looking for innovative thoughts and new, outrageous ideas in our leaders. We elect dreamers and thinkers and worry not about the impossibility."

"What about the economy?"

"It follows that if you're imagining, researching, developing and building you're also selling." She lifted her shoulders in a shrug as if to say, *this is not rocket science.*

"Taxes?"

"Very unpopular. But necessary."

"It sounds perfect."

"It is not. I wouldn't have been exiled to your world if it were. My campaign was good. I wrote the story with all of my imagination of flying into space and going as far as we could go. I performed a play with all the joy and hope, fears and laughter of the human experience and I sang a song of love and heartbreak, healing, faith and family. Then I painted our world in its exquisite beauty so that people loved it more and cared more for it. This is all we do to campaign, and I told the biggest and best dreams, so I won."

"So, nothing about policy or taxes. The economy?"

"If people know to imagine the impossible, all the facets of the human reality, all the rewards of a life of love, and know their world is so beautiful they would not harm it for anything but rather bask in its health, then they will pay exactly the taxes required, find the right policies and politics and science to create all they need to be happy citizens, will they not? Everything starts with what you imagine. You would call this inspiration, and for you, it is separate from politics. For us, that is the foundation. We call it, navgoh or truelife."

"What was this big idea that you had, that got you elected and tossed out into our realm?"

"It wasn't any of my big ideas. It was a smaller, much more practical one. I wanted to use these globes, like the one I'm in, for our prisoners. Give them quality of life even while isolated. Right now, they are in cages and dungeons. This technology was dreamt of by my predecessor, built by his team and launched shortly before he retired. I wanted to utilize it further and make more humane prisons out of them. To give people worlds to live in that were interesting and healing for them."

"Wow! That's advanced thinking. I would think it a big idea."

"Perhaps, though we already feel that people who do wrong aren't necessarily unable to contribute. And they are still people. So perhaps it's a bigger step in your world to this idea, than to ours."

"And who decided this wasn't a good idea?"

"The people who own the prisons, naturally," Corie said.

"Naturally." Cassidy rolled her eyes. Not so very different after all, she thought. "So, this place isn't perfect?"

"Nothing is perfect, and that's never the dream we imagine. People will always get sick, have heartbreak, do wrong, be wronged and feel all the things people feel.

They will give birth, and die, and in between there will be problems. If that changed there'd be no more need for imagination and creativity would there?"

"Do you think it is possible that your friend, Eryn, threw you into our world to save you? Or to be rid of you?" The question had been on Cassidy's mind since their first meeting and asking it was imperative. If Eryn were not the hero Corie thought he was, then she needed to know.

"Eryn is the person who got me elected. He was also in line to govern with me as deputy president. I think he is trustworthy."

"Think, but not certain?"

"Nothing is certain."

"I guess we have no choice but to trust that then, until we know better." Cassidy slipped under the covers of the bed, fluffed up a pillow and yawned. "I'm gonna get a bit of shut-eye. Good night, Corie."

"That is true. Sleep well, Cassidy Cane," Corie said.

"I'll try. I don't know if I've ever slept well on a mission."

"You will sleep better than you have ever slept before, for eight hours at least," Corie suggested from her spot on the table.

And interestingly enough Cassidy awoke, exactly eight hours later, as rested as she'd ever been in her life.

CHAPTER SEVEN

And it was good she was well rested and in peak form because peering through the window into the cottage was a tall man with long wild red hair who appeared as though he was ready to break through the glass and kill her.

Cassidy leapt from the bed and reached over, fumbling for the earpiece. She jammed it in her ear, never taking her eyes off him.

He waved.

"Corie, there is a man. Do you see him."

"Of course I do. He is the caretaker of my cabin. His name is Galon. He is harmless."

"He doesn't look harmless!"

"He just isn't expecting you to be here. You must go and invite him in. Don't tell him I'm here."

"What will I say? How will I explain my presence?"

"You're smart, Cassidy Cane. But I'll help. Put on your sunglasses. The light—" She was right, the sun was starting to brighten out beyond the caretaker's back and Cassidy reached over and put the black-framed lenses on her face.

Grabbing a robe as Corie directed her to, she walked

over to the door.

"Galon?" She queried, repeating the name Corie said.

"Yes, but who are you?" He scratched his head, his expression still somewhat murderous.

"I'm a friend of Corie, she told me to use this cottage any time I travel through the area. And yes, while I know my friend has disappeared, I had hoped the cottage would still be available for my use and here it was, vacant. So, I stopped for the night. My apologies."

"Yes, this is a personal property of the president. President Corie." Galon's face softened as he spoke.

"He called me *president*," Corie said, her voice shocked. "Not president-elect. Ask him why. Galon is always very proper."

"I am interested, why do you think of her as president?" Cassidy arranged her face in a perplexed expression.

"Because she is. Certainly, you know she's been given the title in absentia? You do not know recent news?"

Galon motioned as though asking permission to come in and Cassidy stepped aside. She glanced at the table where Corie's globe had been set the night before and then realized it pretty much matched the decor of the space anyway. White sculptures were in various places around the cottage, the art supposedly dark and morbid to a culture that valued light and colour so much.

"What?" Corie screamed in her ear.

"What?" Cassidy yelled back.

"Are you okay?" Galon inquired, his face returning to its scowl.

"Sorry, I was just shocked that's all." Cassidy darted

her eyes away at the fib.

"Careful," Corie whispered.

"It's your fault," Cassidy whispered back.

"What's my fault?" Galon asked, wide-eyed now.

"That I'm so easily shocked and that, er, that I'm awake so early."

"You need to be careful," Corie advised.

"I am!" Cassidy said.

"You're what?" Galon's expression now indicated that he thought her a few colours short of a full palette.

"I am unaware of the recent events. My apologies. I've been — er — traveling. That's why I'm here, you know, on my — er — travels. So, I'm...I'm rather tired. And I've had this annoying buzz in my ear..."

"Hey!" Corie exclaimed.

"I understand." Galon gave a half smile, and he wasn't nearly so wild looking when he did.

"Please, catch me up on any news." Cassidy pulled her robe closer and indicated a chair to Galon who pulled it out and settled down into it.

"Thank you. So you see, when President Corie disappeared, there were many who thought the second place winner should be president but Eryn said no. He said that until she is found, she shall remain president as declared by the senate, in absentia. So, without the reversal of the vote of the senate, the parliament will run without a president until the next election."

"And they can do that?"

"Yes, nobody knew the president would be gone this long or I'm sure the senate would have voted different. Only a few voted to put her opponent in place."

"Okay, so she is president still."

"Yes. The opponents are naturally perturbed and are pushing for a new election. Eryn's fearful for his life of course. He gained nothing by opposing them but to become their newest target. And to become the president's Regent."

"Regent? So, acting president. Why do you think the president would disappear in the first place?" Cassidy asked, leaning in, hoping for some insight from this simple man who looked after the property. She knew of course, but what did the people think?

"Most think she was disposed of, that the opponents made her disappear to get the job which is why they're not supportive of the in-absentia decision."

"And the rest?"

"Think she took the key for nefarious purposes and ran away. I cannot, however, think what those purposes would be. But it has vanished as well." He looked pained now. Cassidy noted, this wasn't something he wanted to believe at all.

"What if she were to come back?" she asked.

"If she were to return to us now, she'd be fully the president but, of course, that doesn't help with the key."

"Tell me about the key?"

"The key of Impasto? It disappeared with the president and she is accused by her opponents of stealing it. It would be very difficult to prove she didn't take it."

"What would happen to her if she came back without it?"

"I'm afraid she'd be president but without the key, she would stand trial for stealing it. You really have been travelling a long time?"

"Yes, very long. So, what is this evidence that she has the key?"

"Well, there is the letter supposedly wrote saying she stole it."

"I wrote no such letter," Corie said.

"I don't believe she wrote any such letter," Cassidy said.

"Why not?" He rarely found somebody who thought this way.

"Because if you steal something you don't tell everybody. You hide it," Cassidy said.

"That's right!" Corie said.

"That's a very good point. And one I've made myself. But disappearing made her look even more guilty," Galon responded.

"Can't deny that." Cassidy's mind sifted through the new information.

"Would you like to be imprisoned for life? That's what's going to happen to me, and our prisons are not pleasant places." Corie's voice was sad.

"No," Cassidy said.

"What?" Galon eyed her suspiciously.

"No, problem," she replied in Danch, shaking her head. So Corie had been accused of a crime at the moment of her election but she'd told Dr. Gamgee she was thrown into our world because she was in danger from the opposition. Something was rotten in the State of Denmark. Or rather, Ashlen Der Tenth. And she needed to get to the bottom of it before she went any further.

CHAPTER EIGHT

Galon walked down the pathway and Cassidy watched him leave through the big windows, mind whirling at this recent turn of events. She turned on her heel and went back towards the living room.

"What are you thinking, Cassidy Cane?" Corie's voice jarred her from her thoughts.

"I am thinking that you lied to me." Cassidy whirled around and went to the table, picked up the container holding Corie and turned it so she could see its inhabitant, face to face.

"I did not lie. I just did not say it all."

"It is very important that I have all the information I can when embarking on one of these journeys."

"Well, you do have more than usual, no?" Corie spread her hands, palm up as though to convince her.

"I did not know I was traveling with a person who lies!" Cassidy's eyes flashed with annoyance. "I needed that information."

"I left out a bit of detail. Would you have still brought me if I had told you I was accused of theft?"

"Probably. No, most definitely. Because you still

needed to get back here. Now though, not only am I an outsider but I'm aiding a person charged with criminal activity. Even here, surely that's a crime?"

"Well, your being here at all is a crime," Corie responded. "And if I am president, I can pardon you of everything."

"I have a question. What happens to all those who jump through without glasses? What do your guards do with them?"

"Oh, they receive the worst possible punishment," Corie answered.

"Your prison? Or are they—?"

"They're caught immediately due to their entrancement, then immediately tossed back into your rather dull world."

"Our world isn't dull!" Suddenly Cassidy's affection for her own plane of existence welled up. They had problems, sure, it got boring at times, yeah, but it was a pretty spectacular place, earthside.

"If it is not dull, Cassidy Cane, why do you spend so much time jumping out of it?" Corie inquired.

"That, President, Thief of keys, is none of your beeswax." Cassidy walked across the room, exasperated. This place *was* enthralling, its odd bright and colourful scenery, a blazing glory of beauty unlike any that existed on earth, but it was also *too* jam much. At least for her. For someone like Corie it likely did seem like their world was a muted version, but it suited Cassidy just fine. So why did she spend so much time out of it if it did?

She pondered the question as she dressed, then flitted around in the bright kitchen making food. Why was she here anyway? This was the first time she'd brought something back to a world rather than fetching something. It should have been an advantage having a guide, but it was becoming a challenge, especially since President Corie's instructions interfered with her own very well-honed intuition.

She relaxed her shoulders, inhaled a deep breath and thought about it some more. She pondered how she'd felt the moment before the caretaker had been identified, then after, during her entire conversation with him, she had been fraught with tension. A stress that left her wound up. That tight, agitated feeling had woven itself through her nervous system like a subway winds its way through a maze of tunnels. And she had *loved* it. That's why. It wasn't her preference for other worlds that had her leaving her own so much, it was her love of a good adventure and these adventures were the ultimate rush. Jumping into the unknown, using all her talents, knowledge and skills to retrieve, or replace whatever needed to be retrieved or replaced was the ultimate thrill and she needed it like she needed the water that filled her glass as she poked at the food she'd heated. It was oddly familiar, if a brighter yellow. She picked up the bright purple earthenware jar that had been zapped in some sort of oven as Corie had instructed her. What was this anyway? The jumble of letters assembled into sense during her interpretation of the alphabet, and she snorted. Some things never change, she thought as she pulled out a spoonful of the super bright, and delicious pasta.

CHAPTER NINE

The mac and cheese was excellent for preserved food in a foreign dimension, Cassidy thought. And, as ticked as she was at Corie, they needed to get moving to the presidential residence and return this stupid key that Corie insisted she didn't steal, then somehow reinstate her to her rightful place as president, convince this Eryn guy that she was safe there and to not bottle her up like jelly anymore and then get herself home. Cassidy found it heartening that they only threw interlopers from other paradigms out of the world and back into their own realm, rather than a more permanent solution but, of course, in the past they never got past the lazy guards at the portal. They might not be so merciful with someone aiding and abetting a thief, even if the person they aided happened to be president of their country.

"Snow! It's snowing!" Corie's excited voice exclaimed.

Cassidy grabbed the earpiece and yanked it out. "Don't shout, you'll burst my eardrum!"

"I'm sorry," said a distant voice.

Cassidy replaced the Bluetooth. "That's okay, look,

I'm not pleased you lied about the key and I'm going to need the truth from here on in but what is so interesting about snow? I noticed it had snowed when your caretaker showed up. It's a problem." If Cassidy knew anything, it was that any plans made were always made more difficult, if not impossible upon the arrival of the horrid stuff.

"Look at it, Cassidy. It is the most spectacular thing. You are too far away, go to the outside, open the door!"

Shrugging her shoulders and heading outside, Cassidy braced herself for the cold. The morning sun was masked by the white flakes that flew to and fro outside the door of Corie's cottage. It had already started accumulating and Cassidy was about to close the door and complain about the goose bumps rising on her arms when her eyes caught the glint of colour in the swirls of the flurry. She put her hand out and allowed a few flakes to land on her open palm, then pulled her hand back before they could melt on her warm skin. Each snowflake had the geometrical uniqueness of any snowflake she'd ever observed but instead of being white and silvery the tiny flakes sparkled with colour that glinted and shone in the bright morning light. Then she looked more closely at the blizzard that blew about them and saw within the veils of the cold precipitation, swirling ribbons of rainbows, arching and twisting in the air.

"Oh, my—" Cassidy forgot the cold and stepped outside, nearly as mesmerized by the snowstorm as she'd been by the scene inside Corie's habitat before she'd started wearing the sunglasses.

"It's lovely, is it not?" Corie's voice in her ear asked. They'd not added snow inside her own habitat, there being no time to figure out how to create seasons. "Bring me out!"

"What? Oh, yes. No. After. We can't stand here staring at the snow forever. We need to get moving, get you where you need to be."

"Okay, but you'll need the fast-tracker for the snowy roads, Cassidy Cane. It has snowed all night and piled up."

"The fast-tracker?"

"That's a machine like a scooter but for on the snow."

"So like a snowmobile?"

"Yes, perhaps like that. And you'll need winter wear. The hall cupboard has all of my winter clothes. Take what you need. It will get colder as we go up the mountain, but the snow is timely. We can traverse the winter trail instead of the roads. It'll be a few hours longer but so much more pleasurable and that is the most important thing."

"Is it, Corie? Is it really?" Cassidy rolled her eyes.

"It most certainly is."

"You'll explain some more about the key of Impasto on the way, I trust?" Cassidy asked as she closed the front door, reluctantly blocking the brilliant glitter of shiny flakes outside. She swerved towards the closet and found herself with several one-piece snowsuits in yellow, red and blue. "So much for being camouflaged." She rolled her eyes again and grabbed the red one. This place and it's bright colours. Now she would be whipping up the wintery roads shining like a beacon to all and sundry who saw her along the way. Might as well paint a bullseye on her back and shine a spotlight on it. Why not white? With some pretty sequins to match the outside but oh, no, we must be as bold as a zit on a teenager's nose.

"Are you okay, Cassidy?" Corie asked. "You've been quiet for a long time."

"I'm just thinking how lovely and bright this snow-suit is, Corie." Her voice dripped sarcasm as she finished putting it on and turned to get her backpack for the trip ahead.

***

The snow machine, or Fast-tracker as Corie called the vehicle, looked like a snowmobile with a few variations. It was, of course, a bright scarlet. Its front was pointed, like a snowplow blade. The visor was clear and large and from what Corie told her, did not allow the falling snow to stick to it. The gears were similar to the scooter and after a few runs around the significantly large garden, now blanketed with multicoloured snowbanks, Cassidy had figured them out. Despite her concern over having to travel trails, instead of roads, on an unfamiliar machine, and the pending intrusion of past presidential protectives services, she couldn't help but feel awed by the marvelous precipitation. This place, with its over the top beauty, and weird political priorities, was as fascinating as any place she had ever visited.

And while the miracle that they'd figured out how to create small places that were bigger on the inside, or smaller on the outside if you were the type to borrow prose from popular television programs, was incredible, even that seemed insignificant in moments when the sky burned with red, amber and green and the snow fell in flakes of multicoloured glory.

"Are you ready to go, Cassidy Cane?" Corie asked.

Cassidy had wedged her tiny miraculous habitat between windshield and handlebars and lashed it firm with a rope Corie had directed her to in an out-building.

"I am ready to go. So, I am to head straight down the trail and you'll guide me from there on?"

"I will be your guide to the residence, and I will tell you the story as we go."

Like the scooter, the snow machine was quiet. After navigating for ten minutes or so Cassidy felt like she had the driving down pat.

"I'm ready," she told Corie as she sped up a little, eyes fastened on the trail ahead, heart fastened on the beauty of the snow that fell in colourful patterns as she accelerated through the bright purple and blue trees.

"In your world you have computers and things called servers to keep all the information on, true?"

"Yes, that's correct. Pretty much all is digital now. Though we still do have paper files. Wait. Is that what the key of Impasto is?"

"It is a repository and contains all the government files for all of the people. It's the government itself. The president is presented with it upon the showing and induction ceremony. It disappeared before I was due to be presented as president. I was accused of stealing it."

"Why would you steal something you were going to have access to in a few days?"

"They did not notice the theft. A fake was put in its place. That was my defence. But then it was proposed that I had won by taking the key before my election therefore that's why I won, I had an advantage."

"So, there is information in the key that could help

you win?"

"Possibly. You see, it holds all the favourite dreams and wishes of all the people, their favourite colours and places, the stories they wish to hear. So having it before the election might well be a big advantage."

"But wouldn't they have noticed it missing before the election?"

"It was replaced so nobody knows exactly of the theft's time. It may have been taken at any time. It was when they went to ready it for presentation that the curator of the files discovered that it was a fake."

"How big is this key of Impasto?"

"It is as small as my hand," she replied.

"You people are good at making small things hold bigger things."

"We call it reductivity. You find that very interesting don't you, Cassidy? I'm glad you do. I too think it is. We have been working on it a long time. Our great President Avvignon Ghenct was really the imaginer of it though. And directed the scientists to create it."

"So, reductivity, not smallerization?"

"It is both. Reductivity is the process whereby smallerization is achieved. It is easy with information. Harder with people and places but we've succeeded."

"Will I be able to learn how it works before I leave?" Cassidy asked.

"I don't even know how it works, that is for the scientists to handle. But I can introduce you to one of them if we're successful."

"You're not interested?" Cassidy asked.

"Once president, I won't have time to be interested in simple science. I'll be too busy imagining the things I need them to create."

"You know what? You have a strange culture, Corie." She accelerated and the snow machine picked up speed. The reduction helmet kept her ears warm and the wind whipping around her face was brisk. Now that she was getting the hang of it, she realized that this entire part of the journey could be quite fun.

"Faster," Corie encouraged, catching onto her enthusiasm.

Cassidy required no such encouragement. She increased her speed even further, the ungroomed trail smooth beneath the tracks. The wind in her face, the multi-coloured snowbanks on either side of her had her shouting with glee as she took a large turn around a clump of forest.

"Whoohooo!" she bellowed.

Corie laughed in her ear. "I thought you didn't like the winter," she said, wishing she were seated and not encased in a small container like some display statue.

"I like this part," Cassidy yelled, zooming past an outcrop of rock and straightening onto a long, open field where the colourful snowflakes were picked up by the pastel winds and made to dance around before her.

"Corie, who the honeysuckle is that?" she asked at the realization that she'd spoken of her enjoyment far too soon.

"Oh, no, this is not good," Corie said.

"I suspected it wasn't," Cassidy replied wondering what to do next. For there, in the distance stood a shadow that appeared to be a tall man with a weapon slung across his shoulder. And he was waiting for them.

CHAPTER TEN

Surrender!" Corie screamed. "I'm shutting down. Pretend I am but art.

"Surrender? What? Wait, no! Who is it?"

"Pretend you can say you learned about sunglasses from a returning explorer. Whatever you do, they must not see me."

"Perhaps I can escape," Cassidy's words trailed off as another stepped into sight, then another ten, followed by at least another hundred.

"Corie, are you there? Corie?" Cassidy asked, voice desperate as she geared down the machine as the growing army filled her view.

"Great. Just great. Now you shut up." She slowed down the machine, coming to a stop right in front of a woman who appeared to be some sort of military person given that she was surrounded by people wearing identical outfits, bearing arms. The bright blue suits with their sparkling gold buttons were quite attractive, if you managed to ignore that the people wearing it were about to arrest her.

"I am a captain with the president's guard, and you

are an interloper on presidential property. We had a call from Galon, caretaker of Lamartine Cottage," the woman stated. "Come with us."

"But, the machine," Cassidy said, indicating the snowmobile. "And my, er, art." Is that really what you call something that looks abstract, and pretty and completely inanimate and useless, she thought. Well, yes. Good art always had a message and, for certain, Corie could certainly talk your literal ear off, so yeah, art is what it was. Now the question was how to convince the guard to let her take it. Cassidy had forgotten where she was for a moment but was instantly reminded when the guard spoke.

"Art? Of course, you cannot leave your *art* unprotected. Please. Leave the machine, someone will take care of it for you, and you'll come with us."

Cassidy pulled out the receptacle and slipped it into her backpack. The side-eye glance from the guard suggested that she wasn't impressed with Cassidy's particular artistic taste. And that was fine. The less interesting it was the better for both of them.

Cassidy pushed her sunglasses up. Her helmet hid the Bluetooth in her ear for now, though it would appear Corie was implementing radio silence just when she needed her the most. "Thank you. Where are we going, precisely?"

"We are going to the presidential headquarters." the woman said. "I'm Captain Emile Branad. We'll escort you there to investigate your invasion into our territory and decide what to do with you until then."

Cassidy nodded. This was good. She'd be inside the palace which was their ultimate destination though it would be better to have infiltrated on their own terms, not to be a prisoner. And Corie was useless now, her mini-TARDIS had gone black and now it looked like a paper-weight with some fancy embossing instead of an entire mini-world. She picked up the *art*. It truly fascinated her that a world so art-based in its philosophies could be so good at science. This thing weighed no more than a five-pin bowling ball but carried a person the size of herself in it. And that person's whole environment. Perhaps she'd get a chance to meet the geniuses who had created the world imagined by a previous president that allowed for the development of this technology. Sure, Corie was president now, but she wasn't the brilliant mind that cre-ated big worlds in small places, she just decorated them well with pretty colours and lovely music. And enticing stories.

There were shadows on the cliffs and hills, as Cassidy followed the militia of presidential guards. They caught a gentle breeze and Cassidy, despite the amber vision glasses, found the colours on the snow mesmerizing par-ticularly now that she wasn't driving. The winter chills were diminishing as they descended the mountains. Soon enough they reached a parking lot where she was escorted to another vehicle, this time a boxy car of cornflower blue with a red line across the side. The air was much warmer there and after a few hours of driving the snow disap-peared altogether. They drove through the farmland on a brown road that wound its way through fields of grass of blended greens. The grasses were interspersed with rows of flaming flowers that blazed across the landscape and disappeared into the china blue brightness of the hazy sky. Clouds swirled overhead, a blend of violet and lavender, like puffs of pale purple smoke. Champagne and amber grains rose up, waving in the wind, tiny brushes at their tips that seemed to paint the air that changed hue in the swirling breezes.

Cypress-like trees, reaching upwards of a hundred feet in height and created wind-rows along the roadway and leaning against them were tufts of purple irises. The only people she spotted were a group of women in a potato field, and here and there people were binding wheat or picking what appeared to be olives if Cassidy's observations were correct. She couldn't be sure, given her experience with agriculture here was limited and this was an entirely different place.

"Are we there yet?" a voice whispered into her ear and it took a moment for Cassidy to realize that Corie was back online. She glanced at the receptacle in her hand.

"No," She darted a look at the driver. He seemed to not hear her.

"Get to Eryn, he will help. Meanwhile, get news from the guards, talk politics."

"Can you hear me?"

"Yes, I can hear, but I am going quiet again because they must not hear me." Corie's voice trailed off and the globe vibrated in her hand as it shut down once more.

Cassidy checked out the guard who was not totally unfriendly. "So, tell me. I've been out of the loop for a while, what has been going on politically?"

The driver's eyes met Cassidy's in the mirror. "What do you mean? Politically?"

"Well since our president, er, went away, how has it gone? The running of the country?" She had some of this information already, but more was always good, Corie was right on that.

"Oh, that. Terrible. It's a grey time for us. We are ragged men in ragged clothes in the fields. We need to be able to have a new president, but Eryn will not allow it. He says that things must stay as they are until President Corie is declared dead but you can't declare her dead because we don't know if she is."

"Ragged men in ragged fields?"

"What? You do not get a metaphor?"

"I don't get *that* metaphor?" Cassidy said, mulling the words over.

"Are you a scientist?"

Confused, Cassidy considered her answer. The militia leader had called her an interloper. So, she'd assumed she'd been found out as being from another realm. But perhaps not. Perhaps just another country in this realm? Was she still undercover?

"No, just an explorer who has been away." Perhaps bluffing would work. It was worth a shot.

"The ragged men in ragged fields, those without purpose, without light, without art. Once we were ragged, our fields were ragged, nothing was aesthetically pleasing or visually stimulating back then. Until the Anacin seers dreamed of *colourization*. After that things became beautiful, and we advanced greatly. How could an explorer not know these things?"

"Oh, I knew, I just forgot them. So busy, you know, *exploring*."

"Where did you explore?" the driver asked.

"The, er, south," Cassidy responded with the first thing that came to her.

"Oh, lovely there. All those periwinkle beaches."

"Yes, those. Lovely." They *did* sound spectacular. Wow.

"So how does this work? The president is absent, this Eryn is now ruling?" She played dumb.

"With the senators and governors, yes. He's in charge, at least until they figure this out. But people are growing impatient. He hasn't the imagination of the president, he was, after all, just her campaign associate."

"So can't they replace her?"

"He insists she isn't dead. And if she isn't, we can't do anything. It's in the constitution. So it befalls him to govern. But such limited scope and vision. You won't believe this. He wanted to talk about budgets one day. There was much laughter at that. Can you imagine? It was even trending on Squeaker. So embarrassing for us! Anybody can tally numbers. What is required are ideas and creativity. But of course, you know this much. May I ask, why the eyewear?"

"Oh, I have a, er, condition. My eyes are not very pretty to look at, at the moment, so I thought nobody should have to look at them."

"How thoughtful! It's temporary, I hope. Eyes are always the most beautiful part of one's self, don't you agree?"

"Yes, that's why I covered them. *So* embarrassing." Some of this was far too easy now that she was starting to understand. These people loved art and beauty and if she focussed on that she should be able to slide through. She hadn't been picked up for being other-worldly but rather being at the president's cottage. Surely, she could manage to get to Eryn once inside the presidential residence.

CHAPTER ELEVEN

The remainder of the ride was uneventful and enjoyable as far as rides while under arrest went. Cassidy marvelled at the exceptional beauty of Corie's world, particularly this new rural region with fields the colours of gold, yellow, and red as though autumn had grown up from the ground. Further along their drive, more people were out and about. Brightly dressed workers sang shanties in the vast meadows as they laboured, broad smiles on attractive faces, children running through the multicoloured sheaves lain against brightly painted farm tractors. They crossed over a long white bridge that spanned a river of such an exquisite cerulean that Cassidy audibly gasped at its glorious blue then glanced at the driver to see if she had noticed. After all, as a 'local' and an 'explorer' perhaps she shouldn't be as surprised by the beauty of the place as she was.

Soon they entered a city with the most spectacular highways that Cassidy had ever traversed thinking that if she'd driven them herself, she'd have gone off the road, so distracted as she was by their unusual colour. For they were not the dismal grey of asphalt like back home but rather an unusually pale yellow with ribbons of pink and white twisted throughout so that it too was visually exquisite. The painted lines on the roads were a deep red and the rails, where required, were also scarlet and completely visible such that what was entirely a safety feature also beautified the city.

The buildings were also very colourful, but it seemed they were limited to all the hues of blue and green in the world with few variations of bright yellow for contrast. *I'm in a cartoon*, she thought. Except it wasn't cartoonish at all. It was incredibly interesting and beautiful and, yes, artistic.

And entirely dull compared to what came into view a short while later.

For out of the misty clouds that had settled over them in the last fifteen minutes of the drive arose the spires of a castle of silver and crystal that danced and sparkled in the daylight despite the lack of full sunshine. She could see now why they called the presidential residence the Crystal Castle.

"Wow," Cassidy whispered, mouth open in disbelief. And then the sun broke through and suffused the castle in a golden light that sent shards of spectacular colour out from the magnificent building in all directions. The car drove on and Cassidy continued to stare, wide-eyed and mystified at the sheer opulence and glory of the architecture. "They bedazzled the castle," she said aloud. It was as though Disney's castle was amplified by light a million times over into a spectacular display too beautiful for mere humans to even comprehend. She expected fireworks at any moment to explode behind it.

"Have you been here before? On a tour or anything?" The driver asked, knocking Cassidy back to reality.

They approached a tunnel and their vehicle slowed and as it neared the entrance the boxy little car was locked into some sort of rail. The driver cut its engines.

"No, I haven't. I mostly explore the countryside."

"We'll be transported by rail into the presidential residence. It's a security feature, of course. Prevents people from unauthorized entry. Once inside you cannot leave unless you're cleared by the guards to let your vehicle back onto the tracks and only official vehicles can pass through. Everyone is escorted in and out, for safety reasons."

Cassidy was thankful for the tunnel. While it was a lovely shade of mint green it seemed quite boring relative to the exterior of the castle and that was a good thing. She needed to regain her wits. If they need to escape, the only way out was in an official vehicle, she thought. Good to know.

Suddenly the car came to a stop. "Here we are," the guard said. "Follow me."

Cassidy slid out, noticing an item on the dash of the car. With a glance at the guard who was walking away, she reached her hand through the window and nicked it. She wasn't sure what it was, precisely, but if it was what she suspected it might be, it could prove to be very useful at some point in her journey out of this place.

CHAPTER TWELVE

Cassidy had followed along, 'artwork' tucked into her jacket down long corridors that became less and less colourful as they walked, the lovely vine and floral decor giving way to a dull grey as they approached a door with a large box on it. The guard placed their hand in the box and a red light scanned it, then turned green and everything clicked.

With trepidation, she continued. There was nowhere else to go, the hallways seemingly completely sealed off and private. The guard stopped beside another door, repeated the hand scanning and it swung inward.

"In here. You will wait."

"Wait! What?" The room was obviously a jail cell.

"It's where you must wait. Until you are processed."

And then the door shut, and Cassidy was alone in a well-lit room with nothing to see. Except a low cot and another door. She opened it and inside were bathroom facilities but nothing more. She closed it again.

She walked over and sat on the cot. How long would she be here? Was it safe to take the glasses off? The guard didn't seem to object to her wearing them.

She pulled Corie out of her coat and set the globe? on the bed. "Corie. We're here in jail. Can you Open Sesame or something?"

A few moments later a slow buzz was audible and a second later Corie appeared in the little window. Cassidy adjusted it so that soon it appeared that Corie sat before her.

"You are inside the presidential residence?" she inquired.

"Yes, I'm here in a jail cell it appears. How do I get them to take me to Eryn though? I have no idea how to make that happen. To them I'm just a lowly prisoner who is in jail for trespassing on your property. Surely, they won't let me speak to him. It'll be all judges and juries and such, right?"

"Yes, that is a good point, Cassidy Cane. But it is Eryn I must see."

"There is no escaping this cell. The only thing I can think of is to confess to a crime that gets me an audience with your old pal Eryn. What is the crime that would do that? Or is there such a thing?"

"I don't know. Perhaps treason? Yes, I think that is the only one."

"Treason, oh boy. That sounds serious."

"It is. If found guilty it will get you locked alone in a dingy room forever."

"So I'm risking being locked up forever on the odd chance it might get me to see Eryn?"

"Yes, I am afraid so."

Cassidy mulled it over. She had to do something, but this was awfully risky. What if there was no way out? They didn't even know she was from outside but what if they discovered this. She supposed she could throw herself on the mercy of the court. It wouldn't be treason if she wasn't from the place she was accused of it in, right?

"I have an idea! You need to pretend to know of a treasonous act, offer to tell them all about it but say you will only tell Eryn?" Corie said.

"That *is* brilliant! Yes, that might work. Well done, Corie!"

"I'm not just a pretty faceted snow globe you know," Corie responded.

Cassidy laughed. "Who knew you had such a sense of humour! That's funny!"

"It is?" Corie asked. "Why?"

Cassidy's laughter tapered off. With a final chuckle, she said, "another time. Now, how do I call somebody?"

"There should be a button to summon the guard."

Cassidy stood and walked to the door. She patted the walls until she found a slight depression in the wall almost like a dent but subtler. Of course, switches weren't aesthetically pleasing so they hid them.

"This?"

"That's it," Corie said. "I shall shut down. You may have to push two or three times to get heard."

Cassidy pushed on it and nothing happened. She waited a while before she pushed again. Then she heard steps outside in the hallway. They stopped and then the door slid open.

"How may I assist you?" Captain Emile Branad asked.

"I need to see Eryn." Cassidy demanded.

"You can't see Eryn. You will be processed soon and sent to community court."

"I need to report a treason against him, and I need to do it now. It is of vital importance and I will not tell anyone *but* Eryn."

"Treason?" The guard's eyes opened wide.

"Yes, of the worst kind. A coup. Yes, that's it. Somebody is trying to take over the country and I need to tell him before it is too late. I was sent on a diplomatic mission from...er...another country to tell him."

"Say it's Saged." a voice said into her ear.

"Saged. The country of Saged. Gades, its mayor is the problem."

"City!"

"City of Saged, I mean."

The guard's eyes narrowed.

"Why were you at the cottage of President Corie, then?"

"Tell them because Galon invited you there." whispered Corie.

"I was invited there by Galon. He is good friends with president-elect Corie, and I must see Eryn now. To tell of the coup. It's an emergency." Cassidy stood tall, trying to look imposing and important, whatever that might look like in this country.

"I'm no fool. Galon was the one who called us and told us you were there. And if this treason was the case, why not say so at the cottage?" asked Captain Branad.

"Yes, because, er, I told Galon to call you. Because I needed to be sure I could get into the residence first. I also had to know that you could be trusted. You seem like an upstanding and loyal guard. And remember, I did not realize you would lock me in jail."

"Where did you think we would put you for trespassing? In the kitchen?"

"So, everybody's a comedian now?"

"Well, it was a silly thing to say." A twinkle flecked in the guard's eye.

"Okay, it was." I think I'm getting through to her, Cassidy thought. "Will you please take me to see Eryn. Imagine what will happen if you don't and this terrible coup occurs. It will be on your shoulders. I can't even—"

Cassidy turned away from Captain Emile Branad and sat on the bed. She waved a hand as though to dismiss the guard who was pondering the choice before her.

The guard thought carefully. If she took this prisoner to Eryn and it was nothing she'd be reprimanded and perhaps lose rank or even her job. However, if she didn't take her and it proved to be such a terrible thing, well, she might end up in the grey dungeon for her entire life. A coup would destroy the country, ruin everything and things were already bad since the uproar after the president's disappearance.

"Okay, bring your things and follow me to Eryn's quarters. He *is* in at the moment but may be busy. Be patient and wait. And please keep on those glasses. He does not need to see imperfect eyes today."

"Yes, certainly." Cassidy grabbed Corie's receptacle and placed it inside her coat. She followed the guard who walked briskly down the corridors. It took a long time to get to the elevator and then another ten minutes to get to the end of the elevator's journey at the very highest floor of the residence.

Once there, Captain Branad entered a series of numbers, placed her face in a scanner and responded, "transporting a witness for review by Regent Eryn."

"We were not expecting anybody," a voice said.

"Picked up today. Says she has word of a planned treason. A coup. By Gades, mayor of Saged."

"What? A coup? That's very serious. Of course, yes. Absolutely, please, bring her in."

"Keep me hidden," Corie whispered in her ear. "I want to listen to what Eryn says before I am freed. Also, look for a pedestal. It is very important to find a stand upon which I can belong."

"Okay, got it."

"Pardon?" Emile Branad asked.

"Just practicing in my mind how to tell Eryn about the problem," Cassidy said looking around at the beautifully decorated walls. The interior of the building was extraordinary yet somehow subdued relative to the natural environment outside its walls but wasn't that normal for all places? Gathering intel on the structure and searching for ways out, should escape be required, she noted there was an exit and large windows. The windows were useless as they were so high up, but perhaps the door would be a way to leave if she had to run.

"I will let the APO know you're here."

"APO?"

"Acting president's office."

"Oh, yes. Thank you." She noted the difference in labels. Not regent but acting president. Was Eryn a beneficiary of Corie's disappearance. It was worth considering that he might actually be the bad guy here.

"Sit over there."

Cassidy was directed to a chair and then the captain went to a corner and picked up some sort of communication device. She couldn't make out the words.

"They're arguing. I'm not sure if we'll get in," Cassidy said, knowing Corie could hear.

"You're in," the captain said. "Let's go."

"Oh, well, never mind then. I mean, sorry, yes of course. Let's go."

This time the door was opened from the inside and she was told to enter without Captain Branad.

"The president's secret service will take it from here," a guard in bright yellow uniform said. "Come through. The acting president wishes to see you now. You have five minutes to state your case."

"Thank you." Cassidy's heart thumped. This was it. Now, what the heck was she supposed to say. She'd just have to wing it.

Cassidy was led to a large door and the new guard, a stern looking older man, walked to the screen. His face was scanned, and the door slid across. He took Cassidy by the elbow and guided her through.

A siren sounded and Cassidy put her hands over her ears although they were somewhat protected from the earpieces she wore.

"What is that?" she yelled.

"The security alarms. What do you have with you that set them off?" The guard yelled at her.

The alarms stopped suddenly.

"I know what she has," a man's voice said in the sudden quiet.

"You do?" Cassidy asked, taking her hands off her

ears.

"Yes, I do. Would you come with me?"

Cassidy followed him inside. There was a half-dozen people in the room, it appeared that a meeting had been in session. "Give me the room," Eryn said as though they were in an episode of a TV show and it worked. They all stood and left with a curious glance at Cassidy and a handshake to their acting president.

Once they were gone, Eryn looked at Cassidy.

"So, where is she?" he asked.

"Who?" Cassidy responded, confused look on her face.

"Don't play with me. You know who."

"He knows. You will have to let me out. But you must put me on the stand beside his desk. I can only extrapolate from there."

"Well?" Eryn asked folding his arms across his chest.

"I am Cassidy Cane and I came to tell you about a coup against you by Gades, mayor of the city of Saged. Sure, I don't even know what you're talking about. But wow! What a nice place." Cassidy wandered, feeling Eryn's eyes on her back. She looked at a painting of a tall woman. "Is she your wife?" she asked knowing darned well it was Corie in the painting.

"She is our former president. She is no longer with us." Eryn's sad look could easily be a ruse. These people were artists and acting was an art form. She reached into her jacket and placed her hand on the container with Corie in it. Out of the corner of her eye she saw Eryn lunge and knew the jig was up. Reflexes sharp as a cat she leapt forward, and Eryn went sprawling past her. Spinning on her heel, she turned and headed towards the large, red desk.

"On the stand. I must go on the stand!" Corie said. "It's imperative."

"Shut up, I've got this," Cassidy said, making a dash across the large room towards what looked like a tall candle holder with four corner pieces in which the canister that held Corie would fit perfectly. No time to think, a movement out of her eye had her barrelling towards it.

"What are you doing?" Eryn sped towards her but, globe clenched in her fist Cassidy reached out toward the stand with it just as Eryn grasped her by the tail of her jacket.

"No!" She wrenched forward and escaped his clenched hand. In the moment before he grabbed her again, she placed the faceted globe that held President Corie inside it, on the ornate stand as requested.

"There, you're back!" Cassidy screeched as she was hauled back by Eryn and pushed aside while he ran forward screaming, "No!"

But a great cloud of white smoke and an explosion that vibrated through the room sent him flying backwards.

He grabbed Cassidy and twisted her arm behind her back. There was a loud whistling noise. Cassidy struggled to free herself while Eryn held on tight. Cassidy's struggle stopped and Eryn's grasp loosened as the fog cleared.

The voice in Cassidy's ear now filled the room. Corie stepped forward and stood before them, once more in her own real world and ready to take her role as president of the country of Impasto.

"I am back," Corie's voice was strong and she shocked Cassidy when she said, "And you, Eryn, are under arrest for high treason against the president and country of Impasto."

CHAPTER THIRTEEN

Eryn twisted Cassidy's arm and she pulled hard to try to escape.

"Treason. Guards, guards!" Corie shouted.

Several presidential guards rushed into the room. They brought up short at the sight of President Corie and Eryn holding Cassidy in a vice-like grip as she struggled to free herself. They took a step, in unison, as though to go towards Eryn.

"I am not a criminal," Eryn claimed. "Let me go, we can sort this out."

Corie raised a hand. "I am the duly elected president and I have the right to take my place as such. Eryn only stood in my absence and law must decide who is rightful, not guards. Stand down now. Cassidy has brought me back, you must protect her, grab Eryn who cast me from this land, and remove him to the grey room."

The guards looked at Corie, then at each other, nodded at each other and moved towards Eryn.

"No! Please. Corie, I did what I had to do. Then we shall work it out. Please, guards, for now, I am president."

The guards stopped to consider his word. They looked at each other again, seemed to come to some agreement and moved towards Corie as if to grab her.

"No! Stop! He is a liar. He threw me into the canister of smallness, to hide me, perhaps until he could get the key. He claimed there was an impending coup and that I was in danger. Yes, he fooled me, and now he's trying to fool you." She insisted. "I thought he was a friend, so I did as he suggested. Now I realize he probably just wanted the power himself. Again, *I* am the president. People voted for me, *not* Eryn. And I am the one who must oversee the search for the key of Impasto. It is not in my possession, but I am the president. Take him away. Now!"

The guards again looked at each other, sizing up the situation. A few moments seemed eternal until they finally nodded and seemed firmer in their decisiveness. They marched towards Eryn who still held Cassidy by the arm.

"What of the other prisoner, President Corie?" The tallest of the two guards asked.

"Release her to me. She aided my return and is a very important person to help locate the key."

"Stay away from me," Eryn ordered helplessly, pulling Cassidy closer. "Corie, you have it wrong, I—"

"Oh, enough," Cassidy said. She stomped her foot down hard on his. He let out a howl of pain and loosened his grip on her. Cassidy maneuvered herself free, turned and grabbed his thumb, and twisted it until he released her arm fully. She kept winding it until he went to his knees begging her not to break it off from his hand altogether.

The impressed guards moved in and lifted him off the floor as Cassidy stood by, rubbing the ache in her shoulder from where it had been wrenched. She watched as Eryn was led out and the door shut behind them.

Finally, alone in the room, Cassidy turned to Corie.

"Are you okay? I wasn't sure you understood that Eryn was likely not honest with you," she said as she noted the greyish tinge to her skin and an expression of angst on her face.

"Yes, it's unfortunate he turned out to be a crook. But mostly I feel bad from the extrapolation. Largerization is not pleasant. I must lay down. I will summon my senators soon but before I do, please search the cupboards for absinthe. I need a restorative drink.

Cassidy opened a few cabinet doors, and it took only a short while to find a bottle and glasses. She filled a goblet and returned it to Corie who lay on a long settee propped against a large window overlooking the city.

"Thank you, Cassidy Cane, for this and the return. Will you not join me?" She sipped on the absinthe and closed her eyes in ecstasy at its taste.

She wrinkled her nose. "I think I'll pass. So, that's it? You're home and you're president, just like that? I can leave?"

"Not quite, Cassidy Cane. Your work here is not done. We now need to find the key. I don't have it, so where is it?"

"Oh right. This makes things difficult. Because whoever took the key doesn't appear to be in cahoots with Eryn."

"And also, they're not working with him."

"But that's the same — nevermind," she pulled the earpiece out of her ear. She didn't need it anymore now that Corie was right sized. She pushed the glasses up, however. Just in case, because this room was awfully bright and pretty.

"We must return it to me. From whoever has it."

"The question is, who has it? Any ideas?"

"Yes, unfortunately I think I do know who might have it."

"Who?"

Corie sipped the absinthe drink, gave a big sigh, and pondered before answering. "I can only think of one person who would have taken the key."

"Who? For the love of cookie dough, spit it out."

"Gades. The mayor of Saged."

"Explain further please. That's the name you asked me to use to get out of the cell," Cassidy said, moving about the room, looking at books and art. "I'm dying to know who he is and why he might have the key."

CHAPTER FOURTEEN

"Gades, the mayor of Saged, was my primary opponent in the presidential election. A man of very small imagination and you know, in presidential elections, the size of a man's *imagination* is very important."

"I *imagine* it is," Cassidy said, stone-faced.

"He lost. The defeat was large. But he didn't lose well. He was angry although he acted as though he was conciliatory, I could tell."

"And you suspect he's tangled up in this? Do you really think they're possibly in on it together and maybe Gades double-crossed Eryn?"

"I can't say for sure. Eryn acted as my friend, told me that a coup was coming. That Gades was angry and wanted to contest my win. He was accusing me of cheating, of all sorts of things but would he feel better if Eryn were president? It gives him no power."

"But perhaps the power is in having the key. Wouldn't it be too obvious if he jumped into trying to be president. Perhaps he was in on you being sent out of the realm, into ours, and then the goal was Eryn to act in your stead until they had an election to replace you. But Eryn got greedy and decided to stay, claiming you would come back. But without the key, he couldn't function properly. To tell everyone Mayor Gades had it would be to admit being a traitor?" Cassidy paced the room, thinking.

"Perhaps. Something isn't right though, but I can't think what I'm missing here." Corie said. "But then, I trusted Eryn, so I'm not reliable anyway."

"So what's next? Go after Gades?"

"I think so, yes, but after I meet with the senate. They must be addressed first, to let them know I've returned, and that Eryn is no longer in charge and, in fact, is incarcerated."

"Surely, they know now, right? I mean there were people here who have probably spread the word."

"Yes, but I must formally invite them. I will do that now. An emergency session." She drained the remainder of the absinthe from her glass with a huge sigh of appreciation. Then she stood and walked to the large desk in the middle of the room and picked up a round object.

"Principal Senator Theo, this is President Corie. Please direct the other senators to attend to the chambers immediately for an emergency meeting of the senate to discuss my kidnapping, return, and the arrest of Eryn Shrub." She clicked a button and laid it back down. A knock came on the door.

"That was fast."

"Too fast."

"Stay here," Cassidy instructed striding towards the door. "Who is it?"

"The PSS. We are here to help President-elect Corie."

Cassidy looked towards Corie who nodded her consent. Cassidy opened the door a smidge and peeked out to see the two guards from earlier.

"You are alone?"

"Yes, and we are here to protect President Corie. We recognize her as the true and proper inhabitant of this office. Please allow us to continue our jobs as her protectors."

"Come in then," Corie said, her voice strong and presidential.

"Thank you, Ma'am," the taller guard said. "You may not remember me, but I was there when you were elected. It was a happy day."

"It was for me too," the other guard piped up. "I voted for you."

"Shhhh, we are to be impartial," the first admonished.

"That's okay. We'll let propriety go for now. I need loyal guards to protect me, and our democracy, and I appreciate your vote. And your help. I have a senate meeting now. But I am reclaiming my power and my first action is to promote you both as my official guards. I don't know why, but I trust you. You made the right decision when you were called on to do so and that bears rewarding. Now I require you in your new official capacity as bodyguard to the president duties to escort me and my adviser, Cassidy Cane of America, Earthside, to the senate chambers. There we will start to sort out this entire mess. Does that sound fair?"

The two guards puffed up and stood straight. They touched their chins in unison, something Cassidy presumed was a type of salute and nodded.

"I am delighted to accept your promotion and will guard you with my body and soul," the shorter guard said.

"Thank you, what is your name?"

"I am Raph and this is Micho," he replied nodding to the taller guard.

"Pleased to meet you both. Let's go, shall we?"

"Wait, Ma'am, I don't mean to interfere but should you not, you know, apply the sash of incumbency?"

"Oh, yes. You are correct. Thank you."

Cassidy watched, curious as Corie went to a small table near the window where an ornate box sat. She flipped open the lid and pulled out a folded length of fabric, unwound it and slipped it over her head, brushing the front of it with her hand. She closed the lid and turned with a broad smile.

"Feels official now," she said. The sash read *President* and naturally, was adorned with embroidered sunflowers and stars.

"That's very nice. Shall we go through?" Cassidy said, not quite so taken with the pomp of things as the two guards who again did their strange chin salute which Corie returned with grave reverence on her face.

"Yes, yes. Of course. Guards. Lead the way, please."

Raph walked out and Corie followed. Micho indicated that Cassidy should go next, and he brought up the rear as they made their way to the chambers where Corie would take back control of her country and Cassidy would try to figure out who or what had the darned key of Impasto that she was supposed to return to President Corie.

CHAPTER FIFTEEN

The senate chamber room was as ornate as the sash and decorated in a similar style with gold trimmed murals of amber fields of wheat and bright yellow sunflowers bedecking the walls. The windows were broad and high and overlooked the city and Cassidy shoved her glasses up on her nose as she was escorted into the room to prevent her from falling into a trance over it all. The massive room had benches on both sides for the senate to sit at, but Cassidy was led on through to another room with a long boardroom table and collection of chairs that were now mostly filled. The brightly dressed senators, animated and loud, went dead quiet when the four of them entered the room. The guard stepped aside and allowed Corie to lead. She strode across the room and sat in the chair at the head of the large table. Gone was the nervous passenger in a strange canister depending on another to bring her home. There, instead, sat a strong woman ready to take back her rightful place as president of her country. Cassidy chewed the inside of her cheek and pondered the transformation as she stood with the guards on the sidelines. Perhaps smallness inside the pod had created smallness within Corie. She sure seemed larger than life at the head of the table now.

"You, there. Move! My advisor will sit there," Corie instructed a senator who stood, and moved to a vacant chair with a look in her eyes as though she'd been ordered to move by a ghost. Or perhaps a demon. Either way there was no disputing the authority Corie now carried.

Cassidy slipped into the chair feeling all eyes in the room on her. She tucked her hands beneath the table and clasped them tight to help resist the urge to remove her hair from its ponytail to look more formal and governmental, given the serious looks she was being sent. She was an archaeologist, not a presidential adviser, which might not be a popular vocation in a room that might contain enemies of that president.

"Call to order," Corie said, her voice strong. Every head turned towards her, anxious to hear what she had to say. They knew she weaved a lovely tale and part of it was curiosity but part of it was the anticipation of a good long story.

"Please just ask me questions. That's what I request," she said, solemn.

"Why did you run away?"

Cassidy jerked her head towards the speaker, a short woman with long brown hair and a serious expression.

"I ran for my life. At least that's why I thought I left. I was convinced that it was best for the country if I left for a while. Perhaps that was the right choice, perhaps not, that remains to be seen but it was at the encouragement of my former adviser, Eryn, who has now been arrested for treasonous acts."

"Why? Where have you been? How did you escape?" the same woman asked.

"Your question is valuable, LaFont." she skipped over it and answered in her own way. "It's difficult to admit that I was duped. I trusted him completely, he had helped me become elected and I believed his lies about a coup and so, when under the guise of protecting me, he suggested I run, I reluctantly agreed. He promised to fix the problem and return me to power. Now it seems that in my absence he blamed me for stealing the key of Impasto and acted as president. But he has not been a good or rightful president. And as the legal president I have taken back my position and Eryn will remain in the grey room until his trial."

Cassidy glanced around as Corie talked. Eryn must not have acted alone, and she scanned the crowd for anyone who didn't seem surprised by this story.

"Where *is* the key then? It's gone and it disappeared when you did!" A man with stark white hair interrupted and his question was echoed by the rest of the gathered assembly.

"Tonem! I do not have the key! I never had it."

"But there was a letter of confession. Eryn showed us in the senate. And if you don't have it, who does? Where is it?" Tonem asked. He seemed to have a leadership role and the others waited for Corie's answer.

"I did not write that letter. It was forged and I repeat, I do not know. And the interesting thing is I don't think Eryn knows either."

"You don't?"

"No, he would have been a better leader with it." She

looked at Cassidy who nodded.

"So, we are to believe you now after you ran away and deserted us?"

"I had bad advice. I will get better advice from here on in." Corie's voice was strong.

"From your new," he gave Cassidy a derisive look, "advisor?"

"Yes. From me," Cassidy said. "And my advice right now is to end this inquisition and instead we go question the prisoner, Eryn."

"I think we get to say who gets to—"

"You get no say at all," Corie told him. "Cassidy Cane is right. We're going to see Eryn and we're going to do it now. Dismissed."

The senators looked open-mouthed from Corie to Cassidy, then to Tonem, then slowly rose to do as they'd been ordered.

"Corie, you're bossy as heck as president," Cassidy said.

"I'm a leader, Cassidy. Bossiness is a requirement. Come on, let's go see Eryn."

CHAPTER SIXTEEN

Eryn sat in the small grey room, face in his hands. The door slid open, and President Corie walked in with Cassidy Cane at her side. He looked up at them, bright blue eyes awash, red-rimmed. He wiped his eyes and stood.

"Cor — President Corie. Why are you here?" He waved his arm around to indicate the cell.

"To question you. Where is the key, Eryn?" Corie demanded, hands on her hips as though she were his mother scolding him for leaving a mess about.

"I do not know. I swear."

"I do not believe you. I have no reason to."

"I really do not, Corie. And if you don't, I must truly and humbly apologize. I truly thought you might have stolen it. The letter was *so* real. It looked to be in your beautiful cursive. I was absolutely certain you tricked me. When I removed you for your own safety, I thought I was doing the right thing. Then the letter came and I was sure you had it."

"What good would it have been to me in another world?"

"That's the part I couldn't figure out." Eryn

shrugged.

"So you saw this as an opportunity for you to take power?" Corie asked.

"Power? Corie, I've never desired power. I have only ever desired — well, I decided to stand as your regent, then acting president, because I was hopeful someday, I could get to you, perhaps get you back. And I did try. I went out into the other realm, I searched all around the area but there was no sign, no clue as to where you had gone."

"I'm guessing Professor Gamgee already had picked you up by then." Cassidy propped her forefinger under her chin, contemplating his explanation.

Eryn looked at Cassidy with renewed interest. "You are from the other realm and you are helping President Corie return to her place as president?"

"Yes, that's the goal. Which is complete but I'll stick around to find that key of yours as well. It seems like Corie won't get to be president for long if it's not found."

"Without it there will always be suspicion. If we don't find it whoever takes the presidency is doomed, I believe," Eryn said.

"Yes, I can see that. Plus all those people's private information in the wrong hands—"

"Wait! You believe him, Cassidy Cane?" Corie looked shocked.

"I — well it sounds plausible. I'd like to hear his entire explanation before I decide."

Eryn nodded and encouraged, continued. "I knew you were resourceful and would come back if you could, President Corie. And I was right." He looked at Corie as though he still couldn't believe his eyes that she was there.

Cassidy noticed something else about Eryn. An expression in his eyes. What was it? Then it dawned on her. This was a man smitten. Eryn was in love with Corie. And she seemed clueless to that fact. And if he was, did that make him more or less of a suspect? If he loved her, he'd hardly betray her, but if she rejected him, revenge for an unrequited love could be a motive.

"But then when I arrive you attacked Cassidy and tried to prevent my extrapolation?" Corie snapped.

"Because of the letter. It came after you were gone. I thought you had betrayed me — the country, I mean. I thought when you returned you would have the key, would have had it all along, and had stolen it like they said. And that you possibly had used it to cheat to win the election."

"If you thought she was a cheater, I mean, cheated to get the election, why didn't you just let the opponent take power?" Cassidy leaned in, looking closer at his face to see his answer in his eyes as well as hear it.

"Because I still — I didn't want to believe it. I thought I was better for the country because I am not under the thumb of Mayor Gades and even if I am not a good president, I am better than he would have been."

"I have heard that the people are not satisfied with your governance," President Corie said.

"Of course they are not. I can't inspire like you. A president needs to be a muse to the people. I'm not that. If I were, I would have run myself. I know my flaws. I just wanted to support the best person to run the country and that was you. My — our afflatus president."

"Afflatus?" Cassidy ran the word through her brain. She had amazing translation abilities. Unfortunately, a dictionary hadn't come with that upload.

"It is another word for a muse. It's the best kind of president to have. One who is both artist *and* muse and Corie was held up as the first candidate to be such a president in a long time. Perhaps that's why they framed her, stole the key, sent the letter and tried to stop her from becoming president."

"Perhaps," Cassidy said. "Here is my confusion, Eryn. If you thought Corie was going to find her way back, and would figure all this out, why did you encourage her to leave in the first place. Why couldn't she have stayed and together you could have figured this out? Surely the guards could and would have protected her."

"I didn't know which guards to trust, and the threatening letters suggested that the only way to protect her was to hide her away."

"But Eryn, your job was not to protect me, it was to serve the country," Corie said.

"I know but you were my priority, and yes the country was also a priority, but I put you first. Perhaps I made a wrong choice, I probably should have listened when you objected. I know it looks like I tried to steal your presidency, but I did not. I just thought I could protect you and figure this out before you arrived back. Instead, I've been so distracted by taking care of the country and saving the presidency that I've failed to make this place any safer for you."

"Oh, it's safer for her," Cassidy said. "I'm here now

and we'll get this sorted before I leave. That is a guarantee."

Eryn and Corie looked at Cassidy and then back at each other. A look passed between them, a flicker like a tiny firefly dancing just out of reach then disappearing. But Cassidy caught it before it vanished.

These two were far more than candidate and campaign manager and she would get the rest of this story from Madame President Corie as soon as she possibly could.

CHAPTER SEVENTEEN

"So, you and Eryn, in love huh?" Alone with Corie again, Cassidy leaned back and looked around the office, nonchalant as she asked the question.

"Cassidy Cane!"

"Oh, come on. I've been trying to figure out why you would listen to him when you could have stayed behind and defended yourself. And I've been trying to figure out why he was so determined to save you by doing that if he wasn't after your power. And that has to be it. You're in love with each other. Admit it. Fess up."

"It is personal."

"You brought me here to find your blasted key. There is no such thing as personal. I need to know everything. Are you in love or involved in some other way?"

"I need a drink." Corie made her way across to the absinthe bottle, poured a generous glassful and sat back down at her desk. Cassidy was lounging in the big armchair on its opposite side, leg draped over one arm trying to figure out their next move.

"You have your drink. Now tell me."

"I confess I do have certain feelings for Eryn that may

have impacted my judgment."

"Ha! I knew it!" She sat upright. "You two were locking lips and looking for votes. Was it a scandal? Or did you manage to hide it away?"

"We were not, locking the lips! We were completely professional. As his superior it was not right for me to entertain a romantic relationship. It would be completely wrong."

"But you fell in love all the same. And he has feelings for you as well. It is the only thing that makes sense unless he really does want to be president, but he doesn't seem to."

"If he has such feelings, he hasn't said so. So, you think? Do you really think he does?" Corie was casual in the question, but her eyes were eager.

"He's smitten like a kitten."

"What does that mean?"

"That he likes you. He '*like*' likes you." She wiggled her eyebrows. "For real, in a romantic way. But also more, I think he truly cares for you and that even if romance is off the table he really loves you, so he did what he did to protect you, as misguided as that was."

"Do you think he really searched for me in your world?"

"I imagine so. He seemed sincere and it is true, you were gone fairly quickly after."

"That would have been dangerous, we've never been sure we could survive out there. There were stories, though some say they were made up fables to keep us from trying."

"Maybe he cared enough to risk it?"

"Wow. I never thought of that. Should we let him out of jail maybe?"

"No, we have no proof. We need to figure out who has the key and prove him, and you, innocent. Then you guys get married and have little presidential babies."

"Cassidy Cane!" Corie giggled. "You are a tease."

Cassidy grinned. "Perhaps so. Anyway, this is all interesting but still doesn't help us figure this out. Our prime suspect is Mayor Gades of Saged. Would you agree?

"Yes, so how do we get him to confess?"

"Well, by now he will be aware you are here. Maybe we need to pull a bluff," Cassidy thought.

"What is a bluff and how does one pull it?" Corie asked.

"I will explain. Then we will start to implement the plan. Do you have something similar to a press conference here?"

"Where we call the media and they come and hear announcements? We have those."

"Can you call one?"

"Yes, of course. I'm sure all the media is eager to hear about where I've been and why I'm back."

"Okay, then here is what we're going to do. And we may need one of your artists to help out."

And Cassidy set about explaining her plan to a very skeptical president.

CHAPTER EIGHTEEN

The crowd had gathered before the dias. Microphones surrounded the podium. It was very much like a press conference back in the earth realm except for the microphones being painted in bright colours with intricate patterns and the podium glittering with crystals that sparkled in the sunlight. Cassidy pushed her shades up to ensure she was not distracted by all the colours and glittery sights. The media room was all windows and the view over the city was breathtaking and likely spellbinding to a non-bespectacled Cassidy.

"Okay, I am ready. Eryn will surely hate me for this when I am finished."

"He will not. But even if he were to, country first. This will help you and Eryn. Now get out there."

Corie entered the room. The chattering voices stilled at her entrance and all was quiet as she made her way, flanked by her two loyal guards to the podium. Cassidy followed behind, standing just to the left of the stage in order to keep a wide look at the gathered reporters.

"Good evening fellow citizens," Corie began. Cameras snapped as she began her address.

"I have returned to take over my position as president of the country. My decision to be away for so long was improperly advised and I apologize for my absence. I could give a big, long speech but I sense you have questions for me, and I think that we are best to proceed with those without hesitation. Just know that I am here to answer as best I can. Please go ahead."

"Where were you?" The first question came from a lady with white hair in the first row.

"I was in a safe place until things settled down. It was so safe that I do not want to reveal it in case others need to be protected in the future."

"Did you steal the key of Impasto?" a young fellow with a bright yellow jacket asked.

"I did not," Corie responded.

"Was there really a letter from you confessing that you stole it?"

"There was a letter saying that, but it was a forgery. I did not write that letter."

"Nonsense, you wrote the letter, and you stole the key and used it to win the election."

"Does that make sense? I stole the key to win the election, then after winning I disappear with it instead of becoming president, then I write a letter confessing that I did that. To what end? What would I have to gain?"

The reporters became silent. They were logical thinkers, and she was right, it didn't make sense.

"So why have you called us here today? There was to be some sort of announcement?"

"Yes, I came today to announce that the key of Impasto has now been located and will be returned to us very shortly."

Cassidy watched the room. Several senators who were present sat near the back shuffled about. One of them slipped out. She nodded at the guard who left the stage while the reporters shouted words at her.

"Where is it?" One asked.

"Why was it stolen?" Another shouted.

"Has anybody been arrested?"

Corie handled them all like a pro, tossing out answers as best she could while giving absolutely nothing away. "Definitely a politician," Cassidy thought as she slipped from the stage.

She rushed around to the foyer where the guard was engaged in a discussion with the man who had slipped out. He looked vaguely familiar, and she remembered him from the meeting with the senators.

"I will be reporting this to the president, she'll have your job for treating me this way," he said.

"What do we have here, Raph?" Cassidy inquired.

"You! Who are you, anyway, that you are suddenly advising the president? Do you know we can't find out who she is? We do not know where this traveller comes from? Her name does not exist in—"

"In the key?"

The man's eyes darted back to Raph, then Cassidy.

"How could you even search my name if it's missing?" Cassidy asked.

"Yes, Senator Zwart. How could you?" Raph asked.

The senator looked from Raph to Cassidy and back again. Then he darted away.

"Oh, no you don't," Cassidy said as she took a dash

towards the door after him. Raph made chase as well but the senator was faster and was through the door as Cassidy came up to it. She rushed through and picked up speed with Raph just a few feet ahead of her. Then suddenly her legs were shot out from underneath her and she tumbled like a bowling ball, rolling to bring herself upright to her feet but instead of continuing the chase she stood stock still, mesmerized by the crystal glow of the walls of the presidential palace, the cornflower blue of the sky and the opulent marvels of a nature that was so incredibly beautiful it left her in its enthrall, sunglasses having been knocked clear off her face in her fall.

Raph continued his chase but Cassidy was unaware as she leaned forward to smell a fragrant blossom, her thoughts only on the scene around her.

"Cassidy!" Micho shouted from behind her. She did not acknowledge him.

"What is wrong with her, Madam President?" He asked, circling around an entranced Cassidy who stood marvelling at the flowers.

"She dropped her glasses. Grab them. Put them on her face."

"Corie, look at the pretty flowers. They smell so nice."

"Put them on her, Micho, fast!" Corie ordered.

"You're very handsome," Cassidy said to the guard, placing a hand on his cheek. "Isn't he particularly adorable?" she asked to the dismay of the mortified guard.

"Quick, put the glasses on her now!"

"Yes, Madam President." The confused guard placed them on Cassidy's face as she looked at him adoringly.

"You're just one of the best looking guards I ever saw—" Cassidy pushed up the glasses and suddenly she could focus again.

"Oh, my God," her hand dropped. "I let him get away!" She turned, already recovered, unlike the guard, Micho, who she'd been complimenting moments earlier.

She took off towards where Raph had disappeared only to see him coming with the senator, hands locked together with what appeared to be a bright yellow strap.

"In the back door. Before the reporters realize what's been going on. You played the video?"

"Yes, we wanted to give adequate time with them distracted but we only have a few minutes, let's take him up to my office."

Cassidy followed behind them, the guard looked at her sheepishly, but she pretended nothing had happened, offering a cool smile as she walked past him. She was as mortified as he was when she realized what had happened, but she certainly wasn't going to address that here and now. No sirree, best pretend the entire episode hadn't occurred. I mean, he was a fairly handsome fellow, plus without the glasses, he was mostly just biceps, and chiselled jawline and…. She shook her head. That was simply unprofessional. She was advisor to the president and on a mission and it was inappropriate, most likely, somehow. She wasn't paid, so technically she could…no, no, no, she thought. She dashed all thoughts of handsome guards from her mind. They finally had a suspect, and it was time to find this key of Impasto and bring this caper to a close.

CHAPTER NINETEEN

"Who are you working for?"

"Nobody, I'm senator Zwart. I work for the people."

"We know that much. Why did you steal the key?"

"I did not!"

"Why was it found in your home then?" Cassidy asked.

"That is impossible."

"Really? Well, here it is. And it was found in your home just this morning. We received an anonymous tip that it was there and so we sent detectives and sure enough." President Corie held up the oblong object, no bigger than a small water glass that presumably held the data of the country inside it.

"Therefore, you are under arrest for theft of the key of Impasto, treason, resisting arrest, and will be brought to a grey room to wait out your trial which shouldn't take more than six months to complete."

"But I didn't take it…"

"We found it in your house."

"It shouldn't have been there."

"Well, that's odd, because it was." Cassidy walked

around him. "So if you didn't take it—"

"It was found in his house—" Raph said.

"Are you saying it was planted there?" Cassidy carried on. She stood back, one finger on her chin.

"I — didn't say that."

"What's the sentence for treason and theft of the key?" Cassidy asked President Corie.

"Life in the grey room. No chance of parole."

"What about for having knowledge of the crime but not actually being the thief, President?" Cassidy asked.

"Oh, if a person had knowledge, they'd get at least fifteen years. Unless, of course…"

"What?" Cassidy watched the prisoner's face.

"Obviously whoever stole it didn't care about you or the country and now they've given up, returned the key to President Corie, and will likely go unpunished while you languish in the grey room," Raph said.

"Well, I say let's just throw him in the grey room anyway. All this talk of setting him up is just a ploy. We have the key, it was in his house, he is guilty. His poor family. The shame they'll face. And losing their home. They can't stay in a senatorial residence."

"See to their removal," President Corie ordered.

The guard, Micho, made movement towards the door as though to follow orders.

"Okay, okay. I'll tell you. It was Mayor Gades of Saged who did it. He was so angry. He thinks you'll implement the pretty prisons and abolish the grey and that you should not have won. He has the contract to run the grey prisons, you know. He stole the key but when it didn't help him win the election, he decided to use it to frame

President Corie which sent his supporters after her. She was truly in grave danger before she left. So, it was good she left, but that's when he wrote the letter. To frame you for it so that he could take over. But that stubborn Eryn refused to allow it and stood as acting president and then he didn't know what to do. He's a terrible president. I guess Gades decided to plant it on me to make you stop looking at him."

"So where was the key this entire time? Before it was planted on you?"

"Right under your nose," Senator Zwart said. Then told them precisely where it was hidden. Both Cassidy and Corie gasped when he said the name of the place.

CHAPTER TWENTY

The Lamartine Cottage was as picturesque as Cassidy recalled. She entered and walked towards the kitchen. Raph and Micho followed her, and she nodded to the cabinet above the stove. They reached in with their gloved hands and pulled it open and took out a biscuit tin. Inside, nestled in a bed of velvet was the key of Impasto.

"It's the real one this time?" President Corie inquired from the doorway.

"It is, indeed."

"I can't believe we stayed here, and it was right there all along."

"Gades was clever. He decided to hide it here. If it were ever found, Corie would be blamed.

"And you got his full confession on tape?"

"Thanks to Senator Zwart."

"What will happen to Zwart?"

"We gave him immunity for his testimony. I will let him remain a senator. He did do wrong, but he helped us find the key."

"I can't believe he didn't question the fake key."

"He knew it was being used to frame you, so it wasn't

hard for him to imagine that he was the victim being framed. Plus, he's not the brightest hue in the palette," Corie replied.

"Well, that's it then. Is this place under police protection as a crime scene now?" Cassidy asked. "I'd love to stay here for a little while, have a vacation, before I return to—" she glanced at the guards, "home."

Micho raised an eyebrow, then turned quickly to follow Raph.

"You must use it. You are very welcome to stay, Cassidy. You helped find the key. It was your plan that created a confession. Please, stay here as long as you want and when you are ready I will send Micho to find you and escort you back home."

She still only trusted him and Raph with Cassidy's origins.

"Cassidy Cane, thank you for all you have done." Eryn walked into the cottage.

"Eryn!" Corie greeted him with enthusiasm.

"So, you're friends again?" Cassidy asked.

"Yes, we are." Eryn replied. He smiled and Corie met his eyes.

"I'm glad to hear it."

"Please, everyone leave. I must speak to Cassidy Cane alone." Corie waved them all out.

Soon the room was empty, and the President of Impasto and Cassidy walked alone to sit. Corie poured herself a liberal glass of absinthe.

"We have been on an adventure, my friend," Corie said.

"Indeed, we have," Cassidy replied.

"I have a gift for you. It is not much. A token really." Corie pulled a small box out of her pocket and handed it to Cassidy.

She untied the pretty ribbon and flipped open the box. There lay a pendant the size of a silver dollar. She brought it up close and smiled. It contained a tiny window that looked somewhat familiar.

"I should only look at this with the glasses on, I suspect." She wasn't much for baubles but it was pretty and a lovely souvenir.

"Yes, indeed. I know you're not a jewelry person, but I want you to think beyond that. It might be a useful tool to add you your bag. If it entrances you, perhaps it entrances some of the others you might encounter on your adventures who might not be so friendly as my people are."

"This is a wonderful gift! Thank you!" Cassidy said. This could have a very practical purpose aside from being remarkably beautiful. And here she was thinking this was one adventure from which she wouldn't be bringing an artifact back.

"I've been thinking, your world is very beautiful, but it has its troubles and its darkness. You can't always hide all that behind enchanting beauty," Cassidy said. "Be careful there."

Corie considered her words for a moment, then spoke. "But Cassidy Cane, you've made an error. The beauty of our world wasn't created to hide the pain. It was created from pain. It is art and isn't that what art is supposed to do? Takes the agony of the artist and their lived experience and make something beautiful from them? We just nurture this to a greater degree, as a priority. That is all.

We know there is pain but from that we draw exquisite beauty. Perhaps our world has more because we have had more pain, not less. Either way, it's a pleasure to live in it. And I will forever be grateful you brought me home. I must go. Duty calls. The *real* key must be placed in a safe location and I must deal with senator Zwart. You see I want his vote on a matter that was held up before I left. If he agrees to vote with me, I will be very successful in my first big decision as president."

"Good luck President Corie," Cassidy said.

"Good luck to you as well. Cassidy Cane."

CHAPTER TWENTY-ONE

Cassidy leaned back, remembering all she had seen at the labs Corie had arranged for her to tour before leaving. The most magnificent being the display of snow globes where big things lived in small worlds. Animals frolicking safely in conservation areas where nobody could hunt them and fields growing food that no pest or storm could destroy. These people were mad, beautiful geniuses.

Things were so different in a world where imagination and visual art led the way. She'd been given an entire library of movies and television shows, so well-scripted and performed by Corie's people, a person felt incredibly immersed in the program. Not entranced like when she went outside without her sunglasses, but close.

She had only noticed one thing missing in their world and when she'd mentioned it to the scientists, they'd gone off in a frenzy thinking about it. Cassidy had noticed that for all the magnificent things in their world, they did not have birds or bats or insects. Pollination happened with just the wind. So it went that they also did not have any flying objects except for the ability of their road machines, under the right conditions, to elevate for short periods of time.

Upon mentioning this oddity, and telling how in her world people travelled by plane regularly and that birds sang beautiful songs and flew like they floated in the air, they'd immediately started designing an airplane-like vehicle that played beautiful music and contained small libraries, and was decorated with beautiful art. The fact that they didn't yet know how to make things fly seemed not to bother them much. It would come. She also warned them that planes caused pollution problems in their world and to design their flying machines to run clean so as not to destroy their air. Corie, now president, had written a legislative bill immediately on that very topic, so there was no risk of their newest technology causing any trouble in that way. "Means only justifies the end if the means causes no harm," She'd wisely said before reading the bill in her parliament.

"So strange," Cassidy said, remembering all that.

"What?" Professor Gamgee inquired from his seat beside her.

"I'll tell you all about it when we get home."

"So, she really is going to change all the grey prison rooms to those pretty worlds?" Professor Gamgee asked.

"She is. Senator Zwart gave the deciding vote as payment to make up for aligning against President Corie. She's got a big imagination but she's a heck of a dealmaker too. Ironically the first prisoner to occupy one is Mayor Gades who was found guilty of stealing the key of Impasto. Quite fitting, given he stole the key and tried to sabotage her presidency in the first place due to his objections to Corie's idea about prison reform."

"Marvelous. Simply marvelous."

"Yes, it is." But he wasn't listening to her anymore. Instead he was reading a letter.

"What is it?" Cassidy asked, glancing at the paper in his hand and recognizing the tone of Dr. Gamgee's voice. Something was up.

"Well, there's this situation brewing that is highly important, you won't believe it when I tell you!" He waved the letter around. "It is the most spectacular thing. I really can't believe it myself."

"Tell me then." Cassidy looked at him with anticipation. Was it another adventure for her? A massive funding grant for his research? A sale on his favourite pens?

Dr. Herbert Gambee opened his mouth, then snapped it shut again. He looked all round the plane that was now full of passengers and shook his head.

"What? After all that buildup you're not going to tell me? You can't just do that!" Cassidy crossed her arms and formed her lips into a pout.

"I'm sorry, Cassidy. Not here, not now. It's much too crowded. You're just going to have to wait until we land to find out." He folded up the letter and put it away.

"Fine, but once we land you better tell me quickly," she said. "You know I simply *hate* waiting."

THE FRANKLIN EXPEDITION

PAUL CARBERRY & JD RYOT

CHAPTER ONE

The extensive capacity of the heat pumps did little to keep the glacial cold conditions in Terror Bay out of her bones. Cassidy Cane pulled her seal skin jacket tighter, her teeth chattering even with the combined animal fur skin lining. Her trek from Gjoa Haven across King William Island had been a thoroughly unique experience. She was still not used to the creeping cold as it engulfed the cabin of her enclosed snowmobile. Spending several days inside the houses, with the fire continually burning, did little to prepare her for this trip. While she enjoyed learning the Inuit culture from the elders and playing with the children, sharing stories of her former adventures with them. Even though she enjoyed the time with them, she couldn't wait to enter the next portal. In her brief experiences with traversing between dimensions, she quickly recognized that every portal was as extraordinary as the destination. She couldn't wait to explore another strange world. She felt goosebumps break out on her arms and anticipation of this new adventure growing in the pit of her stomach.

Blinding snowstorms and complete whiteout conditions were oddly beautiful from the comfort of her enclosure. Cassidy watched as the gale whipped snow and ice pellets in her direction, the heat in a continual feud with the forces of nature. The whistle of the wind as it swept across the desolate, snow covered region was piercing, drowning out the electric hum of the engine. Cassidy had spent three days in Gjoa Haven with the Inuit settlers. Her time there was brief. Cassidy felt a deep connection with those who had called this place home. Doctor Herbert Gamgee had sent her there under the disguise of a nurse at the Continuing Care Facility, his true purpose concealed from the entire world, including Cassidy. She still didn't know the purpose of these expeditions, but she couldn't resist the temptation of adventure. Being able to experience the harsh wilderness through the eyes of the Inuit settlers gave her a new appreciation of the importance of survival techniques. Trading small trinkets and sweets with the children made her smile. Cassidy had always been against the seal hunt, the images shown on the news were horrifying and deeply disturbing. After spending three days in Gjoa Haven, learning how critical the seal was to surviving in the artic, altered her perception of the entire situation. She glanced down at her parka, her slender frame appearing paper thin underneath the abundant furs.

Doctor Gamgee had arranged everything she required to reach the next portal. A state-of-the-art snow machine capable of navigating any terrain, the triangular tracks and wide skis made crossing the rough ice quick and comfortable. The blackened windshield kept the low winter sun out of her eyes, shielding her against snow blindness. The heat pump and warm clothes kept her from freezing. An advanced GPS navigation system displayed her route towards the portal on the high-definition monitor. Her short stature and trim build afforded her stretching room in the enclosed dome of the snowmobile. Cassidy kept going over the words of Doctor Gamgee in her head, over and over. He had given her the strangest GPS coordinates to the new portal and assured her it wasn't a mistake. She was having a difficult time trusting him.

An abrupt, unexpected, change in the weather allowed the sun to shine brilliantly against the white backdrop. Shards of sparkling specters reflected sunlight spread across the horizon. Looking out over the frozen water of Terror Bay, all she could see was the windswept snow drifting over the ice fields. The ice formed jagged, jutting walls as the old sea ice defied the newly formed ice flows. Walls of towering ice made travelling on foot nearly impossible, rendering this part of the world a natural phenomenon. Round, puffy white clouds crowded the sky, the clouds outlined with black edges.

A sharp ding signalled her arrival at the coordinates. "Well, here we are." Cassidy muttered to herself as the butterflies in her stomach fluttered their wings. Here she sat, just eighty feet above the wreckage of the HMS Terror. The failed Franklin expedition had led to the loss of all one hundred and twenty-nine sailors on board. They had lost both ships for over one hundred years in the Arctic Ocean but recently discovered them, garnering a lot of interest. Through the exploration of the HMS Terror, Doctor Gamgee discovered a portal to another dimension beneath the wreckage of the derelict ship. A twelve-foot-thick sheet of ice was the only thing separating her from the portal, or so Doctor Gamgee had told her. Herbert had been vague about what he expected Cassidy to find in this new world. All that he would tell her was that she needed to look for a magnetic anomaly, and that it was vital she brought it back to him. He had been particularly assertive about that fact. Doctor Gamgee had equipped the snowmobile with a special pod, the entire frame coated in Tungsten and durable plexiglass designed to tolerate extreme temperatures. He assured her that the pod was equipped and capable of heating the exterior shell enough to melt down through the ice, while the interior would maintain safe temperatures. Once the pod cut through the ice, it would plunge straight down into the portal. Herbert had the entire ship moved just enough for her to enter before the thick sea ice formed back over the shallow waters of Terror Bay.

All she had to do was press the red button. Her finger hovered over it, the cold plastic brushing against her skin as she struggled to force down the debilitating thoughts racing through her mind. "This is crazy, Cassidy." She tried to talk herself out of pushing the button. The analytical side of her brain warned her of all the horrid events that were possible. What if the heat gave out? She would be trapped in the midst of a sheet of thick ice, which wouldn't thaw until spring in two months. What if she broke through the ice but didn't sink? She would find herself held firmly against the ice with no way back up. What if she couldn't find the portal? She would suffocate from lack of oxygen, powerless to reach the surface. What if the glass broke? She would drown while she froze to death, her muscles unable to function. A white blur rushed across Cassidy's vision, squinting against the bright sunlight, the form slowly began to take shape. A polar fox cub was scampering across the tundra. She was so hypnotized by the elegance of the young Arctic fox that she lost all track of time. She watched it play in the snow, pouncing after a few stray birds but never able to capture one in its tiny paws. Every so often she would lose sight of the critter as it retreated behind a snow drift or behind a jagged formation of ice. Eventually, the fox vanished from her line of sight for good, the animal disappearing into the winter wonderland, its white fur the perfect camouflage for the Arctic conditions.

Cassidy impulsively pushed the button as her irrational side demanded jurisdiction over her once again. Her whole body tensed, not understanding what to expect next, Cassidy held her breath and closed her eyes. She waited for something, anything, to happen. Anticipation escalated, any moment she expected to plummet on a wild descent through the thick sea ice. A wave of heat washed over her, perspiration began to form on her brow. Cautiously opening her eyes, Cassidy was disappointed to find she was sinking through the ice at a snail's pace. The frozen salt water was inching up the windshield, inch by inch the pod was melting the old ice. With her seal skin mittens, she wiped away the dripping perspiration. Cassidy contemplated removing her outer layer as the temperature continued to rise in her pod. Now she wondered if Herbert had made a miscalculation, the enclosure was starting to resemble an oven. Quickly examining the control panel, Cassidy wondered if there was a way to abort the descent. Panic was settling in, a surge of adrenaline flooding her entire system magnified the situation. She realized that no one except Doctor Gamgee knew where she was, and she wasn't sure he would come looking for her. Her breath was laboured, claustrophobia was taking over as the ice completely filled her vision. The melting sea ice turned pure white, bubbled and churned as the pod drifted downwards faster now. The sea water collected above her head, turning back into sheets of ice almost instantly.

An abrupt deviation in pressure jolted Cassidy in her seat, the pod bursting through the last layer of ice without warning. The thick glass slammed hard against the ice once before the hum of the engine returned, bright white lights illuminated the darkened waters all around her. A barren sea opened up before her, void of any marine life, mimicking the world above. Light from her pod only stretched a few feet in front of her, the darkness swallowing everything beyond its reach whole. It took several moments for her eyes to adjust, the underwater world reluctant to reveal itself to her. Cassidy had no sense of direction, she couldn't tell if she was drifting with the current or descending. Everything looked the same to her down here. After several tense moments, Cassidy spotted something swimming near the edge of her vision. She recognized the silver back and pinkish-red belly of the Arctic Char, she had seen several during her stay in Gjoa Haven, in the dining halls. In an instant, the underwater world exploded with life, drawn in by the light. A school of fish swam in all directions around the pod, dancing back and forth in her field of vision.

The blurry haze of a sunken ship started to come into

focus. The wooden frame of the ship was, remarkably still in excellent shape. Seaweed covered the entire ship, the ocean current causing it to sway back and forth in an unending dance. A towering smokestack was still intact, the long pipe listing only slightly to the left as the ship rested upright along the ocean floor. They had removed the three masts during the winter when the ship got stuck in the ice. It was a preventative measure to stop the buildup of ice on the sails and masts from capsizing the ship. They never replaced the masts; the crew was forced to abandon the HMS Terror in the ice during its third winter. The Terror, once thought destroyed by the ice flows, was intact and showed little signs of any damage. Cassidy watched in astonishment as the British Naval ship seemed to stretch endlessly into the darkness.

Suction tugged at the pod, yanking the drifting vessel downwards towards a swirling pit of darkness alongside the HMS Terror. Cassidy's vision began to blur as the pod spun out of control, a gushing roar of water grew louder, the expanding force pinning her into the seat. Her knuckles whitened as she gripped the steering wheel in a frivolous attempt to control the spiraling motion. Cassidy closed her eyes tight, waiting for the nauseous sensation to pass.

CHAPTER TWO

Cassidy felt her mind racing, powerless to tell if the visions she experienced were filtering in through her eyes or if they were embedded directly onto her brain from the portal. Every trip through the portal had a distinct effect on her, and this dimension was toying with her mind. Unable to determine if she was in a feverish dream or trapped in another reality, Cassidy waited for the feeling to pass. A crisp breeze sent shudders throughout her entire body, her knees trembled, and goosebumps sprang out all over her body. She crossed her arms over her chest, rubbing her upper body to generate warmth.

Visions of the past, present and future blended together. The overload of information caused her brain to pound, every detail flickered in her head just long enough to register. She couldn't concentrate long enough to comprehend any meaning, the torrent of memories flooding over her like a waterfall. Images of old British-style ships sailing through rough waves laden with large pans of ice were dominant over all other pictures being painted in her head.

"What are you doing here?" A man's voice reverberated in Cassidy's cranium. She glanced around in all directions, but all she could see was blackness. She closed her eyes and the impressions of the ships and frozen world returned to her.

"Where are you?" Cassidy questioned. She had encountered nothing like this in the other portals. Was this dimension entirely in her mind, or was she now only realizing that fact?

"That is not relevant right now." His commanding voice was void emotion. "What is critical is that you comprehend why you are here."

"What do you mean?" A pair of ships trapped in the ice came into focus, a line of sailors walking away from the ships stretched far. The men were pulling sleds, overwhelmed with supplies as they trudged across the ice.

"Do you know why you have come to this wretched place?" Somehow, Cassidy knew the voice belonged to one man on the ice.

"I don't even know what this place is?" Curiosity and intrigue captured all of her attention, drawing her focus towards every detail she could discover. The men's faces were veiled from view, everybody had their faces shrouded in scarves. Their outer winter slops were frozen stiff and covered in filth.

"Creation of this dimension was born of heroic tragedy, the lost souls here doomed to live out their lives defending a tragic secret. The origin of their suffering is also the source of your salvation." A man on the ice stalled, lifting his head up towards Cassidy. She felt his eyes upon her, an ice-cold sensation coursed through her veins.

"Salvation of my planet?" Cassidy studied the man's

face, his clean-shaven face riddled with ice burns. Time aged his eyes far beyond the man's years, his brown eyes saturated with immeasurable misery.

The man now stood alone of the open ice, the silhouette of the two ships prominent in the background. "Not just salvation for your planet. Rather, it can be the redemption for all mankind, in the proper hands." As he spoke, Cassidy noticed his yellow teeth and bloodied gums.

Cassidy opened her eyes and was startled to discover herself surrounded by the sailors she had seen on the ice. They trudged past her on both sides, neither man glancing up from their desolate journey to pay her any attention. "I don't understand. Who are you?"

"I was once someone to you, now I am no one of any importance. My great discovery led to my terrible fate and the damnation of my crew." Underneath his thick, wool jacket Cassidy noticed golden buttons on his dress uniform. She recognized the style of his garments, once dawned by the British Royal Navy. He stood tall and proud, a stoic figure underneath the many layers of clothes protecting him from the extreme cold. "My pride would not allow me to let go of our extraordinary discovery. It remained until the bitter end, and now we are here waiting for liberation."

"I still don't understand," Cassidy called out, the swarm of sailors pushing her away from him. They carried her away from him without saying a word. She struggled against them, never able to elude their grasp even though she couldn't feel them touching her. "I can help you." Cassidy felt a blast of frosty cold air and a blizzard of snow clouded her vision. She covered her eyes with her hand, squinting against the golden light that loomed over her. The silvery glow grew outwards, an explosion of pure white forced her to clench her eyelids shut. When she opened them again, she found herself in an officer's berth aboard a ship. The bed was narrow and short, even for her. Drawers underneath utilized every inch of space. The sheets were neatly folded, the thin pillow placed neatly at the head of the bed. A tiny nightstand next to the bed had a drained glass and a bottle of black rum, the residue of the black liquid remained from the finished drink.

A tiny window faced out over an infinite ocean; the white-capped waves rolled into the horizon in a perpetual ripple. Cassidy turned around and narrowly avoided bumping her head against the low door frame. She stepped into the corridor, careening into the wall as her legs still adjusted to the swell of the ocean. "Hello," Cassidy called out, her voice echoing back to her. It was eerily silent aboard this ship. The melodies of crashing waves were distant, as if she was far removed from the middle of the ocean. The hallway was lavishly carpeted, the red and blue colours resembled the union jack. At the end of the hallway was a solid oak door, the brass knob polished to a glorious luster. Swaying back and forth with the cadence of the ship, Cassidy made her way towards the exit. Something was calling her towards it, drawing her in.

On the wall next to the door, an oil painting hung prominently on display. She paused to admire the painted image. A British Officer in his dress uniform. Golden shoulder boards accented his black tunic, buttons resembling gold coins ran in pairs down the center of his double-breasted jacket. Medals and crosses affixed to his chest spoke of courageous deeds and boundless loyalty to duty. A stiff white collar covered most of his neck, reaching to his chin. Vibrant, hazel-brown eyes looked proudly into the future with a smug sense of accomplishment and self-worth. Cassidy couldn't help but crack a smile at the man's hair, it didn't suit the stature of the portrait. Hair stuck off the sides of his head in curly lumps, the top of his head bald. Her lips curled into a gentle grin, a faint chuckle escaped her throat. Her soft laughter seemed to disappear into thin air, the echo that should have existed was replaced by silence. The door at the end of the hallway began to demand Cassidy's focus. Somehow, she knew that where the echo had vanished. She ran her fingers over the solid oak door, she felt an immense power emanating from the other side. Now she understood that this was a dream, and once she walked through this door, she would appear in its awaiting dimension.

Again, her heart raced in her chest as her rational side tried to reason with the situation she was facing. Her growing concern was the fear of coming out of the other side of this portal underneath the frozen ocean. Reaching out for the brass handle, Cassidy clenched her muscular frame in anticipation, not knowing what awaited her on the other side. With her eyes shut, she yanked the door open and felt herself falling.

CHAPTER THREE

Cassidy had her eyes clamped shut, but she recognized she was on a ship. She felt the wooden boards of the weathered decking. Underneath her, the swell of the waves shook the ship back and forth. Roaring waves crashed back into the ocean as a mighty wind filled the sails of the ships, the canvas fluttering above her. A strong scent of brine filled her nostrils. The sun was bright, the warm rays beating against her skin and negated the biting sting of the wintery winds. Below her hands, the boards were waterlogged and slick from the melting frost. She leaned backward on her knees, stretching out her abdominal muscles.

"You there, how d'you find yourself on my ship?" A deep, booming voice startled Cassidy. "Answer me or find yourself overboard." She noted a thick, British accent coated his speech.

Opening her eyes, the gleaming white light of the sun shrouded her vision. She shielded her eyes with the back of her hand, the looming shadow of a tall man slowly taking shape in front of her. "Where am I?" Her voice was flat and feeble, the side effects of travelling through the portal still had control over her.

"Do not dodge my questions with those of your own. I demand an explanation as to why a youthful lady would stow away on the Lord Commander's ship?" The luster of the sun began to fail, slowly revealing the features of the man standing before Cassidy. A sense of déjà vu washed over her, as if she had met this man somewhere before as she peered into his hazel eyes. A triangular brimmed hat propped on his head; locks of white hair coiled into tight, eccentric circles flowed out from underneath. "I grow impatient."

"I can't provide an answer to that." Too drained from traversing the portal, Cassidy couldn't even come up with a false excuse. With tremendous exertion, she forced her exhausted legs to stand. Every muscle fiber twitched and knotted. Painful daggers pierced at her body from within.

"Count yourself lucky that I have neither the time nor the heart to punish you." The man snapped his fingers, stomping footsteps pounded against the decking as two sailors approached. "Whatever your reasons, they are of little concern. Where we are heading is punishment enough." A frosty burst of sea water showered over the deck, the droplets of water beading on her seal skin parka. Something caught the interest of the captain, his stare fixed on a point far behind her. Cassidy turned her gaze to join the commander. It was as if the ocean had frozen instantly, the white caps curling upward toward the splendid rays of sunshine. A howling wind cut across the snow, hiding the source of the captain's amazement. Nestled into the horizon, a white castle, sprouting from the ice like a dazzling crystal, towered high above them. Low, growling roars carried in the wind from the prodigious structure.

"You summoned us, Sir Franklin." An inexperienced, nervous voice broke Cassidy's concentration.

Two young sailors, dressed identically, stood at attention in front of the captain. Their wool knit hats pulled down to their eyebrows. Both men wore heavy, cotton tunics that had become frozen stiff from the salty mist. "Young lad, Francis, if I'm not mistaken."

The taller of the two seamen stepped forward, bowing his head. "Yes, sir." His feeble voice squeaked, the poor young man still progressing through adolescence. His face still riddled with acne and scars.

"Very good then. Take…" Sir Franklin's face flushed with embarrassment, turning his checks a bright red. "Excuse me, young lady, I've not behaved like an honorable gentleman. Please forgive me but I am Sir Jack Franklin, Commander of the HMS Fear," he held out his hand. "And who do I have the pleasure?"

Cassidy tried to shake his hand, but he took her hand in his, and bowed down to kiss it. Before she understood what was happening, he tipped his hat to her. "Cassidy Cane," she responded sharply, outraged by his abrupt action, drawing her hand backward.

"Well, Francis, please escort Miss Cane below deck and make sure they feed her," Sir Franklin turned his attention away from Cassidy. "And you, young man, tell Sir Irving that we will make our way to the shore. Make sure that a crew informs the Erebus of our intentions. I shall accompany the party to explore this castle. Maybe this is where my father landed."

"Aye, aye, Sir." The young lad clicked his heels together and carried on about his duties.

Young Francis grabbed Cassidy's arm, but she defiantly yanked it away. "I will accompany you." She was not about to be left on board this strange ship.

Shock furled Sir Franklin's brow, he was not a man who accepted defiance. "Miss Cane…"

"Call me Cassidy, and this is not up for deliberation." she asserted herself.

"This is my ship," Jack raised his voice.

"I am not one of your sailors," Cassidy cut him off. "They will not treat me as such."

The wind was silenced like a scolded dog. Cassidy stood in defiance of the Captain, the tension between them rising swiftly. Young Francis bowed his head down to look at his boots, not wanting to make eye contact with his Captain. For what seemed like an eternity, Sir Franklin pondered his next words. "Have it your way then. It makes no difference to us."

"Sir, what would you have me do now?" Francis asked.

"Go help the men gather provisions for the night," Sir Franklin barked without hesitation. The young sailor scurried off to join the commotion rising from behind them.

Cassidy stepped forward. "What would you like me to do?"

"You are not one of my sailors." Sir Franklin tried his best to sound cordial, but his finest effort did little hide his indignation. "I will simply propose that you remain out of trouble. I do not have the men to spare looking after you."

Cassidy felt insulted. Cassidy was more than capable of taking care of herself, and she was positive the men aboard the HMS Fear could learn a thing or two from her. "You don't have to worry about me." She spit out each word, the sting of the insult still fresh.

"There you are Sir Franklin." An exceptionally tall man snuck up behind them, not sensing the tension between them. He was clad in the same clothes as Jack but looked different from his counterpart. His jacket wasn't stiff, but dangled loosely from his broad shoulders, the fabric dancing in the breeze. His cheeks were rosy and an extreme contrast to his pale blue eyes. "I need to speak to you."

"What is it, mister Irving?" Sir Franklin sounded annoyed by the younger man.

"If it pleases you, a private counsel may be beneficial." Irving spoke gently. His wig, while comparable to Sir Franklin's, appeared to be of poorer quality. The white curls hung loosely just above his shoulders with messy, stray hairs going in all directions.

"I don't have time for that," Sir Franklin rolled his eyes at the proposition. "Just get on with it man."

"Well Sir, there appears to be a problem with the compass. The dial just spins around in random directions." Irving presented the facts.

"Gibberish, that compass is brand new." Sir Franklin shook his head. "It employs the latest technology available, just like every other piece of equipment under my command. I guarantee you it is not a malfunction of the equipment."

"With all due respect Sir, it operates based on its capacity to detect magnetic fields. There is no human error possible because it's purely mechanical." Irving spoke calmly and ignored the Captain's irritation. He reached into his pocket, retrieving a pack of cigarettes and matches. He shielded the smoke and struck a match in his hand with practiced expertise, drawing in a slow puff. "I can give a rough bearing to Sir Coizer on the Erebus, but I'm not able to provide him the exact location. I recommend that we wait here for him. They are not that far behind us, anyway."

"I will take it under advisement. In the meantime, Sir Irving, I suggest that you try to fix that compass of yours." Sir Franklin turned his nose at the acrid odor of cigarette smoke. The breeze blew it right into his face.

"He will not be able to fix it." Cassidy interjected.

"What do you know of it?" Sir Franklin chuckled. "I have serious doubts you are privy to the knowledge of this invention." He shot Irving a sly grin which the other officer did not reciprocate.

Not wishing to expose her identity, revealing the fact that she was an inter-dimensional traveller, choosing her words carefully. "I know just as much as any member of your crew. I've seen this happen before."

"Seen this happen before?" Sir Franklin didn't wait for an answer. "This is the first time we have used the invention aboard any vessel."

Cassidy felt her heart racing, both men gawking at her quizzically. She had vaulted into the midst of an argument she had no benefit of winning. All she had to do was keep her opinion to herself, and she would have discovered the magnetic anomaly, anyway. "This new technology isn't much more advanced than putting a leaf in a puddle of water." Both men remained still, a bewildered look plastered on their faces.

"I've never heard of that method being employed except by the unsophisticated savages." Sir Franklin scoffed. "Hardly reliable and inconsequential to our situation here."

She may have fooled Sir Franklin, but Irving's gaze remained glued on her. Cassidy felt warm, she could feel the perspiration beading on her goose bumped flesh. "I'm just trying to say that people used to believe that it worked." Cassidy knew the truth, she had stumbled upon her destination without having invested in any effort. By saying anything, all she did was put her chance of discovering the artifact at risk. Irving continued to study her with untrusting eyes. "Now we have a new compass that we believe works without fail."

"Sir Irving, please send a message to the Erebus immediately. I do not want to delay any further than what is necessary." Sir Franklin brushed off Irving by waving his hand theatrically. "Now, Miss Cane, will you escort me to the mess hall for a glass of whisky?" Irving left quietly, keeping the line of sight between them until he vanished through one of the doors.

Cassidy turned her back to Sir Franklin, admiring the natural beauty of the tundra. Looking closer at the white castle, she could see the weathered grey stones underneath. "I don't drink whisky."

"Well, I could offer you some of my personal black rum." Sir Franklin softened the tone of his voice. "The others will be envious."

"Did you say black rum?" That triggered Cassidy's subconscious. She recalled seeing a bottle of black rum on the nightstand in the officer's berth. That feverish dream must have meant something. It had to be connected to this world somehow. Was this all part of some puzzle she would have to piece together to discover the artifact Doctor Gamgee required from this realm?

"Very well then, I will fetch my steward and have him prepare us two drinks before we depart." Sir Franklin turned to leave. "If it pleases you, we could take our drink here on deck."

"That will do just fine, Sir." Cassidy replied graciously, relishing in the opportunity to collect her thoughts alone. The captain's footprints could be heard echoing into the cold air. Four giant towers had been erected into each corner of the castle; each pillar was a near perfect circle. Each tower had windows sporadically placed throughout the structure, with a canopy covering each landing from the elements. The stairs at the front of the building had been drawn out as far as they could, each step about four feet wide. Broken off the hinges, one side of the double wooden door lay battered against ground. The iron frame twisted and distorted from some horrific struggle years ago. Layer upon layer of ice had built up over the stones from previous winters. The ice was so white it looked blue in the shadows. It appeared to be vacant, there were no signs of activity outside in the snow-covered courtyard.

"Your drink, my lady."

Cassidy could feel the warm breath on her neck. She spun around immediately, coming face to face with a scruffy-looking sailor. Long strands of black, greasy hair clung to his face. His breath reeked of salt fish and whisky. He held out a glass half-filled with the black rum Sir Franklin had offered.

"Thank you." Cassidy took possession of the glass, wondering if it was the same one from her vision. The sailor brushed back a stray clump of greasy hair, grinned a toothless smile and took his leave without uttering another word. She placed the drink on the rail, looking back out over the ice-packed waters separating the HMS Fear from solid ice. The water was virtually black, making the ice stand out even more against the backdrop.

How deep was this water?

Footsteps approached the rail, the clank of Sir Franklin's glass against the rail startled her. He didn't say a word, he just leaned against the rail and glanced out over the water. "I've been chasing after my father for years. So many I've actually lost count now." He raised his glass. "To Sir John Franklin." They clinked their glasses together. Cassidy wondered what the failed Franklin expedition had to do with this realm. The further she dug into this mystery, the deeper the layers went. Somehow, earth's dimension was directly connected to this realm. Events that took place aboard the HMS Terror and HMS Erebus had shaped the structure of this alternate world.

Or was it the other way around?

The black rum burned all the way down, the liquid splashing into her empty stomach. She coughed, holding her forearm up to her face to stifle the sound. "That's strong."

Sir Franklin nodded his head. "It's from my private

cache." He tilted his glass towards the water, letting a drop tumble out of the glass and join the dark water below. "Straight from the casks of the gods they say." He bowed his head towards the water and raised his glass to an imaginary figure. "I used to believe that the gods watch over us." His voice was bitter, filled with a deep hatred that Cassidy could feel. "Until the first time I lost a man at sea. These dark waters contain demons that reach up from below the shadowy depths and drag us down in the cold grave." He turned towards her, placed his hand on her shoulder and stared directly into her eyes. "The sea will always win. It takes our loved ones, our friends and the people we work with. It will take everything from those who try to defy it. These waters are so black because of the souls it has devoured."

Cassidy took another sip of her black rum, this time the burn didn't last as long. The dark liquid caused a warm tingle to radiate throughout her body. The words of Sir Franklin were heavy with regret, a deep pain coursed through his veins. Water and ice were not the normal area of study for Cassidy. It was at this moment that she realized she missed being an archaeologist, she missed being a teacher. She finished the last of her drink, slamming the glass down on the rail in triumph. "Thank you for the rum." Cassidy was determined she wouldn't let these darkened waters consume her.

"Thank you for listening to this old man ramble." Sir Franklin finished off his own drink, taking both glasses as he turned to leave. "Follow me to the mess. The rations for our meal have been prepared. Once we finish eating everything else should be ready."

Now that she had discovered her sea legs, Cassidy

could navigate the slick deck with ease. She could keep pace with the veteran sailor, she walked into the galley with him. The tight entrance was deceiving, the room expanded into a much larger space than she would have thought possible. Furnished with lavish art, high-end furniture and a giant dining room table, Cassidy assumed that she was in the officer's mess hall. A rush of hot air surrounded her; the room was being heated somehow. She hung up her hat on a coat rack nestled in the room's corner and took off her jacket. Every eye in the room gave her a quick stare, her clothing must have seemed odd to the crew of the ship. She wore a beaver skin vest over a loose-fitting white blouse, her feminine figure expertly hidden from the gawking men.

A chair was pulled out for her, young Francis held the chair for her with a curt smile on his face. After being in this new dimension for a short time, she realized that the sailors were trying to be gentlemen. She tried not to take offence to their gestures, but she didn't appreciate being treated this way. If the men aboard this ship knew all the things she had accomplished in the last few weeks since exploring the dimensions, they would look at her differently. She sat down in the sturdy wooden chair, the blue cushion surprisingly soft. The dining table was long enough to seat eight people on either side, the darkened mahogany wood was showing the signs of being at sea for too long. Cassidy found herself to the left of Sir Franklin, she sat with her back to the wall. She could watch as all the officers filed into the room. The men shared small talk as they went about their business of hanging up their winter slops.

Servers wearing white jackets and chef's hats brought

out plates filled with steaming hot food. Having prepared it below deck, the stewards entered the room from a set of stairs off to the left. Cassidy knew that the officers tried their best to hide the higher quality of food from their sailors. Jealousy and envy could cause a mutiny, even though everyone knew that the officers ate better. Mounds of creamed potatoes, carrots and peas smothered in gravy made her mouth water. The pork roast beneath it all looked succulent. "Thank you," Cassidy said as a steward placed a plate in front of her. After only a few minutes, everyone sat down at the table had their dinner in front of them. The waiters brought out fresh baked buns with butter, and they had placed bottles of red wine and whisky on the table.

"Father, Praise You for friendship and family.

Thank You for bringing us together today to share a meal. The people in our lives bring us such joy, and we are grateful for time spent in fellowship together.

Help us use this time to bond closer as a group and learn to love each other more.

Bless our appetites, both physical and spiritual, to honor You in all we do. In Jesus' Name, Amen."

Sir Franklin said grace, the other men at the table all bowed their heads. He spoke with conviction but with a subtle softness required of a clergyman. The words he spoke flowed graciously off his tongue. Practiced time and time again, he didn't stutter once. The sound of cutlery clanging off the plates rang out throughout the dining hall. Most of the men didn't even bother to look up except to accept a glass of wine. Cassidy met eyes with Irving. He was leaning towards a shorter, older man. They were definitely talking about her; Cassidy could see Irving pointing at her with his fork as he spoke. She leaned towards Sir Franklin. "Who is that man Irving is speaking with?"

Sir Franklin finished chewing his food, washing it all down with a large gulp of red wine. "That is ice master Peglar."

"What does an ice master do?" Cassidy asked curiously.

"They are precious members of any ship sailing through the arctic waters." Sir Franklin said. "They are experts in navigation, fishing, hunting and survival on the ice. He will accompany us to the castle."

Quickly looking around the table, Cassidy couldn't help but wonder who else would join them. "Are we leaving soon?"

"We will be headed out onto the ice as soon as possible." Sir Franklin responded quickly, abruptly turning his attention away from Cassidy. She sat there, listening to the different conversations taking place around the table. The atmosphere was buzzing with rumors and gossip. Everyone had their opinion about what they would find in the castle. Some men thought it would be empty, others believed it would be haunted, while some people thought an ice princess lived there. Cassidy did her best to listen in on the conversation that Irving and Peglar were having, but they must have realized she noticed that they were talking about her. Both men had remained huddled close together, their voices hardly rising above a whisper. Anticipation started to build; the thrill of adventure was edging closer. Sir Franklin rose and the rest of the men stopped eating, rising to join their captain. "Well, let us head to the skiff, we want to make sure we get to the castle before sunset."

CHAPTER FOUR

The boat's gunwales dropped inch by inch, each jostling descent interrupted by an abrupt halt. Groans and grunts from the men lowering the ship grew louder with each passing moment. Strain forced the rope to dig into the sailor's hands, with each drop the boat sank further down before they caught the ropes. Cassidy bounced around on the hard wooden platform that served as her seat. Once they reached the water, the sailors used their ores to navigate towards the coast. Men with large spikes pushed away loose fragments of ice that threatened to damage the hull. The water was as black as oil, the pure darkness threatening to engulf anyone foolish enough to enter. The waves rocked the much smaller whaling boat, the sheer force of the ocean on full display. With every surge that raised the boat, a nauseous sensation would rise in her stomach. Fear would drive that feeling aside as they crashed back down into the ice-cold water.

None of the men showed any fear. They all went about their business, not paying any attention to the strong waves beneath them. Cassidy was glad that she didn't have any assigned duties. She didn't have her sea legs and years of being an archeologist made her miss standing barefoot, with the earth beneath her feet. Sir Franklin stood in the center of the whaling ship, expertly directing his crew as they performed their services. She watched Peglar and Irving as they concentrated on the shore, concocting a strategy to reach the shore. Ice had built up against the rugged coast, the silvery wall towering seven feet above them in some places. The other unnamed members of the crew worked faithfully to paddle and maneuver the boat to the shore. Sailors struggled with the effort, beads of perspiration dripped down their foreheads as they toiled relentlessly. Overheated by their heavy outer layers, some men removed their coats despite the stinging cold chill rising from the water.

"Mr. Peglar, what is our best option here?" Sir Franklin's voice lifted above the anguished cries of the struggling sailors.

"Sir, just order the men to bring us alongside the shore," Peglar pointed straight ahead. "Mr. Irving and I will take care of the rest."

"You heard the ice master, men," Sir Franklin shouted passionately. "Not much further now."

The tired sailors moaned a half-hearted hurrah, before returning to their duties. It was a tedious, strenuous process as the men paddled towards the coast. They had to slow down every time a sizable block of ice threatened to damage the boat. High waves lifted the colossal sized shards of ice dangerously close to the edge of the boat. If just one of those miniature icebergs landed in the ship, they would capsize in an instant. One man jabbed at a hunk of ice, the sharp edge of his pike dug in deep. He tried to yank the head out, but it lodged in tight. A wave raised the schooner up as the iceberg fell down on the other side, nearly ripping the poor, young sailor clear out of the boat. Cassidy leapt forward, catching him around the waist just before he tumbled out of the boat. Embarrassment swept over his face as the pike jerked out of his hand, slipping into the blackened waters.

Everyone aboard stared at the young man, snickering laughter erupted from the other men as they attended to their business. Cassidy knew they directed the laughter towards the unfortunate sailor who nearly fell overboard and had been saved by a woman. Still holding her arms around his stomach, Cassidy released him from her grip. He spun and acknowledged his gratitude towards her, having earned his respect. A shadow crept over the boat, the towering wall of ice loomed ominously above them. A sudden chill gripped her, the sun fading behind the elevated ice wall.

Knelt down at the edge of the boat, Irving and Peglar dug through a bag stuffed with various tools. Peglar retrieved an axe, the dull blade full of indentations and scrapes. "Maintain the boat as steady as possible now boys." Carefully lifting the axe above his head, Peglar starting hacking away at the ice wall. Broken fragments of ice scattered across the deck and back into the sea. The sailors held the ship as steady as they could, but the bobbing water made it challenging to strike the same place. Once the hole was deep enough, Peglar planted one foot into the ice and used it to steady himself. As the waves caused the boat underneath him to shift, the ice master bent his knee in cadence with the rolling waves. Peglar continued to hack away at the ice with the dulled blade, chiseling out a set of steps into the bank. "There, that ought to do it," He proclaimed through laboured breathing. He ascended the makeshift stairs and peered down at them.

"Do you see anything?" Irving called out, gesturing for the others to remain aboard the whaling boat.

With his back turned, Peglar disappeared from view temporarily. His footsteps crunching in the crust as he moved around. "Nothing of any danger, Sir." His voice sounded remote, the wind carrying it away from them.

"After you, gentlemen." Sir Franklin ushered the sailors up the ice stairs. One by one, the men dashed up the stairs. Cassidy took notice of the silver spikes at the bottom of the men's boots, the grips digging into the glistening surface. Irving, Sir Franklin and Cassidy were the only people remaining in the boat. They tossed lengths of rope back down into the ship, Irving tied knots into the handles of the bags carrying the party's provisions. Steadily, the sailors hoisted the supplies. The rope fell back down into the waiting arms of Irving, who secured the ends to a five-foot-long toboggan.

"After you, Miss Cane." Irving offered Cassidy his hand as they hauled the toboggan up over the ridge.

Cassidy placed her boot into the foothold, discovering it troublesome to find her footing. Frigid cold sensations ran up her arm as she placed her hand in the gaps. Something deep inside the ice seemed to percolate out of the carved holes. A cold unlike anything she had ever experienced washed over her, draining the warmth from her very essence. Her hands struggled to grasp a firm grip, but she didn't want to show any shortcoming in front of the sailors. Cassidy worried, her feet slipping out from underneath her, she scampered up the makeshift stairs hurriedly. As if anticipating her endeavors, the youthful sailor she had saved earlier, graciously held out his hand for her, hauling her up onto the shore. "Are you all right?" The young man asked.

Cassidy brushed the sleet off her pants. "Yes, I am, thank you." His pale blue eyes were so light, they appeared to be grey. A thin moustache rested on his lip like a black rim left behind from a glass. She stood up under her own power, finding herself uncomfortably close to the young man. "What is your name again?" Not remembering if she had ever known it.

With a tilt of his hat, the young man revealed a scruffy mop of curly black hair. "My name is Tommy Seeley."

"Ordinary seaman Seeley." Irving's head poked above the ice. "Stop lolly-gagging around and help Sir Franklin up." Irving pulled himself up and joined Cassidy. Tommy rushed over to help the Captain over the ledge, Sir Franklin was out of breath from the effort. "Well don't just stand there, gentlemen, these supplies need to be loaded aboard the skiff and brough to the castle. Seeley and Edwards, scout ahead and make sure we aren't walking into any trouble." Irving barked orders at his men. "We don't want any surprises when we get to the castle now."

"Yes sir." A harmony of voices responded in unison. Everyone scurrying about their business without hesitation. Years of obedience drilled into them, encouraging them forward as a company.

A large, long ranging mountain chain appeared behind the castle. Cassidy had not noticed them from the ship, but the jagged formation reached far into the sky not too far from where the castle nestled. She thought it would be the perfect location to defend, the mountains and shorelines offering great protection from all angles. Giant formations of ice and snow blended into the horizon, merging into the clouds above. Loud scraping caught her attention, the men had loaded the toboggan with all the supplies and were hauling it towards the castle. She could see Tommy far ahead with Edwards, their bodies blurring into two black specks as they scouted ahead. A low melody started to rise from the sailors as they worked in unison to pull the skiff across the crusted surface.

"Stay close to us. If the wind picks up, we could all get separated if we are too far apart." Peglar startled Cassidy. His speech was low and throaty, it was the first real time she had heard him speak directly to her. "I've seen people get twisted around in a matter of minutes. Stumbled across the frozen carcasses of my friends I had been walking alongside." Wisdom and experience weathered Peglar's soulful, emerald eyes. There was a deep sadness saturating the iris of his eyes, his black pupils mirroring the ocean water. Cassidy nodded her head, acknowledging his warning. She made sure she kept pace with Peglar, who was leading the two officers, making certain she remained in the midst of the pack. She had been trapped in a sandstorm before, the dynamic force of mother nature wasn't something to oppose. Sandstorms could materialize out of thin air and without warning, not unlike the fickle weather of this frozen wasteland.

"How long do you think it will take to uncover any evidence in there?" Irving asked Sir Franklin, his voice distorted by the approaching wind.

"If my father is here, we will know immediately." Sir Franklin's voice carried more heavily on the wind. "He wouldn't have any reason to hide from us. He would recognize our sails."

They followed in the tracks left behind by the skiff. The trail already beaten down. Without warning, the wind's intensity increased and whirled the snow around in blinding swirls. Cassidy lost track of the men pulling the sled within seconds. She had to squint against the pelting snow, the ice pellets hurt her eyes as the wind whipped a torrent of tiny daggers into her face. She closed her eyes for a second to protect them, when the gale passed, she opened her eyes again. Barren, white tundra stretched out for as far as she could see. "Hello?" Cassidy yelled out nervously against the white-out conditions. The tracks were gone. "I'm over here." She took a moment to compose herself and tried to remember her training. After taking a moment to survey the ground around her feet, she realized that she stumbled just a few feet from the tracks. She tucked her head into her chest, bracing herself against the barrage of snow pellets.

"Stay close, Miss Cane." Peglar reached out from the blanketing wall of snow, escorting her towards the rest of the party. "Until this storm passes, wear these." The ice master handed her a pair of wire-framed goggles. Placing them over her head, she found the straps dug into the sides of her skull. Able to see without squinting against the wind, she kept pace with the sailors as they trudged across the tundra. After several minutes, they arrived at the staircase of the castle.

A loud creaking noise groaned out as Irving opened the door, the metal hinges screeching high pitched wails. Cassidy followed closely behind Sir Franklin, accompanying him up the stairs. The faint flicker of torch light danced down the stone passageway. They followed the source of the light; The hallway protected them against the wind and pelting snow. They rounded the corner and felt the scorching heat from a torch, left behind in a holder hung on the wall. The corridor opened into a grand chamber. Irving gathered all the sailors around the giant hearth, fumbling with matches and logs trying to light a fire. They had already lit several of the torches placed around the corridor, the shifting light casting their silhouettes across the hall.

A roaring boom engulfed the room as a giant flame illuminated the murkiest corners of the great hall. The once smooth stones, now distorted by harsh weather, pitted and scarred them over the years. Beneath the whistle of the wind that ripped through the open window, Cassidy heard a melody of birds chirping in the rafters. Trees sprouted up from the earth, roots reached out across the fractured stone floor. Grime covered the once brilliant red tablecloths. Ancient wooden tables and chairs scattered across the room by the wind, long abandoned by the former inhabitants. Whispers of the past echoed from the walls. They recounted tales of past hardships, lives lost and of agony suffered out here on this desolate strip of earth. A wave of warmth from the fire fought against the savage chill, the warmth unable to stall the seeping coldness from the windows. The sailors huddled near the roaring blaze in the hearth, Sir Franklin joined them. Cassidy huddled into the circle; everybody did their best to shake the coldness out of their bones.

"It appears the castle has been long deserted, Sir." Irving broke the silence first.

Disappointment and resentment lingered on Sir Franklin's expression. "It would appear so," He replied wistfully. "But we have the whole night to explore and gather any evidence there may be." With a twist, he shifted towards his company and positioned himself at the center of their huddle. "Sir Irving, have the men set up the stoves. We shall clean off the tables here and eat near the warmth of the fire. We will also need to set up a place to rest for the night. Have two of your men scout out a suitable location."

"Aye, Sir," Irving replied. "Seeley and Edwards, take one shotgun with you. Have a look around and after lunch we shall set up camp for the night. The rest of you prepare the stoves and rations." The congregation became much smaller as the men went about their tasks.

"Mr. Peglar, please board up the windows and doors as best as you can. I would like the men to be comfortable for a change," Sir Franklin ordered.

"I am able to help with that," Cassidy offered. The three remaining men looked astonished, exchanging astounded expressions with each other. "I'm positive it would make things easier, Mr. Peglar."

After some consideration, Sir Franklin finally responded, "If you insist, you can go with him. Irving, I want to discuss some concerns in private with you."

"Come along, Miss Cane, let's look at those windows and see what we can do with them." Peglar didn't wait for Cassidy. He was a good five feet away from her before her legs started to churn, she had to sprint to catch up to him. "Help me search for anything we can use to block the windows. I'd prefer not to use our own supplies, that will make it easier when we leave tomorrow." He sauntered towards a door; the stone had designs engraved into the archway. Peglar stopped to observe them. Perplexed by the illustrations, he turned towards Cassidy with a concerned expression on his face. "Have you seen these before?"

Cassidy leaned in closer, trying to detect any correlations with the Egyptian hieroglyphs she had spent years researching. The only connection she observed was the use of animals, but the characterization of bears and wolves dominated the carvings. "They appear to be telling a story." She discovered a logical sequence to the drawings. Wolves appeared to be in an eternal feud with a giant polar bear that walked on its hind legs. The bear had developed some traits of man, with its paws taking on the shape of hands and its defined musculature gave the creature a humanoid appearance. At the tip of the archway, a single stone had a disc-shaped object carved into it. In every image, every beast was bowed down in worship, with the bear above the disc and the wolves sprawled out in a circle. "Are these carvings on all the doorways?"

"We will have to look into that later," Peglar said as he pushed the door open. The cold, damp air flooded out of the room, wrapping its fingers around Cassidy. A tight spiraling staircase led down below, the dimness gave the impression of twilight in the absence of the glowing torches behind them. "Let's search elsewhere. I don't have time to go down there right now." Peglar closed the door behind him and shuffled over to the next room. Something in that place was calling Cassidy, imploring her to explore further. She turned back to find Peglar, who had already stopped to wait for her. "Are you coming?" he said impatiently.

Cassidy felt the urge to explore. Somehow, she knew something important was buried into the darkness of that room. "Just a second." She turned to glance over her shoulder, one last time, at the staircase before running over to join Peglar. She needed one of the torches from the wall before she could head down into the darkness. Peglar walked into another room; Cassidy took notice of the archway. Just stones and weathered markings, no hieroglyphics over this door, or anywhere else nearby. The former occupants filled the room with lumber and ancient wooden doors.

"Perfect, just what we are looking for," Peglar exclaimed excitedly. "I will fetch some men to carry over the boards." He pushed past Cassidy and wandered back into the great chamber.

Cassidy grabbed a torch from the holder on the wall and bolted towards the darkened passageway, eager to explore what lay beneath the castle. She closed the door behind her quietly, making certain not to draw attention to herself. Despite the brilliance of the flaming torch, the dimness of the staircase gave the impression of gloom, keeping its secrets carefully concealed. Carved into a solid slab of rock, the stairs spiraled downward into the madness below. The irregular steps and rough landings made it a hazardous descent. Cassidy couldn't see much further than a few steps in front of her. A musty, damp smell awaited her at the bottom of the steps, an encompassing layer of cold cut through her jacket. She was chilled to her soul. The bottom of the stairs led to an empty room, the light did little to illuminate the space, but she found torches hung in place along the wall. As she lit the first torch, the shape of the room came into view. It was a complete circle, Cassidy walked along the edge, lighting the torches spaced equally throughout the circumference of the room. Each torch lit illuminated a new detail that had been sheltering in the obscurity.

Now that all the torches were lit, Cassidy was disappointed to find that there was no other way out of the room but back up the stairs. Fully illuminated, the details carved into the floor virtually appeared out of thin air. It depicted an enlarged version of the hieroglyphics that decorated the archway upstairs on the floor. Except now all the images were centered around the mysterious disc. All the wolves appeared to be after the artifact and the bear-like creature was defending it. Slowly walking over to the center, she cautiously avoided stepping onto the disc. She took notice of the positioning of all the groupings of wolves; they mirrored the locations of major landmasses on earth. Centered in the middle, the disc marked the location of the magnetic North Pole. Was this drawing a map?

Accidentally stepping onto the disc, a low rumble moaned in the room. The ground started to shake and shift underneath her feet. Before she could run back to the stair, Cassidy felt the floor open up beneath her and she collapsed into the unknowing darkness below.

CHAPTER FIVE

Sharp pain radiated from her elbow and back, tumbling down the angled shaft left scrapes and bruises all over her body. Luckily, she had dropped out of the tunnel feet first, bracing herself against a painful fall. The torch had fallen on the ground behind her, but miraculously remained lit. The pale yellow light twinkled in the puddles collected in the gravel along the narrow passage. Somehow Cassidy avoided breaking any bones during her fall. She dusted off her clothes, realizing that she had several scrapes over both of her hands. With a heavy grunt, she bent down and massaged a knot from her back as she stretched out for the torch. An intense pain threatened to collapse her as her back muscles cramped. The torch weighed tremendously more than it should have, the burden to straighten up unbearable.

Cassidy looked up towards the hole in the ceiling, finding it pitch black. The light from the torch too feeble to shed its glow upon the trail. "Now what?" She murmured to herself, discovering herself in yet another avoidable situation. The walls of the underpass were black, jagged rock. Moss grew upon the surface all around, mushrooms sprouting up from the tiny cracks. As painful as it was, Cassidy twisted her neck to examine her two options. The tunnel led straight ahead in either direction, both paths looked forlorn. Disoriented by the fall, Cassidy wasn't certain which direction was north. She remained silent, evaluating her options. A delicate breeze rushed past her face. Barely noticeable, but just enough for her to distinguish which direction it flowed. She turned to face the breeze and began to wander down the passage. Condensation wet the soil beneath her feet, she watched the beads of water dripping down the rocks. With every passing minute, Cassidy could feel the current growing stronger. A low whistle began to form softly in her ear.

Grrrrrr

A low, deep growl echoed through the caves. It was too far away for Cassidy to determine its origin. Her heart started to race, pumping blood to her leg muscles, strengthening them to perform their next move. Curiosity, as it invariably did, got the better of her. Without hesitation, she proceeded down the narrow tunnel. Her only escape was to turn and run down an unexplored path, not sure what awaited her on the other side. With every stride she took, the light reached further into the uncharted, towards the source of the potential menace.

Rrrrrr

A guttural snarl froze Cassidy in place, the sound much closer than before. Vibrations of the low grumble trembled the ground beneath her feet. A stiff wind blew out the torch, casting her into seclusion. It took a moment for her eyes to readjust. A distant radiance from the end of the tunnel provided just enough light for her to find her way down the trail. The tiny dribble of sunlight had just enough influence over the darkness to guide her. Cassidy looked over her shoulder, finding nothing but darkness behind her. Forced to proceed forward, Cassidy found the determination to press on. Her heart pounded in her chest with anticipation. With every step towards the exit, the daylight's power grew stronger. The ground was dryer here than it was further into the grotto, the fierce bitter winds of the tundra lashed out at her. A reminder of the frigid temperatures awaiting her. Cassidy could see the pure white tundra just outside of the opening. A flood of relief washed over her, drawing her out into the opening.

The usual blustery noises of the tundra came to an unnerving halt. Not a single sound existed around her, Cassidy stopped still, the hairs on her arms rising in alarm. Silence replaced the boisterous wind, setting her on edge. A loud crunch in the snow echoed from the nearby forest, a branch snapped followed by a low, guttural grunt. She remained frozen, alarmed by the extraordinary, throaty growl rising around her. The sound was low and menacing, it filled the primal animal savagery with hunger. Another harsh growl ripped from the creature's throat as it sauntered out of the tree line and into view. A polar bear, standing on its hind legs, was taller than any man she had ever seen. Sharp, white daggers protruded from the creature's moist jaw. The creature's front paws crashed back down into the snow, sending a thunderous crunching sound booming across the desolate earth between them. The dying light of the sun captured in the creature's fur, giving the beast a yellow aura.

Cassidy didn't stand a chance in the deep snow against the bear, she could scarcely maneuver in this untouched environment. She turned and raced back into the seclusion of the cavern. Blinded by the bright light outside, her ability to see in the dark was temporarily diminished. The low rumble of the bear as it raced across the tundra at her propelled her legs forward. She kept stubbing her toes against the craggy rocks. As she slowly pushed further into the cave, the low grumble of the bear approached rapidly, gaining ground on her at a threatening pace. Adrenaline fueled Cassidy's body, preventing her from tripping on one of the derelict rocks in her path, her legs pumping faster now. A faint flicker of light guided her. It was coming from far away, but it was all she needed. Cassidy squeezed through a narrow opening, forcing her slender frame through.

From the shadows, the predator appeared with a ravenous expression on his snout. Cassidy let out a shuddering gasp, she could feel the creature's warm breath from the other side of the tiny opening. She watched as the creature curled up its gums to reveal the stained teeth, letting out a low rumbling growl. Pacing back and forth, the polar bear beat its claws off the rock wall in frustration. Shards or rock scattered across the stony path below. Cassidy slowly started to withdraw, never taking her eyes off the fearsome predator. The bear let out one booming, angered roar before disappearing back into the shadows. Somehow, Cassidy knew that the creature wasn't done with her, she felt a curious attachment to the beast that she couldn't explain. After a few deep breaths, Cassidy remembered what had led her down this path. Quickly turning around, she saw the dancing torch light in the distance. It's flickering flames casting men's shadows on the wall. "Help!" Cassidy screamed out. She strained to hear a response, but none awaited her, she had to keep moving. Lost in some network of caves below the castle, Cassidy had never felt so alone.

With her arms outstretched, her hands braced her against the wall, the dim light guiding her towards her purpose. Every step allowed the yellow flame to illuminate the tunnel a little more, she could almost run now. She cupped her hands, "Hello." her voice rang softly off the walls.

"Miss Cane?" Sir Franklin's voice responded. Cassidy rushed forward; the harmony of his voice calmed her mind. She could see his shadow spread out on the cavern wall about one hundred feet in front of her. The narrow corridor opened into a larger chamber, she scrambled towards it. An empty void separated Cassidy from Sir Franklin, an ominous hole between them. "There you are."

Cassidy noticed the relief in his expression from across the void. A giant pool of water lay thirty feet below them, rugged rocks sticking out of the surface of the tranquil water. "How am I going to get across?"

"I don't know." Sir Franklin scratched his chin. "The gap appears too wide for any ladder we have. Have you explored the caves yet? Maybe there is another way out."

"There's a giant bear down here." Cassidy shuddered at the thought of the terrifying creature. "And I don't even have a torch." Her voice seemed to be swallowed by the water below, her words falling into the treacherous chasm. She looked around the room, the stonework that made up the foundation of the castle had seen better days. The lack of sunlight and neglect had allowed large clusters of mold and algae to form. Bricks lined with cracks and chips poked out from underneath the blackened mold.

The corners of the room lay in shadows. Sir Franklin began to pace along the edge of his path, allowing the yellow torch light to reach the corners of the room. Tucked away in the far-right corner was another passageway, a torch posted to the wall right next to the exit. With a jump in her step, Cassidy rushed over to the doorway. Only the rusted hinges remained, the door a distant memory to the space. As she picked up the wooden torch, spiders scurried away, disappearing into the algae. Cassidy had seen far worse in the caves in Egypt, the sight of the arachnids not bothering her.

"I will send my men outside of the castle to search for a hidden entrance." Sir Franklin shouted, his voice a distant echo.

All Cassidy wanted to think about was finding her way out of this underground network. "There is an entrance along the backside of the castle." Cassidy remembered. "You will need the shotguns. There is a large polar bear lurking about." Sir Franklin tipped his hat to her before retreating up the stairs to the main level of the castle. She stood in the darkness, trying to think of a way to light the torch. After several minutes of deliberating, she remembered what the elder chief at Gjoa Haven had placed in her pocket. She reached into her pocket to fetch the lighter. With a flick, a tiny flame sprouted up in the darkness. Damp cloth didn't make lighting the torch easy, she had to stand there for several minutes before the embers grew large enough to generate light. A set of stairs spiraling downwards waited for her. Echoes of the men's voices carried above her, their feet stomping around on the stone floors caused dust to fall from the ceiling. The low, gruff rumble of the polar bear sounded in the distance below.

CHAPTER SIX

Flickering glints of light illuminated brilliant high-lights etched into the wet stone walls. The pitch blackness below engulfed all the light from the torch, not allowing the light to penetrate it. Cassidy shivered against the seeping cold, her breath floated past her vision through her pressed lips. After having identified the exit to some elaborate underground network of tunnels, the echoes of men's voices faded. The staircase seemed to go on forever in a never-ending spiral. Every rotation around the center sphere brought her deeper into the frigid darkness. It threatened to consume her.

Etched into the walls, hieroglyphics of animals told a grand tale of some ancient battle or discovery. Dominant over all the animals, the polar bear appeared to be the guardian to the great disc. The prospect of solving this riddle distracted her from the growing coldness that enveloped her, penetrating through her furs and into her bones. Whatever that disc represented, Cassidy knew she would have to find a way past the polar bear. Thoughts about the creature's ancestry raced through her mind. Was this bear a direct descendant of the beast portrayed on the wall? Part of a long line of guardians? Was it the same bear?

At the bottom of the staircase, the splintered remains of a wooden door lay strewn about. Violent claw marks marred the fragments of timber. Cassidy walked over the abandoned remains of the door, forcing her way into the darkness. Somehow, the darkness seemingly sought to reach out and capture her, fighting against the pale yellow of the torch. Coldness surrounded her like a mausoleum. It was an overpowering sensation, far removed from anything she had ever experienced underneath the scorching dessert. The musty smell of moss and rich earth was heavy. Once she passed through the opening into the next room, she recognized the source of the earthly aroma. Bare earth replaced the stone and trees sprouted forth from the soil. High above the trees, a slight opening in the roof allowed sunlight to nourish the wildlife that called this cavern home. Birds fluttered their wings between the branches, flying amongst the trees, humming their soft tune. Cassidy stood in awe of this slice of heaven buried underneath an unforgiving tundra. Snow filtered in through the hole, falling harmlessly to the ground below. A giant pool in the middle of the cave had steam billowing off the surface. A natural hot spring providing warmth and shelter to everything dwelling in the cavern. Beads of perspiration began to form on Cassidy's forehead from the heat, her backside still chilled by the glacial climate of the castle hallway. She moved deeper into the cavern; the ground was soft, her feet sinking into the soil. The trees were all slanted towards the opening; they appeared to be reaching out for the sunshine. Taller trees near the middle blocked out the sun, the trees behind them got smaller as the darkness consumed them.

What lurked in the blackness?

Cassidy moved closer to the water, towards the origin of light. A beam of light appeared to be striking the ground just beyond the pond, on the other shoreline. A fish breached the water, the small arctic char made just enough noise to catch her attention. With lightening reflexes, a bird swooped down from its perch and plunged into the water with a big splash. It emerged from the water, the arctic char still wiggling within the bird's beak as it disappeared back into the tiny forest. Cassidy cringed as she heard the bones of the fish snap. She unzipped her jacket as she approached the warmth of the lagoon, embracing the change in temperature. The coldness left her body, gratefully replaced by the humid steam. Another splash rippled the waters on the pond. Cassidy stepped onto the muddy bank, her winter boots slipping in the muck. Crystal clear water filled the pond. Every detail was on display, the pond filled with varied species of fish. Speckled rocks and seaweed covered the bottom, a layer of slime built over everything.

Upon closer scrutiny, Cassidy realized that this body of water wasn't a pond. It belonged to an underground river, the current could be observed beneath the surface. Wildlife from the Arctic ocean passing through the covered rivers must stop here for a rest during their migration. She bent down to place her bare hand in the water, finding it much colder than she expected. With her cupped hands, she scooped up the ice-cold water and drank. Untouched by the influence of humankind, nature at its finest. The source of the heat wasn't coming from the water. It had to be coming from something else. Whatever source produced the heat, it wasn't coming from the lake. Something else in this cave was generating a tremendous amount of heat. All of that didn't matter right now, Cassidy allowed herself to bask in the warmth. As her entire body began to get back to normal temperature, she allowed herself to momentarily forget about the problems she faced. It allowed her to refocus, turning her attention to a solution. If she could climb one of these trees, it would be possible she would be close enough to exit this cave through the opening above. With any luck, the polar bear would still be hunting for her far beneath the castle and she would have enough time to get back to Sir Franklin's group.

With her neck strained, she looked up towards the exit. She was discouraged to find that none of the trees were close enough for her to make her escape. There was no way she would risk falling into the frigid waters from that height. If the fall didn't kill her, the ice-cold waters would finish her. Maybe there was another way out of this cavern. Another tunnel or escape route nearby, hidden in the darkness surrounding her. After several moments of deliberation, she determined the best thing to do for now was to examine the other side of the pond. She certainly wasn't in a rush to exit this warm cave and head back into the blistering cold. The edge of the pond was treacherous, her feet slipping in the slick mud. She headed back onto the grassy bank that bordered the pond. The ground was still damp here, but it was manageable. Every so often, Cassidy would notice animal prints in the softened ground. She bent down to inspect the paw prints.

Her heart leapt into her throat when she realized that she was looking at the imprint of the polar bear that had been stalking her. With giant claw marks that dug deep into the earth, the size of the paw amazed Cassidy. She stepped down into the print, the paw twice the size of her own foot, even with the winter boot.

Silence settled over the clearing. Birds stopped chirping. The water was deadly silent. A booming roar rattled the cave, the birds fluttered their wings and made a racket. Even though the grumble was far away, panic began rising in her chest. Her lungs constricted, robbing her muscles of the oxygen they craved. The realization of the monstrous breadth of the bear crippled her. Frozen in place, she awaited another thunderous growl to signal her demise. At any moment the alabaster bear would emerge from the darkness. Cassidy wouldn't stand a chance. For what seemed like an eternity, she stood still in silence. There were no more growls or groans. Slowly, the birds began to chirp. The rush of water trickled back into existence. Her thoughts escaped the panic that had taken hold, the muscles in her legs found the courage to keep moving. She laughed out loud, her hearty chuckle in cadence with the melody of the fowl.

With new-found energy, Cassidy rushed towards the sunlight. Snow falling through the cracks melted before it could touch the ground, the precipitation turning to rain. The light struck the ground just beyond her vision, the bank veering downwards just beyond the tree line. Once she stood at the edge, she could see down a stone structure at the bottom of the hill. The light shined directly into the building through an opening. She could hardly

believe what she was looking at, the stone temple erected to collect the light from above. The bank was steep,
but Cassidy didn't have the patience to find a better way
down. With an agile leap, she pumped her legs to keep
herself from falling over. Nearly tripping up in her own
feet, she scrambled towards the stone wall of the temple
at breakneck velocity. It didn't take long for the features
of the stone to fill her view. She reached out her arms to
brace herself against the wall; the stone was cold and slippery. Unable to stop herself with her hands, she used her
forearms and shoulders to break her fall. The pain radiated up her shoulder and deep into her back. Cassidy
cursed under her breath. Cold to the touch, the stones
sent shivers through her body. The building stood about
ten feet tall with a square base, styled in the fashion of a
shrine. Something about the way they laid the rocks reminded her of the structures the Inuit built. Stones laid on
top of each other, the same way they built the Inukshuk.
Somehow, the structure was sturdy without the benefit
of any bonding agent. The ground surrounding the structure was dried out; the grass burned down to the roots,
Cassidy cautiously made her way around the side of the
structure. She rounded the corner, the blackened caverns
now to her back, an opening in the middle of the stones
allowed entrance.

Cassidy eased her way to the doorway, not allowing
herself to take her eyes off the darkness. With her back
to the door, she stared at the cave wall. It reminded her
of staring into a pitch-black night sky, void of any stars
or moon. Oblivion, that's what it reminded her of. Serene
sound caught her attention, she turned towards the open-

ing, a gentle melody played from deep within the structure, drawing her into the sunlight. A comforting warmth embraced her, the pleasant aura of cardamon and ginger greeting her. Clay bowls laden with treasures rested along a ledge that ran the length of the entire room on all sides. The middle of the floor opened into a stairwell leading down, the beam of sunlight following the stairs. Dream catchers hung from the ceiling, dangling in the darkness. The light funneled through the opening above her, the beam intense and golden yellow shined brilliantly in the room. An extraordinary sensation of exhilaration washed over her, everything in the room was charming. The scent, the warmth and the beauty enticing her to explore further.

Enveloped by the refreshing environment, Cassidy closed her eyes and allowed herself to become absorbed in the experience. Something remarkable was waiting for her in this building, but that could wait just a little longer. She felt as if her wounds were being healed. Mental and physical exhaustion disappeared; the weight of the world lifted from her shoulders in an instant. It wasn't often Cassidy felt this euphoric; it was a rush of adrenaline and endorphins being released into her bloodstream. All she wanted to do right now was stay in this state of euphoria, lost in a momentary paradise.

ROOOOAAAARRRRR

The resounding roar violated the peacefulness of the room. Cassidy twisted around and confronted the opening, materializing from the obscurity was the polar bear. It raced towards her with prodigious velocity. White teeth protruding from the creature's jaw, it only opened its mouth to let out a thunderous grunt or deep snarl. Cassidy backed away helplessly, her only chance was that the creature could not fit though the opening. Before she could realize, her back foot didn't find any footing, and she tumbled head over heels. Everything spun around violently in her vision as she fell down the staircase. She reached out to brace herself, but her fingers slipped off the slick stairs and walls. Hitting the landing hard, Cassidy found herself staring straight back up the shaft. It wasn't as long as she thought; the fall taking much longer than it should have. Every bone in her body ached. Instantly, bruises started forming on her ribcage and legs. The ground rumbled as the bear galloped towards the stone structure. Cassidy held her breath and waited for the beast to appear at the top of the stairs.

BOOM

An exploding blast bellowed above; a faint flash lit up the room above her. The ground trembled as something above her crashed into the ground. She heard someone shouting something inaudible. A tall, black shadowy figure emerged at the top of the stairs. "Cassidy, is that you?" Peglar's voice cried out.

"Mr. Peglar," Cassidy responded with glee. Finally, she wouldn't have to run from that cursed polar bear any longer. Blood thirsty, the animal chased after her with conviction but without purpose.

"Are you alright?" Peglar started to walk down the stairs, the sunlight catching in the metal of the shotgun barrel.

Cassidy pushed herself up, forcing the muscles to work. "I'm a little sore but nothing serious." Cassidy brushed the dust off her trousers and jacket in an attempt to disguise her pain. Stiff and tense from the fall, her legs trembled beneath her. The thundering echoes of the polar bear's paws started up again. Peglar turned towards the sound and charged towards the noise, the shotgun raised to his chest in front of him. "Mr. Peglar," Cassidy yelled out, not wanting him to get hurt. No response, merely the sounds of the creature's gnarled roar and their footsteps echoing above her.

BOOM

Another roaring boom ripped through the cavern. Cassidy could feel the tremble in the ground growing smaller, but there was no crash this time. An anxious moment passed by quickly before Mr. Peglar appeared once more. "The fool got away, but he'd be a bigger fool to come back." Mr. Peglar held up his weapon with satisfaction. He scrambled down the stairs with grace, the slippery surface no match for his agility and steel-spiked boots. "I only grazed the beast, but I think he gets the message."

"I hope so. That thing has been chasing me since I fell through the floor." Cassidy choked back a tear, filled with relief and grateful for the presence of Mr. Peglar. Awkwardly, he stood in front of her. He didn't know how to acknowledge the quiver in her voice. Cassidy took a moment to regain her composure. "We need to explore this structure."

Fear shrouded Peglar's features, a deep terror pouring from his eyes. "This place is cursed." he shook his head, "we need to leave now." He reached his hand out and nodded his head towards the exit.

Cassidy took a step backward. "No, there's something

down here and I need to discover what it is."

"There's nothing down there but misfortune and sorrow." Peglar hushed his tone. "There's a reason the people who lived here built this place. They had to make certain that no one else ever stumbled upon that evil creation."

"What are you talking about?" Cassidy questioned, softening her voice to match his. She took a step forward, they huddled close together. "If it's so evil, why didn't they just destroy it?"

"I'm talking about something from another world. The last time they tried to destroy it, terrible things happened." Peglar's voice shivered with dread. He was uncomfortable being so close to the source of evil. "The only thing they could do was bring it here and try to ward off the curse."

"How do you know it's cursed?" Cassidy needed to learn as much as possible about the artifact. If she was going to find it, she preferred to understand what she was dealing with.

"Sir Franklin's father discovered it during his expedition to find the North West Passage. They had got caught in the ice north of King William land. Once they recognized they weren't going anywhere, Sir John Franklin sent a crew out in search of land where they could take refuge from the storms." Peglar's voice was filled with apprehension. "The men don't remember where they were when they discovered it, but they mentioned being stalked by a polar bear the moment they took it into their possession."

"The same polar bear that has been trailing me?" Images of the hieroglyphics rushed through her mind. A polar bear was guarding the artifact from the wolves — were mankind the wolves?

"Your guess is as good mine, but they say that bear tormented the crew. Sir Franklin maintained the metal disc held tremendous capabilities and refused to abandon it. Half of his company committed mutiny, many perished during the struggle for power. It forced those that remained to abandon the two ships in the ice."

"What was the name of those ships?"

"The HMS Fear and, Sir Franklin's ship, the HMS Erebus." Peglar answered. A realization that this world was bound to her own shook Cassidy to the core. Sir Franklin's failed expedition had gone unexplained for over a century. The recent discovery of his sunken ships only added to the mystery. Many people had once believed the thick Arctic ice smashed the two ships, but both ships were discovered unscathed. Both ships were located far from where they had been abandoned. "Sir Franklin held onto that disc until the bitter end, convinced it would benefit humanity."

"What made him so certain?" Cassidy was intrigued by Mr. Peglar's every word. This ancient mystery was intriguing, filling her with conviction. She needed to solve this mystery.

"No one is sure. They came across a village of Inuit people. When they discovered the device, they informed him it had been left behind by the people who came from the sky."

"Do you mean aliens?" Only Cassidy Cane could feel this much joy located so close to an artifact filled with ancient alien machinery.

Peglar paused for a moment, perplexed by the question. "Alien?"

"People from another planet," Cassidy said matter-of-factly.

"What other planet? We have never seen people from another planet." The question troubled Mr. Peglar, he responded as if she had insulted him.

"Just continue your story, forget I said anything." Filled with regret, Cassidy craved to learn more about what happened to Sir John Franklin's crew.

"The Inuit people told him that the artifact needed to be transported back to where they found it and buried. Mankind was not ready for the powers left behind by the sky people. Once they were ready, the artifact would help salvage mankind." Mr. Peglar gazed into Cassidy's soul, his eyes fixed on hers. "In the right hands. If the disc falls into the wrong hands, it would be a powerful weapon." He examined her, as if inspecting her. "Why are you so resolved on discovering what rests beneath this room?" Peglar raised his voice, making sure she heard his every word.

Not knowing what to do, Cassidy decided her only option was the truth. No benefit would come from trying to make up a lie. "I have been sent here from another dimension." She expected a shocked expression on Peglar's face, but he remained stoic. "To retrieve the artifact for a scientist in another realm. A dimension not unlike your own."

"You're the one the prophecy spoke of." Peglar continued to study her, looking for some unknown sign. "Perhaps you work for the evil forces spoken of by the Inuit."

"I can assure you, I'm not evil." Cassidy almost laughed at the notion, she may have been a lot of things, but evil? Certainly, she was adventurous, but never evil.

A hearty laugh escaped from the belly of Peglar. "Miss Cane, I have no doubt that you are nothing but virtuous."

"Then what's so ridiculous?" Cassidy joined in the laughter.

"You don't see it yet, do you?"

"Get what?"

"Who sent you here?" Peglar stopped laughing.

"Doctor Herbert Gamgee," Cassidy explained.

"And how well do you know this man?" Peglar pressed the question.

This wasn't the first adventure she had been on for the doctor. "I've worked with him before." Maybe she let the thrill of his missions cloud her judgement. "I don't know him much beyond that. His motives are a mystery to me."

"Have you ever thought that his intentions are not for the greater good?" Peglar paused, looking deep into her eyes. "Is he the prophesied evil the Inuit spoke of?"

CHAPTER SEVEN

"I honestly don't know." Cassidy pondered Peglar's question. Unable to think clearly, she had doubts about what would happen next. "All I know is I need to find the artifact." Driven by the rush, she would worry about the next step once she arrived there.

"I won't stop you," Peglar said with compassion. A deep, implicit understanding between the two. "But I won't go down there with you. I will wait for you here." He held out the shotgun to her. "Do you know how to use this?"

"I've fired one a long time ago." Cassidy remembered the bruise that had formed on her shoulder after firing the weapon. The kickback of the gun nearly breaking her collarbone. "I don't need it." Cassidy pushed it away from her.

"Are you sure I can't persuade you to take the shotgun with you?" Peglar held the gun firm in his hands. "I'd feel a lot better knowing you have protection."

Cassidy shook her head. "I really don't want it. Besides, if that polar bear comes back, you will need it. To protect us both."

Peglar nodded in agreement. "If you insist. Just holler out if you need my aid. I won't leave until you come back up. Be careful."

"You too."

Cassidy turned around and walked down another set of stairs. The sunlight fading into the obscurity, the torchlight flickering off the walls. The stones vanished into the natural rock that formed the network of caverns. Someone had taken the time and effort to burrow deep into the earth, smoothing the walls as they descended. Before the sunlight completely faded, Cassidy turned to face the top of the stairs. It was comforting to see that Peglar stood watch over her. Darkness waited for her beyond an arching doorway carved into the rock. She crept past the entrance, finding a narrow path in front of her. The edge of the rocky path dropped off abruptly. Cassidy could hear waves roaring beneath her. The dynamic force of the Arctic current remained invisible but felt as the crashing waves smashed against the rock wall. Salty sea air occupied the room with a briny smell, it was so dense she could savor the ocean on her tongue. Cassidy noticed a kerosene lamp hung from a hook. A luminous flame erupted in the glass lantern as she passed the flame of her torch underneath the opening, casting light further into the cave. Lanterns had been placed around the room. She trudged along the path, igniting the beacons along the way. A single rocky pathway stretched out into open water. The emerald-green water only ten feet below. Drops of water splashed over the path as the waves broke on the rock face below, the ocean slowly eroding the narrowed pathway.

Darkness hid the path, the passage continuing on into

the misty abyss that seemed to stretch on into eternity. Rocks fell into the water below as Cassidy transferred her full weight onto the path. The roar of the waves drowning out the sound of the rocks entering the water below. She peered over the edge; the whitecaps of the waves rolled past. The raging waters had chiseled a tunnel through the rocks and passed through the other side, time had created an unstable bridge. As she wandered further from the safety of the shore, Cassidy became more determined to find where the path led. The artifact she was searching for remained entombed in the shadows. Beneath her feet the stones trembled. Every step brought her closer to the end of her quest. The flickering light of her torch revealed a metallic object nestled on an alter about twenty feet away. Adrenaline flooded her body. Her legs compelled to purpose, she dashed down the path. Raw energy emanating from the plate vibrated through her body. The alter carved from the rock with hieroglyphics etched into it.

Cassidy stood in front of the alien artifact, close enough to reach out and touch it. Deep down inside, she realized she should turn and flee. Something else was compelling her to reach out and touch it. A force beyond her own comprehension, more powerful than anything she had ever experienced. Without reason, she reached out and picked up the metallic artifact. It was heavier than it looked. The disc fit in her palm, its surface ice-cold, yet it emitted a tremendous source of heat. It pulsated pure energy through her body, she wanted to throw the disc into the waters below, but it wouldn't let her. She couldn't explain the sensation, she placed it back down on the altar. The immense surge of electricity left her body the moment she set it back down on the altar. She grabbed her pair of gloves, hoping that thin fabric would somehow protect against the unexplained power. A low, growing rumble rattled the chamber. Rocks cracked and broke off, falling into the emerald waters below. Something beneath the water began to rise from the depths. Before Cassidy could see what it was, she snatched the artifact, surprised to find that the electrical surge was dampened by her winter gloves. It was still present, but it no longer consumed her body. She tossed the foreign technology in her pocket and dashed across the bridge as quickly as she could. A deafening boom knocked her down, nearly sending her into the water below. She stared down at the waters below. The emerald liquid swirling into a violent vortex, sucking in large hunks of rock as it grew in size. There was something in the eye of the funnel, rising from the crevasse.

A hand grasped her jacket, yanking her to her feet. "We must leave this place." Before she could see who her saviour was, he was steering her towards solid ground. They ran as fast as possible, the rock bridge crumbling beneath their feet. She could feel the path swaying beneath her feet, ready to disintegrate into the glacial waters below. A boisterous, piercing screech tore through her skull. The sound trying to freeze her in place. As they reached the edge of the bridge, they both leapt just as the bridge crumbled into the ocean below. Cassidy landed on solid ground. Her guardian angel was not so lucky. She twisted around to find a hand desperately clutching the side of the path. A figure developed from the water, the waves carrying it towards them. Cassidy reached out and snatched the man's hand just as he lost his grip, his weight dragging her closer to the edge. She stared down at Mr. Peglar, his panicked eyes staring back up at her. The shotgun was grasped tightly in his hand, he refused to let it go. He dug his boots into the rock face, taking the burden of his weight off her shoulder. She got to her feet, the floating figure drawing closer as she pulled Peglar up with all of her might. He tumbled on top of her as she wrenched him over the edge.

Peglar leapt to his feet, pumped the action of the shotgun and took aim at the mystical creature closing in on them. A deafening boom burst from the shotgun, an intense spark illuminating the complex underground cavern. The figure riding the waves wasn't slowed down by the blast. It was closing in on them now. Slowly, the features came into view. Tall and elegant, the mysterious figure took the form of a woman. Her onyx hair danced in coils around her round face, her tanned skin free of blemishes. Big, walnut brown eyes stared down at them, her pouty brown lip curled upwards at the corners. Peglar pumped the shotgun once more, raised it to his shoulder and took aim. "Stay back," he yelled in vain, the woman hovered just a few feet away from the ledge. Peglar turned to face Cassidy. "Run you fool." Fear rattled his voice, his entire body trembling.

Cassidy stumbled to her feet and darted forward, grabbing ahold of Peglar's winter slops. She dragged him towards her, urging him towards the exit. "Come with me." He fought against her grip and freed himself. "I'm not leaving without you."

Peglar turned towards the woman, the wave inching

closer to the shore. Her arms outreached for them. Cassidy knew she was reaching for the artifact, she sensed the woman's gaze upon it. The disc in her pocket surging with electricity, sending waves of heat coursing through her body, her muscles engorged with strength. She reached out once more, grabbing Peglar by the elbow and hauling him backwards. Her newfound strength shocking herself and Peglar, he tripped over his own feet as she yanked him. She caught him before he fell and led him towards the exit. After a few steps, Peglar decided to join her rather than struggle against her will. Cassidy entered the tunnel first, her feet skipping every second step as she raced up the stairs. The pulsating alien disc providing her with a source of unbridled power. Peglar's footsteps echoed closely behind. Rays of sunlight above marked the exit, guiding her back. She raced through the carved archway and burst out into the open cave, the earthly smell of soil and moss greeting her immediately. Her chest heaved up and down as she struggled to catch her breath, the artifact ceased to provide energy. Peglar exited the stone shack behind her, bumping into her, and sent them tumbling to the ground.

"We aren't done yet." Cassidy got to her feet first, presenting her hand to Peglar and dragging him to his feet. He nodded in agreement and slung the shotgun over his back. The woman was crying out to them, her shrill voice filling the cave. A flurry of wind threatened to drive them back into the temple. Cassidy felt a shockwave of heat erupt from the disc, forcing back the windstorm. Opportunity reared its head, and a slab of ice dropped from the ceiling and landed on the stone structure. In an instant, the man-made building imploded, sending a wave of dust and debris flying in all directions. Destruction and pandemonium reigned all around. Defeated shrieks cried out from beneath the caved in structure. Cassidy heard the thunderous pounding of the polar bear's paws in the distance, approaching them. Likely drawn in by the commotion. Somewhere lurking in the dark, the howl of a pack of wolves rose. "What are we going to do?" Cassidy jumped to her feet, not knowing what problem to deal with first.

"I remember the way out, follow me." Peglar took her by the arm and guided her towards the shadows. The shotgun gripped firmly in his fist, bounced off his hip as they ran.

They sprinted down the bank, the growing sounds of howling wolves surrounded them. Movement caught Cassidy's eye, a pure white wolf dashed across her vision and dissolved in an instant. Torchlight reached the darkness, a pitch-black hole in the cliffside stood out. Cassidy knew where they were going and raced ahead of Peglar, her long strides carrying her towards the entrance. The body of another wolf darted towards them from the left, quickly gaining ground on them. Another two wolves appeared out of thin air from the right, the pack had surrounded them and cut them off. Both of them halted. Peglar raised the shotgun in the air and fired off a round. A shower of ice and rock pelted them from above.

The thunderous boom momentarily scared off the wolves, they retreated into the shadows, buying them enough time to escape. Without hesitation, they ran into the cave. The torchlight couldn't reach the walls of the cave as it gave way to a large opening. "Now what?" Cassidy said with a sense of urgency, discovering herself lost in the open space.

"I think it's this way." Peglar pointed into the darkness. It all looked the same in every direction. A high-pitched howl startled Cassidy. She turned to see the pack of wolves had followed them into the cavern. Peglar pointed the shotgun in their direction and fired another round. The wolves scattered in different directions. "That was my last shell," he said, frustrated.

"Let's hope they don't know that." Cassidy tugged at his sleeve and looked him in the eye. "What way do we need to go?"

Peglar spun around, trying to find his sense of direction once more. He oriented himself with the door, trying to make sure he was composed. "It's this way, I'm sure of it." He guided her off into the darkness.

CHAPTER EIGHT

They hurried through the cave as fast as their legs would carry them. Sounds of paw prints gathering on the rocky floor growing louder behind them. Wind threatened to blow out the shimmering flame. Cassidy followed close behind Peglar, his winter jacket making loud flapping noises as he ran. Out of cartridges for the shotgun, they were running out of options. Cassidy heard the wolves sniffing the air, their wet jaws snapping at the scent. The cavern was a never-ending black void, no matter how fast they ran they couldn't find the edge. "Are you sure this is the way?" Cassidy called out to Peglar.

"I'm positive," Without turning his head, he responded. His voice carrying into the void, no echo returned. Peglar was breathing hard, his laboured breaths growing deep and saturated with fluids.

Cassidy wanted to race past him; his pace was much slower than her own. The only reason she didn't take the lead was the faith she placed in him. She believed that he knew the way, but doubt was clouding her judgement. "Hold up." With a swift burst, she ran ahead of Peglar and spun to face him. "I can race ahead to check."

"There's no time. The wolves will be upon us in an instant." Peglar was frightened. "We need to stick together if we are to stand a chance." Every word had to be forced out between choked breaths. His chest was expanding rapidly. Beads of sweat dripped off his skin. Howls from the wolves rose behind them, precariously close now. Claws digging into the rocky terrain could be heard tearing into ground. "We are almost there."

Peglar led the way, convinced that he was heading the right direction in this black abyss. There were no identifying features to guide them. Only the pale light from their torch to accompany them, they advanced through the darkness. Cassidy ran alongside Peglar now, the urge to dash forward grew greater. She couldn't elude the wolves. Their only chance was to arrive at the exit before those wild animals cut them off.

"We are almost there." Peglar pointed to the shadows. Cassidy strained her eyes, the wandering shadows playing tricks with her view. At the boundary of the light, she saw a wall of rock leading straight up. As they drew closer, a staircase heading up began to form. Adrenaline flooded into her body, giving her a boost. A tiny chuckle escaped her lips, she was too happy to contain herself. She reached out and grabbed Peglar by the elbow, rushing him along with her. Her heart leapt into her throat and she let out a terrified gasp. A single white blur rushed past the staircase, then another crossed its path. Peglar stepped in front of her, protecting her from a frontal assault. She pirouetted around only to discover more wolves. Their circle was getting tighter, closing the distance between them swiftly.

"What do we do now?" Cassidy wasn't ready to give up.

Peglar bent his knee and picked up a handful of rocks, cramming them into his pocket. "We have to act quickly." He gestured to the ground. "Grab as many as you can. We are going to get as close to the staircase as we can before we start to throw the rocks at them. With any luck, we will have just enough time to make a break up the stairs." Cassidy bent over and scooped up a handful of rocks. They were cold and wet, the jagged edged poking her through her gloves. Peglar turned towards her and placed his hands on her shoulders. "Listen, no matter what happens to me you run as fast as you can. Don't wait for me and don't do anything stupid. Do you understand me?" The wolves edged closer; they slowed their movements now. The gaps tightening along the perimeter. Peglar shook Cassidy back and forth. "Do you understand?" A tear rolled down his cheek.

"Same goes for you," Cassidy snapped back. "Don't think you need to be the hero." She palmed a rock and closed her fist tightly around it. "We are running out of time." She brushed his arms off his shoulder. He thrust his hand into his pocket and pulled out a large rock, nodding his head in agreement. All around them, the wolves bared their teeth and snapped their jaws. They lashed out at them with low, guttural snarls. The growls rumbled from deep within the pits of their bellies.

In unison, they both dashed towards the staircase. Cassidy took aim at the wolf closest to the stairs and threw the rock with all of her might. It landed in front of the beast, the resounding bang startling the creature.

It dashed out of formation. Peglar let his rock fly just after her, his projectile much more accurate. It found its mark, banging into a wolf's head, sending the creature scurrying away whimpering. A gap big enough to run through opened up and Cassidy broke into full stride. She reached the stairs and turned around. A wolf was nipping at Peglar's jacket, he turned around and took a swing at the critter. His blow caught the creature on the side of the head. The wolf recoiled away, baring its jaws at Peglar in defiance as it backed away, its head dipped low. Cassidy threw her rock towards another wolf approaching Peglar from the left. It struck the creature in the rib cage, stunning it long enough for Peglar to make a break for it. Cassidy threw another rock in his direction, the loud banging clap providing just enough distraction for Peglar to make his escape. He joined her on the stairs and didn't wait for her to turn around, he spun her around, nearly knocking her off balance.

"We have to keep moving," Peglar screamed as the wolves regrouped. The pack approaching the stairs cautiously. Cassidy threw her last rock into the pack, striking one wolf. It let out an agonized yelp, but the wolves were not defeated yet. They scrambled up the steps together. Cassidy skipped steps but she wasn't as sure-footed as Peglar, her feet slipping out from underneath her. Several times, Peglar had to catch Cassidy before she lost her balance completely. Peglar turned to throw his last rock at the wolves, who were already making their way up the stairs. His throw missed the lead wolf but sailed into the pack and struck another square in the snout, causing him to yelp in torment. The angered howl of the alpha male rallied the others, coaxing them to proceed despite the peril.

"What way do we go when we reach the top of the staircase?" Cassidy noticed the ledge just ahead.

"Turn left and run towards the light." Peglar was falling behind, gasping for air.

Cassidy turned and ran down to yank Peglar forward, she would not let him give up so easily. "Keep your legs moving." With a handful of dirty fabric, Cassidy pulled Peglar up a stair. That seemed to ignite a fire in the older man, his limbs started churning again. For the first time since they entered this cave, Cassidy felt the disc in her pocket. It began to resonate, a slight pulse that beat faster as the wolves got closer. She didn't want to wait to find out what would happen if they got too close. A strange sensation began to throb in her abdomen. Fear, that was the only word Cassidy could think of to describe the feeling growing inside of her. Was this pulsating a warning, an omen? Something told her she had to keep the disc away from the wolves at all costs.

After a few laboured leaps, they reached the top of the ledge. Together, they both turned left and raced towards the torches that marked the exit. "We are almost there." Peglar pointed to a black iron gate. It hung open, swaying with the breeze lazily. The light from behind giving the illusion that the iron bars were growing and shrinking in size.

"Get inside." Cassidy rushed forward, racing to the gate. She grabbed ahold of the cold iron bars, waiting impatiently for Peglar to enter the room before she closed the door. The wolves were nipping at his heels, the back of his foot catching the jaw of the alpha. A painful expression crossed Peglar's face as he let out an agonized cry in unison with the wolves. The impactful blow causing both of them to suffer injury. Cassidy slammed the gate shut just as Peglar crossed the threshold. The alpha wolf leapt into the air, throwing its body against the gate in a vicious act, knocking Cassidy backwards. She fell hard onto her backside, straining her neck to monitor the gate. Peglar struggled with the door as he tried to close the latch. Stunned from the impact, Cassidy could only watch as the wolves pounced towards the door. The pulsating artifact in her pocket let out a high-pitched, piercing wail that cut through the tunnel. The wolves dipped their heads down, covering their ears with their paws. Cassidy jumped to her feet and latched the lock.

The sound ceased; the defeated growls of the alpha wolf pierced into her soul. It paced back and forth, trying to find a weakness in the gate. The obedient pack continued to toss their bodies at the iron, the alpha watching attentively for any hint of weakness or default. "Come, let's put some distance between us before they break the gate down. It's only a matter of time before that happens." Peglar pointed to the roof where the iron cut into the rock, the bars were shaking. Debris and dust falling from the ceiling. The alpha wolf was staring at the same thing, frothing at the prospect.

Peglar ushered Cassidy further into the bleak hallway, the carved tunnel diving deeper into the earth. Loud, crashing bangs erupted behind them as the wolves continued to throw their bodies into the iron gate. "How much further is it to the castle?" Cassidy wanted to take her mind off the disturbing sounds behind her. She needed a distraction, anything to help her ease her mind.

"We still have a way to go." Peglar's voice echoed loudly in the tunnel. "This is the sub-basement of the castle above. It is a network of passageways. A man would easily become lost down here."

"Luckily, I am not a man, and I don't plan on getting lost down here." Cassidy laughed, hoping to ease the tension.

"No one ever plans on getting lost." Peglar chuckled. "It just happens sometimes." They walked into an intersection. Peglar studied the markings on the wall. Cassidy couldn't make any sense of the words written there. It appeared to be some kind of code written in another language. "We have to go left."

"How do you know that?" Cassidy stared at the markings. Some carvings were words, some of them were symbols. Each wall had their own combination.

"Those are common nautical terms, and the symbols represent truth or lies. Sailors during the war came up with the codes to deceive the enemy. If they captured a ship, the captors wouldn't understand the orders they found." Peglar walked down the left corridor, the sounds behind them fading. A solitary wolf howled into the tunnel one last time before they put enough space between them.

"When did you learn about all of this?" Cassidy allowed her mind to wander. The path was ice cold, but the disc in her pocket acted like a furnace, providing enough heat to keep her body temperature comfortable.

"During the great war." Peglar's voice was distant, he

stared off into the distance, looking past the cave and into the past. "I was a boatswain on Sir Franklin's ship during my time in the military. After two years of war, I had been lucky and never had to fire my weapon. I had directed my skills towards other pressing matters."

"What do you mean?" The tunnel forked left and right, Cassidy studied the markings again. They looked very familiar to the ones at the last junction, only a slight variation to the carvings.

"Which way do you think we should go?" Peglar questioned her, avoiding the question.

The drawings had to be the key. She recognized the nautical term for left and right, the trick would be determining the symbols for truth and false. "Should we go left?"

"We should, but can you explain why?" Peglar attempted to teach her.

"Are you avoiding the question about the war?"

"Yes, I don't like to talk about the war." Peglar didn't hide his intentions.

"I don't understand why I chose left." Cassidy wasn't ready to let the subject go yet. "Why don't you like to talk about the war? You said you never fired your weapon."

"There can be worse things than killing a man during war." Peglar responded as he turned down the tunnel. "I'll give you another chance at the next junction to crack the code."

"If I crack the code, can you tell me what happened?" Cassidy kept pressing.

He stopped in mid stride. "If you explain to me how the code works, I will tell you. Not a guess, I want the explanation."

Cassidy held out her hand. "Deal." They shook hands in agreement, a deal brokered between them in the cold pits of the castle. "If you don't want to tell me, you don't have to."

"I will tell you," Peglar spoke softly. "It's not something that I can hide from you forever. Other people understand what has happened to me. It is no secret amongst our crew."

"Then why not just tell me?" Cassidy didn't understand his attempt at secrecy.

"Just because it's not a secret, doesn't mean that it's easy to talk about." Peglar quickened his pace. His entire body trembling beneath his winter jacket.

"Are you okay?" Cassidy asked, concerned. She reached into her pocket and held the alien artifact in her hand.

"I'm just a little cold. All of that running caused me to overheat and sweat. Now that I'm not running, my body temperature is still adjusting. I'll be all right in a few minutes, just need time to acclimatize." Peglar's lips started turning blue, his teeth chattering. His cheeks had turned a pasty white.

"You don't appear well. Are you okay?" Concerned for his wellbeing, Cassidy took the disc out of her pocket. "Take this, it should keep you warm." She handed him the disc. He happily took it from her hands, holding it close to his chest. A soft smile spread across his face. "Does that help?"

"It does." Peglar unzipped his winter slops and placed the disc inside a pocket. They continued walking down the corridor. The curved ceiling covered in frost, the floor slick with ice. Their pace slowed, every step a dangerous adventure for Cassidy. She struggled to gain any traction on the black ice. "Here we are, your final test. Which way should we go?" The tunnel opened into three different directions and wooden signs hung from the ceiling marking each corridor.

Cassidy studied the words carefully. Starboard, port, and head were scribbled on the signs leading left, right, and straight. That part was easy, all the words matched the direction. It was the symbols that didn't make much sense. Three anchors rested beneath each word; those were identical. It was what was wrapped around the anchor that differentiated them. Beneath starboard, the anchor was wrapped with a rope knotted at the top. Underneath head the rope was also knotted in the same fashion but the rope was frayed. The last knot, underneath port, was tied to the right and the rope was free of any defects. "I know that the ropes have something to do with it."

"Very good, you are headed in the right direction," Peglar emphasized the last word, placing a great deal of theatrics with it.

"The knot for starboard is the only one that isn't facing the right direction, so left is incorrect because it's not true?" An educated guess, but still a shot in the dark. Cassidy studied his expression for any sign that she was headed in the right direction. Peglar said nothing, he just nodded his head. Not in agreement, he just acknowledged her heard her. "The other two knots face in the right direction, but the rope facing the head is frayed. You wouldn't want to use that rope, so it is false. We have to take the path on the right, because the rope and knot are true." Cassidy was sure of the answer. Peglar stood stoned faced, hiding a smirk stretching across his expression. He let out a tiny chuckle. Annoyed by him, Cassidy stomped her feet. "Well, am I right?" she demanded.

"Miss Cane you are a very intelligent woman. Perhaps your husband served, and you paid attention to his tales?" Peglar saw the angered look on Cassidy's face. "I meant no offence. I just never experienced this before."

"Experienced what? A smart woman?" She spat back, insulted by his comments.

He shook his head. "No, Miss Cane, I've never seen anyone solve the code so quickly. You are correct, we head down that path." His words were jovial, a look of pride on his face. The same look a teacher has when one of their students accomplishes something great.

"Well, I've held up my end of the bargain, what happened to you during the war?" Cassidy was still upset, her blood boiling.

"Nothing."

"Nothing? That's your big secret?" Cassidy sensed her face flush red with anger. "Why would you hide that?"

Peglar began walking down the tunnel. "If you ask any of the men in Sir Franklin's crew about their experience during the war, they will have something to tell you."

Cassidy picked up the pace, glad to get moving again, the chill was seeping back into her bones. "I don't get it. What are you hiding from me?"

"Miss Cane, I am not hiding anything." Peglar turned his head to face her. "I am ashamed that I never experienced action. The others returned home with tales of bravery and victory," his said, his voice laden with regret. "When I arrived in my home, I had nothing of worth to mention. Even though I never shied away from the action, I was never placed in a position to prove myself." He was no longer talking to Cassidy, his internal monologue spoken aloud for his own benefit. "No one ever called me a coward, they never needed to. Everyone knew that was the only logical explanation. How else could a man avoid such hardship during a war?"

"That is nothing to be ashamed of." Cassidy truly believed those words. War was a terrible thing. It created terrible demons that could ruin people, destroying everything in their path. She had seen families destroyed by the experiences of combat. Peglar remained silent, ignoring Cassidy as they trudged down the path. "You mentioned your skills were utilized elsewhere?"

"I became an expert at navigation. I studied the patterns of ice and how to survive in the frigid conditions." Pride lingered on his tongue, but it was burdened by his shame.

"So, you became an Ice Master, that is a very important position aboard any ship." Cassidy remembered reading about the position in a book she studied in college about the Franklin expedition.

"It is important during times like these." Peglar responded sharply. "Not during a war. The only reason for my position aboard this ship is because Sir Franklin feels sorry for me. He believes that I can still be useful but everyone else would just as soon cast me overboard, they hate taking orders from a man like me."

Every footstep echoed loudly, almost obnoxiously in

the silence. The wall creaked, the ice in the cracks expanding against the stone in an extended battle for position. Without another word spoken, they walked down the long hallway, the moaning of the castle creating an eerie atmosphere. Mother nature had taken residence here, her cold touch decorating the hallways with sheets of ice. At the end of the hallway was another junction. The signs that should have been hanging from the door had fallen onto the ground, and ice had formed over them. Peglar stood over the signs and shook his head. "Damn it, they fell face down."

"So what do we do now?" Cassidy could hear the panic in his voice.

He kicked his spikes into the ice, the hard surface suffering minor scratches but refused to give any ground. "We will have to make a guess. I don't remember which way I came down here."

"Let's take a minute to think this over. Maybe something will jog your memory." Cassidy remained calm. "Was the tunnel very long?"

"I remember it took me a fair amount of time to walk down the first tunnel, if indeed this is the last junction." Frustration clear on his voice. "This damn disc has lost all of your body temperature and has gone cold again." Peglar took the artifact out of his pocket; the metal had lost its lustre. The light no longer catching on its surface, he held it out for her to take.

Cassidy reached out and took ahold of the disc. Instantly, the surface shimmered again, the dull light of the torch dancing across the metal. "That's weird." Cassidy felt the disc spring to life, a warmth spreading through her veins the moment it was in her possession. "It's warm."

Peglar reached out and placed his hand on the artifact. "That is most peculiar." He stared at Cassidy with great interest. His lips opened to speak, but he was drowned out by a terrible crashing sound. They both jumped, startled by the sudden commotion. "What was that?"

ROOOOAAAARRRRRR

A booming growl responded, answering the question. The trembling echo was much too deep to belong to the wolves. Peglar stared at Cassidy with a fear in his eyes. They looked down the three tunnels, not know which way to go. Neither of them knew the correct path. Thunderous galloping shook the tunnel as the polar bear rushed into the underground network.

"Run."

CHAPTER NINE

Their footsteps were drowned out by the pounding paws chasing after them. They ran into the darkness at full speed. Already twenty feet ahead of Peglar, Cassidy had to slow down so he wouldn't be left behind in the shadows. Cassidy heard his laboured breaths from the edge of the torchlight, struggling to keep up with her. A pulsating throb grew stronger with every step she took deeper down the tunnel. If it was a warning, it was too late, there was no time to turn around, they had to keep pushing further into the underground network. She slowed her pace enough to allow Peglar to catch up. "You have to keep up, we are almost there."

"This doesn't seem right," Peglar choked out between panting breaths. He had discarded the shotgun somewhere behind them, the weapon no longer in his possession.

"Just keep your legs moving," Cassidy tried to sound reassuring, but the booming paws were drawing closer. Grunts and groans from the polar bear closing in on them. The intensity of the disc increased; a sense of dread crept over her. "We will get out of here."

Peglar staggered forward, unable to keep moving in a

straight line. Wasted effort, Cassidy did her best to keep him on track. Her leg muscles were cramping, depleting electrolytes leaving her vulnerable to exhaustion. The tunnel opened into another junction. Without speaking another word, Peglar grabbed Cassidy by the shoulder and dragged her into the right path. The signs rushed by too quickly for Cassidy to read. Peglar's laboured breaths betrayed their position, panting loudly he buckled over. "I need a moment." He stopped moving, bending over at the hips he dry heaved.

"No, we can't stop." Cassidy pushed him forward. "Keep moving, no matter what, don't stop moving those legs." Cassidy dug her shoulder into his side, helping take some weight off his legs, they staggered down the long tunnel. The snorts and grunts grew louder, closing in on their position. The polar bear, sniffing at the air, following the lingering body odour directly towards them. She expected any moment to turn around and witness the creature lumbering down the tunnel. The pulsating disc grew stronger, the energy radiating an undeniable power that couldn't be ignored. Cassidy noticed another junction straight ahead that only had two paths. "Left or right?"

"I say we go right." Peglar was still trying to catch his breath.

Cassidy felt the ground beneath her feet tremble, the polar bear was dangerously close now. They only had one chance. They entered the junction and began to turn right. A stabbing pain forced Cassidy to one knee on her left side. Peglar stumbled over her, collapsing into a heap in an effort to avoid falling on top of the smaller woman. An anguished cry escaped her lips. Something deep inside was telling her to turn left. "We have to go the other way."

Peglar got to his feet first, pulling Cassidy up from the ground and taking the torch from her hand. "Then we will go left."

The sharp pain ceased, and Cassidy continued trudging along. The whole tunnel trembled as the polar bear let out a deafening roar, rattling the surrounding walls. As they passed the junction, Cassidy caught a glimpse of the enormous beast's white fur glowing from the darkness. Fear propelled them both forward with newfound purpose, their legs ignoring the fatigue. This tunnel differed from the rest. It twisted and turned, bending left then right as it weaved its way upwards. Fresh air rushed past them as they pushed further into the tunnel. "This has to be the right way." Cassidy's heart leapt with joy. Peglar kept pace even as he struggled to catch his breath. The path sloped upwards now at a sharp angle, the ice giving way to the stone path beneath. Tremors shook the tunnel, the bear's growls rumbled from the pit of its stomach as it chased after them. Cassidy was too afraid to turn her head, she just kept her legs churning towards the exit.

"No," Peglar screamed in anguish. The flickering light reached a dead end. A stone wall greeted them at the end of the path. "This can't be."

"Wait, I think I see a hole." Cassidy found a black opening, situated near the bottom of the floor. They continued to race towards the wall, their only chance of survival was hidden within that tiny hole. A gust of fresh air was billowing from the hole.

"Get in, I'll be right behind you." Peglar forced Cassidy into the small tunnel first. It was pitch black and covered in ice, the tight confines of the tunnel constricting her movements. She crawled on her hands and knees, dragging herself forward into the darkness.

Peglar screamed bloody murder behind her. Contorting her body into a painful position, she watched him crawling towards her. He had dropped the torch outside the tunnel, the faint light catching in the polar bear's pure white fur. Claws digging at the walls in a furious attempt to widen the hole, the creature desperate to follow them into the abyss. "Keep going," Peglar cried out in pain. With all of her weight on her forearms, Cassidy pulled herself forward, dragging her body behind her. Someone had carved the tunnel out of the ice, making it difficult to gain any traction. Her elbows digging painfully into the ice, she kept moving forward as fast as possible. Peglar was following close behind her, his hands bumping into her feet as he pushed himself forward.

Cassidy was warmed by a trickle of sunlight in the distance. "We are almost there," Cassidy said joyfully, a renewed source of energy driving her forward. "We made it, Mr. Peglar."

There was no response. Only the frantic clawing and throaty growls of the bear at the other end could be heard behind her. She twisted her body, barely able to see past her own waist. Desperately, she forced her body to one side to allow the tiny amount of light to illuminate the cave. Peglar laid face down in the tunnel, his jacket had been torn from his body. "Wake up, Mr. Peglar." Out of frustration, she kicked his arm. His chest was still moving up and down rhythmically, she kicked him again.

"Just…" Peglar croaked. "Go on without me."

"What is wrong with you?" Cassidy pleaded. "If you keep moving, you will warm up."

The bear was tearing away at the ice, the hole widened enough to let the creature stick its shoulders through at the bottom. His claw dangerously close to Peglar's feet now. Painfully, Peglar crept his body further out of the rabid creature's reach. The sickening sounds lashing out at them. Shards of ice fell onto the stone path behind the bear as he tunneled his way into the ice. "Don't worry about me." Peglar coughed. "Just go."

Cassidy refused to take her eyes off him, driving herself closer to the exit with her heels. A low murmur drifted into the cave. The sounds coming from the exit. "Help!" Cassidy screamed. "We're down here."

Silence.

"Down here."

Mumbles filtered down to her. She couldn't pick out the words, but she knew they were voices of Sir Franklin's crew. "Mr. Peglar needs help." Cassidy turned to make sure he was still following her. Even though she had only moved ten feet, he wasn't able to keep pace. He was falling behind, his face buried into his chest. Desperate to keep warm, he had forced himself into the fetal position. "Please, we need your help."

"Miss Cane." A young man's voice finally answered. His frame blocking the light from the exit.

"We are in here."

"Hold on, I will get you out." Cassidy recognized the voice. It belonged to Tommy Seeley.

"Please hurry." Cassidy forced herself back towards Peglar. He was barely moving now, his efforts wasted. "We are almost there." Cassidy assured him. He didn't respond, his breathing was shallow. "You can't quit now." She grabbed him by the shoulders, dug in her heels and pulled with all of her might. All of her effort only moved him a few inches, but she refused to let go, straining again, she pulled him even less with the second attempt. Her face bright red from exhaustion, she tried to get a better grip. The bear snarled and grunted as it clawed away at the ice, a constant reminder of the threat just below. "I need help," Cassidy called out to Tommy.

"I'm on my way." Tommy's voice seemed more distant now than before. She turned her head to confirm he was in the tunnel. His outline was slowly making its way towards her. More voices erupted in the background. Frantic sounds of commotion loomed ahead. Dreadful, demonic sounds inched closer from below.

"You have to hurry," Cassidy frantically cried out. The vicious growls below frightened her to the core. Peglar's weight was threatening to pull them back down the tunnel. A powerful, clamping mouthful of teeth eagerly awaiting them. The hot stench of devoured meat oozing from the rabid jaws below, pouring over them.

Cassidy gripped Peglar underneath the armpits, planted her feet and tugged with all of her might. She dragged him for several feet before the white stars appeared in her vision. The surrounding commotion began to blur together, fading into white noise. She braced herself once more, pulling Peglar another foot. Her head began to swim, the stars clouded her vision until all she could see was a single, bright light. Cassidy tightened her grip as she felt consciousness slipping away, refusing to give up. Unable to pull him any more, she locked her grip underneath his arms to make sure she wouldn't lose him.

Cassidy blacked out.

CHAPTER TEN

The tunnel was narrow, a slight slope leading upwards taxed Cassidy's leg muscles just enough to make her groan at the effort. A radiating tingle warmed her back, the raw energy from the disc vibrating through the pocket that had fallen over her back. The polar bear's roar echoed behind her. The mighty bellow booming off the tight walls, enclosing her in boisterous noise.

Cassidy Cane stared at the elderly man, his ice-cold blue eyes and alabaster hair gave him the appearance of a ghost. The long furs draped over his frail frame hid his shaking arm that rested on the mahogany wood cane. In his younger years the man stood head and shoulders above the crowd, but now he hunched over at the hips, barely able to meet eyes with her. She held out the ice-cold metallic disc, the radiating source of energy smothering all of her senses. "What is this?" She demanded.

"I will explain that to you if you wish, but there is so much more that you need to understand." His voice was raspy, each word barely escaping his dried lips.

"I don't have time for games. What is this?" Cassidy's heart was still beating wildly in her chest. A raw surge of power waxed and waned in her hands, a pulsating beat that mimicked the rhythm of her own beating heart.

"That is a source of pure, clean energy." The elderly man made his way towards a small, rounded wooden table. He pulled out the wooden chair, the four legs scraping across the hardwood floor. "Please join me, my legs aren't as strong as they once were." He used his cane to push out the chair.

A flashing image of Mr. Peglar crossed her vision. "What happened to him?"

"Please have a seat." He tapped the chair with his cane, the rattling noise pounding in her skull.

She refused to take a seat. "You have to tell me what happened to Peglar." Cassidy crossed her arms across her chest in defiance.

"Tea?" The old man pushed a white porcelain cup across the table towards her.

"How d'you do that?" Cassidy found herself sitting across the table, she wanted to stand up, but her muscles didn't respond to her brain's demands. Instead, she reached out and took a sip of tea. It was warm, and it replaced the coldness from the tunnel.

"I can assure you that Mr. Peglar is safe. Thanks to your heroic actions, he will live to see another day." Strands of the man's white beard flowed over his neck, his Adams apple bobbing beneath. With shaking hands, he sipped on his tea, the cup clattering against the plate as he placed it down. "That is not why you are here."

Cassidy noticed the sway of the ocean beneath her. It didn't make any sense. "Where am I?"

"You are where you need to be," he stated calmly, not

answering the question. "What is critical is that you comprehend why you are here."

Cassidy recognized those words from earlier. "You are the man from my dreams." The elderly man let out a chuckle, his sly smile curling the long hairs on his lip. "That is not what I meant."

A raspy cough stuck in the man's throat. "I know, it's just not very often this old man gets to listen to a young lady say those words."

"Why am I here?" Cassidy leaned forward across the table. "And I don't want any cryptic answers this time. Please, cut to the chase." Subconsciously, she had grasped the tea and took another drink.

"Search deep within yourself. You should recognize who I am by now." His ice-blue eyes glared through her.

Frustrated by the elderly man's cryptic response, Cassidy banged her fist on the table. "You're Sir John Franklin." Unknowingly, the words spilled from her mouth without thought. "You were the first to discover this disc." She placed it on the table. His ice-cold eyes melted, revealing a deep brown iris beneath. "What is this?"

"Have you spent much time studying the Inuit folklore?" John Franklin's hair turned jet black, the wrinkles disappearing from his skin as his youth returned to him. "Have you ever heard the tale of the god who created the Tuurngait?"

"Yes, the goddess Sedna, the Spirit of the Sea sent the Tuurngait to kill the Spirit of the Air and the Spirit of the Moon. Tuurngait is capable of travelling between the spirit world and the physical world. After a battle with the Tuurngait lasting 10,000 years, the Spirit of the Air and the Spirit of the Consciousness work together to defeat it. The defeated Tuurnbgait attempts to defeat its creator, but the Spirit of the Sea banishes it to the physical realm." Cassidy had listened to the tales told by the elders during her stay at Gjoa Haven.

"That's correct." His voice was filled with youth now, it was strong and steady. "They say that when the Sedna vanquished the Tuurngait to earth, she lost her powers during the conflict. Her ability to harness the power of the sun lost, giving birth to the moon."

"Is that what this disc is?" She reached her hand out, the metal surface responding to her touch.

Sir Franklin noticed the strange reaction. "I have never seen it do that before." He reached out, disappointed to find it had no reaction despite his desires. "You must be the prophet. Your ability to manipulate the disc will be a great benefit to mankind."

"I did not come here on some mystical quest." Cassidy felt insignificant next to the artifact now. "That disc is not for me."

"What are you planning to do with it then?" Sir Franklin stood up, his frame broad and his chest thick with muscles.

Cassidy stood up in defiance, banging her fists against the table. "I didn't ask for this. My job is to bring this artifact back to Docter Herbert Gamgee."

"Did he tell you his purpose?" Sir Franklin bellowed; his words had enough power behind them to knock Cassidy back into her chair.

Cassidy thought long and hard. She still wasn't sure of the doctor's motives, but she had no reason to deny his request. "No, he did not. All I can say for certain is that the disc does not belong in my hands." Doubt muddled her thoughts. Was this just another adventure for her, or was this her purpose? Was she brought here by some higher calling?

"I need you to think long and hard about what you are doing." Sir Franklin snatched the disc up from the table. "I sacrificed over one hundred and twenty men to save humanity. If this falls into the wrong hands, the power it contains would be devastating." He tossed the disc into her lap.

"What would you have me do?" Cassidy clasped the disc in her hands.

"I would have you wake up." He pounded his fist against the table.

Cassidy jumped up in her bed. She awoke to find herself lying in a berth aboard a ship. The ocean tossing the boat back and forth like a child's toy. Her body was wet with sweat, and it took a moment for her heart to slow down and to gain her breath. "It was all a dream?" Cassidy said aloud, not knowing where she was.

"You are still dreaming."

Cassidy leapt up, tossing the sheets onto the bed. Sir Franklin was sitting in a rocking chair next to her bed. "What are you doing in here, Jack?" Cassidy reached for the blankets, pulling them up to her chin.

"Jack is my son, I am John." Creaks and groans filled the room as the chair rocked back and forth. "Like I said, you are still dreaming. You need to wake up."

"What does that mean." Cassidy wanted to scream. She was so frustrated she started to pinch the skin on her arm until she drew blood. "I just want this to end."

"Do you know why that disc reacts to you the way it does?" John asked patiently as she continued to pinch herself.

"I don't know anything about this.... thing." The artifact was underneath the cover with her, she felt it resting against her leg. "I just want you to tell me."

"You want me to tell you?" Sir Franklin chuckled. "You realize that I am a figment of your imagination, right?" He leaned in close to her. "The answer rests deep inside of you, just let it out."

With a balled fist, Cassidy took a swing at Sir John. Somehow, she missed hitting his face from less than six inches away. "I can't do this anymore. I'm done." She whipped the covers off, tossing them over Sir John. The blanket crumpled up into a ball in front of his feet, never once landing in his lap even though it should have. The disc sat in her lap, she stared at the shiny surface. Disgust contorted her expression, her nose crinkled up, sending a wave of wrinkles over her face. "It's because it belongs to my world."

Sir Franklin nodded his head in agreement. "You realize that if you bring it back to your dimension, that anyone could harness its powers."

"This disc can help solves the earth's energy crisis." Cassidy muttered to herself, refusing to talk to her subconscious any more. "Can it be weaponized?" She asked herself, remembering the immense power it was capable of producing. It had allowed her to escape with no knowledge of its capabilities. What if the wrong person got their hands on it? This disc could create something far worse than a nuclear weapon. The atomic bomb would fail in comparison to the raw energy surging within this artifact.

"In the wrong hands this source of energy could be used for terrible things." Exactly what Cassidy was thinking, John's voice seemed faded and distant.

"I don't believe Doctor Gamgee is the wrong person." Cassidy didn't expect an answer. "I should just throw that disc back into that cave and leave it there." Her head was spinning now. "But if he solved the world's energy crisis, it would change the fate of our planet." She couldn't decide what to do. "What do I do?" Cassidy screamed into an empty room.

"Wake up."

CHAPTER ELEVEN

Laboured yelling and frantic footsteps roused Cassidy to consciousness. She wobbled back and forth; the clouds gathered above her head. She strained her neck just enough to turn her head to the side, the wooden walls of a skiff greeted her. "Where am I?" Cassidy's throat was dry, the words catching in her larynx. Ice scraped the bottoms of the skis as she was being pulled away, the castle looming over her as they left. Men were screaming out to each other, the wind blurring their words together. She turned her head to the other side. "Mr. Peglar."

Peglar was lying down next to her. Unresponsive, his body bounced and twitched to the will of the sleigh. Every bump and dip rocking his body back and forth. His chest was rising slightly, the movement barely noticeable underneath the blanket they had thrown over him. A winter jacket and been thrown on him hastily. Cassidy looked down, surprised to find her fur jacket had been removed and replaced by the black winter slop that all of Sir John Franklin's men wore. Purple blotches filled her vision. A constant, throbbing headache made every movement agony. She wasn't able to concentrate long enough to pick out what the men were shouting about. Dried, cracked lips, made worse by the biting cold, made it nearly impossible to speak.

Muffled cries stuck in her throat as she attempted to call for help. She forced her arm to move her hands into her pocket. Agonized by the effort, her fingers searched for the disc. They ran across the cold metal, unable to tighten her grasp on the object. Burdened by the responsibility of retrieving the artifact back to her own dimension, Cassidy mustered her last ounce of strength. "Help." Scratchy sounds that resembled her voice crossed her lips.

"Hang in there, Cassidy, we will get you back to the ship safely." Tommy Seeley's voice appeared from thin air.

Unable to locate him, she decided it wasn't worth spending the energy, he would come to her. "Water." All she could muster was a single word. Anything more would have choked her. She felt a hand cradle the back of her head, tilting it just enough so she could receive a drink. The cold metal lid stung her lip, but it was worth it. The water was graciously received by her dry mouth, the moisture bringing her tongue back to life. It hurt to swallow, each gulp getting slightly more comfortable. "More water." Her throat no longer resisted the words. Tommy leaned in but his smile didn't last. A booming echo forced him to take action, he ran off towards the action.

Deep, heavy moans spilled out of Peglar, his limbs slowly coming to life. Then he rolled himself onto his side. He opened his eyes, dried tears stained his checks, he mouthed the words "thank you," no noise left his mouth. With newfound energy, Cassidy rolled onto her side to face Peglar.

"You're welcome." Cassidy reached out, placing her hand on his shoulder, she laughed. They had been through hell together. Barely escaping the clutches of the polar bear, they had been placed onto one of the skids to be pulled across the ice like luggage. She reached back into her pocket, finding that the object she believed to be the artifact was the barrel of a pistol.

Peglar saw the look of fear in her eyes, he reached out and seized her by the shoulder, restraining her from sitting up. "No." Dry orders delivered from his cracked lips, his eyes seeking to console her.

Cassidy dropped the pistol, thrusting her hands back into the pockets, hoping they concealed the artifact deep within. Empty. "I lost it." She brushed his hand away, forcing herself to sit up.

A dying yellow sun was minutes away from falling beneath the mountains. Dark, heavy clouds loomed overhead, the wind pushing them across the horizon. The barren tundra was cluttered with men accompanying the skid in a long line. Tommy Seeley was running towards her, an expression of dread on the young man's face. "Wait." Cassidy called out as he rushed by. The other men began to rush forward, moved to purpose by something unseen to her. There were no shadows to hide in.

The snarling growl of the polar bear sent shivers down her spine, chilling her to the core. "It's the bear." Cassidy glanced at Peglar. "It's coming after me." Cassidy turned her head and watched in disbelief as one sailor fired a shotgun at the bear. The slug knocked the animal backwards momentarily, the pellets falling into the snow harmlessly. The great polar bear reared onto its hind legs. There was no sign of blood anywhere on the creature's pristine fur. Cassidy turned her head forward as the sled jolted onward.

The men weren't running away. They were rushing forward to help pull the skid with the men in the harness. Men grabbed the ropes, dug their heels into the packed snow and helped. They toiled relentlessly, the skid moving along the snow much faster now as the weight was evenly distributed between the whole crew. The sails of the HMS Fear bobbed up and down in the distance. Wind caught in her sails, rushing the ship dangerously close to the ice. Sir Jack Franklin was leading a group of men towards them, every man armed with a rifle. War cries rose from the men as they raced forward to greet the bear head on.

A clap of thunder rocked the ice. White lightening tore the sky in half. Loud cracks rang out from the ice beneath her, the brewing storm threatening to open up the frozen sheets. The polar bear roared in defiance of mother nature, standing on its hind legs and thumping its chest with its giant clawed paws. The deafening roar challenged the clouds, which countered with another thunderous bang. A bolt of lightning struck the ice between them, sending fragments flying in all directions. A white cloud of fog, ice and water remained between them. Sir Franklin and his crew rushed past the last of the men pulling the skid. They took a knee, aiming their rifles towards the last known location of the bear. A booming rumble erupted from the sky as the men readied their weapons. The polar bear emerged from the mist, galloping full speed at them.

"Fire," Sir Franklin barked the order. Gunfire erupted, flashes sparked from the guns as another bolt of lightning illuminated the sky. Smoke seeped from the barrels, the wind driving it back in the shooters' faces. The polar bear grunted in defiance, baring its teeth at the soldiers. A flash of lightning illuminating the white skin, giving the creature the appearance of an ethereal glow.

"Retreat," Sir Franklin bellowed. His men raced to catch up with the skid. The bear followed closely behind, showing no effects from the gunfire. Not one bullet had penetrated the creature's thick skin. "Reload." Another booming clap quickly followed the command. The bear's claws dug into the snow, flicking up the shredded ice behind it as it barreled towards them.

A blinding flash struck the ice just beyond the skid, the powerful impact shifting the ice all around. Cassidy felt the skid tipping over, she did her best to brace herself against the fall. The sheet of ice hurtled towards her face as she was thrown from the skid, protecting her face with her hands. She slammed hard onto the ice, skidding across the surface like a ragdoll, stopping inches from the edge. The roar of the ocean just below. She inhaled the salt water below, its perpetual power pounding the ice.

"Fire."

Thunder drowned out the sounds of the rifles. A pair of hands pulled Cassidy to her feet. "Hold on tight." Tommy Seeley was holding a rope, squeezing her around the waist.

"What are you doing?" Before Cassidy could say another word, Tommy leapt over the ledge. Chaotic, swirling waters raged below. The grip of gravity tugged at

Cassidy's legs as they swung over the open waters. She screamed out loud until the solid wooden boards of the deck appeared underneath her. Pure joy filled her body as her feet touched the wood, lifting away the fear. Cassidy watched as the other crew members took the leap of faith, soaring across the gap defying the roars of the bear.

"I can't believe we escaped that polar bear." Joy overwhelmed Cassidy. The last crew members boarded the ship as the polar bear reached the edge of the ice. A bolt of lightning silhouetted the bear's dominating figure as it stood defeated. A mighty bellow left its belly, the resounding roar rivaling the thunder.

"That was no bear," Tommy said fearfully. "That was Tuurngait."

CHAPTER TWELVE

"Where is it?" Cassidy demanded, slamming her fist down on Sir Franklin's mahogany desk.

"You mean the disc?" He reached into his desk drawer. "Here, take it." He treated the object like it had a terrible curse, flinging it at her in one swift motion.

Cassidy caught the disc as it bounced off her chest. "You don't want it?" After all the tales that had been told, surely someone would desire it.

"The Tuurngait will hunt you down." Sir Franklin tapped his fingers on the metallic surface. "It will not quit until it has taken possession of it." He backed away and sat behind his desk. Bags had formed under his eyes, the events of the previous day robbing the captain of any sleep he was owed. "My father had buried it away, the inukshuk he built warding off the evil spirit."

"What evil spirit?" Cassidy questioned.

"The Tuurngait," Jack spoke, lowering his voice. "It will swim after us, following the mystical trail left behind by the disc. No matter where we run, we will never escape it."

"Why can't we just build another inukshuk?"

"My father had the help of the elder shaman. With his magical abilities, they warded off the Tuurngait." Sir Franklin leaned back into his chair, the wooden legs groaning underneath him. "My father fled your dimension, hoping to escape the Tuurngait's persistent pursuit. He couldn't close the dimension fast enough, the Tuurngait followed him through."

"What if I take it back to my world?" Cassidy knew after all of her adventures, if there was a way to stop the Tuurngait, Doctor Gamgee would figure something out. If he didn't already. The doctor always seemed to know more than he let on. "Then you wouldn't have to worry about that demon anymore."

"You would take responsibility for this terrible creature?" Sir Franklin didn't sound convinced. "Don't you understand that you cannot simply kill this creature by ordinary means?"

Cassidy didn't know if she could trust Doctor Gamgee completely, but she understood him well enough to realize he would stop at nothing for self-preservation. If she brought the artifact to him, he could harness the powers it contained and defeat the Tuurngait. "You have to trust me. Bring me back to where you found me. My escape pod should be somewhere in that harbour now. The Tuurngait will follow me back to earth and you will no longer have to deal with it."

"Very well. We shall set sail for Franklin Harbour. We should be a few hours ahead of that terrible beast by now. It's not the fastest swimmer, but it never quits. The longer we are searching for your vessel, the more danger we put ourselves in."

"It will not take us long to find what I am looking for." Cassidy chuckled at herself.

"Why would you say that?" Cassidy's light heartedness did not amuse Sir Franklin.

"I assure you, you've seen nothing like this." She winked at him.

Sir Franklin snapped his fingers. "Steward," He bellowed, his voice deep and authoritative. A young sailor entered the room, standing at attention just inside the doorway. His head was bowed to his chest, the young man's face riddled with acne and dry skin. "Tell Sir Irving that we are to change course to head into Franklin Harbour immediately."

"Aye aye, Sir." The young sailor clicked his heels and ran back into the hallway to carry out his duties.

"We should arrive shortly. If my estimations are correct, we are just passing the mouth of the harbour." Sir Franklin stood up, looking out the port window. A slight smile curled the corner of his lips. "Sir Irving tells me you are a Slipstreamer. He recognized that fact the moment he laid eyes on you."

"Why didn't he do anything?" Cassidy pondered. "I remember being chased one time by people who disliked Slipstreamers. I was caught."

"He said nothing because we are all Slipstreamers aboard these ships," Sir Franklin explained. "We had trouble with the people in this world. That is why we stick to the Arctic region. They do not care for it and we don't have the capabilities to battle them. They leave us alone, mostly."

"Mostly?" Cassidy laughed, remembering recent experiences.

"It lifts the spirits to view such splendid sights."

"Is Franklin Harbour your home?" Cassidy asked, unable to see anything but the white clouds in the sky.

"Most of my crew claim their homes in one of the many villages of this harbour." Sir Franklin continued to peek out of the tiny opening. "I am relieved to find Ice Master Peglar reporting for his duties. We had believed the man too far gone to be brought back to us. Yet he stands just two days after the torturous ordeal."

Cassidy rushed out of the room and ran down the hallway. She burst through the door, the salt sea breeze greeting her. "Mr. Peglar," Cassidy called out, relieved to catch him on deck. He turned to greet her, a joyous smile on his face. Cassidy ran across the deck and embraced Peglar. "You are looking much better."

"Much better thanks to you, Miss Cane." Peglar squeezed her elbow. "Tommy told me you never let go, even when he discovered you unconscious in that ice cold tunnel. If it wasn't for you, I would have succumbed to the bitter cold in that tunnel."

"I wouldn't be here if it wasn't for you either," Cassidy recalled the numerous times that he had saved her life. "What are you doing out here on deck?"

"The men spotted an odd piece of ice bobbing alone in the water. They called me out to have a look at it." Peglar pointed to port. "The ice is see-through, like glass."

"That is not ice, Mr. Peglar." Her heart leapt into her chest.

"What is that thing?" Peglar scratched his head.

"That is my way back home." Cassidy wanted to celebrate. "Bring us alongside, I have work to do."

"I will go tell Sir Irving at once." Peglar limped away.

Cassidy leaned over the rail, the winter winds pelting her face with pellets of freshly frozen water from the tips of the waves. The sun died in the sea's darkness. Tiny pieces of ice surrounded the wooden boat, the side of the ship scratched up from the frozen boulders. The howl of the wind drowned out the sounds of the water splashing against the gunwales. A low rumble rattled the decking of the ship as a miniature iceberg smashed into pieces against the side of the HMS Fear. Cassidy could feel the artifact surge with energy, it too, realizing that it was close to heading home.

CHAPTER THIRTEEN

Cassidy stared down at the panel, probing for the knob she had been trained would bring her back to the portal. The artifact rested heavily in her lap. She wondered if the artifact was trying to bring her back home, the extra weight trying to sink her towards the swirling portal hidden in the abyss below. Green, the button she was looking for was green. The memory of her training popped back into her mind. "There it is," She found herself speaking to the artifact, expecting it to communicate with her.

Silence.

Her finger pressed the button. A mechanical buzzing sound filled the compartment, the sea slowly rising, swallowing the capsule whole. The image of the HMS Fear fading out of sight, the dark waters enveloping her as she sank towards the bottom. It didn't take long before the portal reached out, grasping the sinking vessel in its clutches. The pod started to spin head over heel, as the currents pulled the device downwards in a tightening spiral. Immense force pinning her in her seat as she swirled around the vortex, the rotations spinning faster and faster as she neared the portal. Cassidy closed her eyes and waited for the nauseating sensation to dissipate. The artifact pressed down into her lap, the metallic surface radiating heat, the pulsating growing more intense.

Suddenly, Cassidy felt weightless, the force of the spiraling vortex disappeared. She opened her eyes, a dark void greeting her on the other side of the window. Surrounded by nothing but her thoughts, Cassidy anticipated another feverish dream. All of her senses were meaningless here. Touch, taste, smell and hearing rendered useless by the passage between dimensions. She had no control over them. Unable to recognize anything, drifting through the portal aimlessly. Time stood still. She didn't feel cold or anxious, she only existed in this portal. Questions raced through her mind, there was no time to answer them. What if the Tuurngait couldn't be stopped? Should she have brought this artifact back to earth? Did she trust Doctor Gamgee? Was she doing the right thing? What was going to happen to the people living in the other dimension?

The world exploded to life around her. Dark, purple waters gushed over the glass. The mast of the HMS Terror appeared in her vision. Bubbles of air raced her to the surface, the mast falling out of view below her as her pod launch towards the surface. Water rushed by, changing colour as the light reached into the depths to greet her. The force of gravity returned, pinning her into her seat with tremendous pressure. Her stomach turned over, the velocity giving her the phenomenon she was riding a roller-coaster, bursting out of the surface. Water splashed in all directions as the pod breached the surface. Cassidy landed back on the surface of the water with a hard thud, sending a terrible shot of pain up her spine.

It was dusk now, the horizon purging the sunlight into dying flames, the last of the day's heat all but gone now. Bitter cold flooded the cockpit. "Damn it." Cassidy pounded the heat, demanding that it turn back on immediately. She fiddled with the toggle frantically.

"You are back with us, Miss Cane." A voice appeared over the crackling receiver. Bright light emitted from the dashboard as the power surged back to life. Heat began to filter through the vents as the electricity turned back on. "I will have the rescue team extract you from the surface immediately."

"Doctor Gamgee?" Cassidy couldn't pick out the voice over the static crackling.

"The one and only," Gamgee acknowledged. "I assume that you managed to uncover the artifact."

Cassidy wasn't absolutely certain if she was ready to hand over the artifact. How much time would she have to dispose of the disc, and what would happen if the Tuurngait found it? "Yes, I have it," Left with no choice, Cassidy admitted that she had it. "But there's something I need to tell you."

Before Cassidy could respond, Gamgee's voice interrupted her. "I assume that the Tuurngait followed you here. I have measures in place to deal with that creature."

"You knew about that." Cassidy was furious. "Why didn't you warn me about the Tuurngait?" Her face flushed red with anger.

"If I told you about the creature, you would not have gone after the artifact." Gamgee tried to defuse the situation.

Only infuriated by his response, her blood pressure began to rise. She scanned the console for the switch to open the glass covering. Tempted to throw the artifact into the frigid depths, her finger levitated just about the toggle. "I might have died. That creature was relentless. It nearly killed one of us." With a jolt, the glass slid open. A gust of wintery air swept over her, expelling all the heat from the compartment in an instant.

"I had faith in you." Gamgee remained calm. "I still do. I know you won't toss that disc into the ocean. So why don't you close that glass dome and stay warm. We are prepared to handle this."

"How can you tell that the dome is open?" Cassidy blurted out. Shivers took control of her body, she couldn't stop herself from shaking.

"We can see you." A bright flood light shined across the water from an approaching vessel. "Just hang tight, we will be there in just a few minutes."

Cassidy sensed a presence rising from the depths. The disc went crazy. An energy overload spilling from its surface caused the disc to turn bright white. Cassidy looked over the side of the floating pod. An ethereal, alabaster glow was swimming towards her. "It's here," Cassidy tried to call out. Fear gripped her by the throat, asphyxiated by the words as they stuck in her larynx. She watched in horror as the form took shape, the massive limbs of the Tuurngait taking shape in the depths. Gnarled claws stuck out from the creature's enormous paws, gashing at the water as it swam towards her. "Help me." Cassidy was helpless.

"Like I said, Cassidy, we are prepared." Gamgee's

voice echoed from the radio.

Tuurngait erupted from the waters, leaping onto the edge of the pod. Its tremendous weight driving the nose of the vessel to submerge. Water flowed over the ledge, splashing onto Cassidy's legs. Frantically, she scurried towards the aft, desperately trying to escape the vicious snarl on Tuurngait's snout. It stood on its hind legs, letting out a thunderous growl towards the sky.

A flash of green light pounded into the Tuurngait's chest. Paralyzed by the emerald light, Tuurngait fell backwards into the water. The ship rocked back into place as the creature's weight dispersed. The boat puttered alongside the mighty creature, casting an ivory-coloured net over the Tuurngait. The mechanical winches struggled to pull the Tuurngait out of the water. "What are you doing?" Cassidy called out, trying to warn them.

"We have what we came for now." Doctor Gamgee appeared at the side of the boat, his black toque pulled down to his eyebrows and a neck warmer pulled up to his nose.

Cassidy threatened to toss the disc into the frigid arctic sea. "You don't have it yet."

"Oh, that thing, you can do whatever you want with that. I've said it before, Cassidy, I came prepared, and I possess what I wanted." Gamgee motioned towards Tuurngait.

Cassidy didn't know what was happening. "Here, this might be useful too." She tossed the disc at his feet.

Greedily, he bent down and retrieved it. "I will be able to save a lot of lives with this, Cassidy. You've accomplished the extraordinary this time."

Cassidy was cold and tired. All she wanted to do was rest, her part in this was finished. "Just get me out of here." Gamgee motioned towards his crew, who threw a ladder over the side of their boat. Quickly realizing that his plans were far beyond anything Cassidy dreamed to comprehend, she reached out and climbed the ladder. Standing in front of Doctor Gamgee, she watched him place the artifact inside a steel crate before slamming the lid shut and locking it.

"Well, Doctor Gamgee, what are your plans for that creature?" All Cassidy wanted was the next adrenaline rush, she didn't think he was going to spill the beans on his plans.

"I plan to study this magnificent creature. If the anecdotes about it are genuine, it was conceived by the Inuit gods," He spoke excitedly. "Within the genetic structure of this creature I may find the cure for cancer, or any number of diseases."

"What about the disc, you must know of its capabilities to harness extraordinary power?" Cassidy was surprised by Doctor Gamgee's forwardness. She didn't expect an answer, maybe she could probe further into his plan and set her mind at ease.

"I heard the stories, yes." Gamgee nodded his head. "What I have not learned is how I will be able to utilize the powers contained within. Perhaps the answers to all of my questions lie within the Tuurngait. Perhaps the answer lies in another dimension. We must keep searching them."

Cassidy embraced the adrenaline pumping through her veins already. "Where to next, Doctor?"

EPILOGUE

Tallis ran, his black hair bobbing on either side of his head, as a barrage of laser fire followed him. His breath was hot and humid, pushing out into the cold air and becoming vapor that trailed along either side of his head as he ran, like steam coming from a train.

He was wearing a large fur coat over his shirt that was stained with red, its bristles frozen into stiff peaks.

It was always cold on Trallit. Every time he'd been there it had been cold, but it had never once snowed. It sometimes rained the coldest, bitterest rain he had ever felt on any world: but it never, ever, snowed on Trallit. One of the quirks of the meteorology of this strange dimension.

It had taken him a week to discover that, despite snowfall and other strange changes, he was in fact on the third planet from with sun in the Sol system: that this was this dimension's Earth, despite all outward signs. The constellations were what had tipped him off: they had been off at first, until he'd noticed the Southern Cross in the sky. Not only was he on an Earth-like planet, but on the Southern Hemisphere of it as well.

The Trallit people were terrestrial, that should have been a hint. They looked just like the humans of his home dimension Earth, save for the fact that their complexion — at least the group following him — was different. He reasoned that this was the result of different long-term migration affects that were a consequence of the lack of snow patterning.

None of that mattered now. What mattered now was that this particular culture of the Trallit people had invented lasers, and that those lasers were being fired at him with increasing intensity.

Tallis ducked behind a corner and took several pained, deep breaths of the cold air, trying to steady himself. The air was so chilled that it felt like it pierced his lungs. He held his watch up to his ear and then shook it desperately. He smacked it several times and the red LED came on again, slowly facing back from nothing. He smiled and almost laughed with joy, but held onto himself for fear that the encroaching patrolmen would hear.

He depressed the buttons on the watch's sides and it bleeped to life. He looked up across the way to the slot on the wall it was indicating towards, the smile leaving his face as he heard the patrols getting closer.

The slot on the wall beckoned him, and he swallowed. Taking one last deep, full-lunged breath he ran across the open walkway in full view of the Trallit patrolmen. They opened fire, their weapons strafing across the night sky in wide arcs that followed him. He swallowed and kept running, making a bee-line for the alley wall without pausing.

One of the shots caught his fur coat, and he felt it

evaporate clean off of his shoulders as though it were happening in slow motion. Full intensity. They had dialed their lasers up to full intensity, a level they would have had to have called and gotten clearance to attain. Tallis would have cursed at this change in the dynamic, had he not been so focused on getting the exact angle of his approach on the wall.

He hit the wall just as the Trallit patrols were turning to corner to see it, and they watched him disappear into nothing, as though the brick had no substance to it at all.

They followed him, but came up solid against it, and began feeling along the creases in the red stone, finding nothing they could pass through. After a moment they became convinced that one of their blasts had in fact struck him, and began to phone in their reports.

***

Tallis landed on the grassy knoll of the park from where the portal opened several feet in the air, the sudden change in orientation making his inner ear do a flip and disoriented him. It was also day here, and the sudden change to cloudless brightness and warmth was a sudden shock as well — like having cold water thrown into the hot bath you were enjoying, suddenly.

He scrambled into a nearby tree line out of sight and waited there, eyeing the gap in the world he'd fallen through, waiting to see if anything but a cold breeze would follow him. After a long moment when nothing did, he smiled and started to laugh with relief.

Wiping tears of joy from his eyes, he checked the readout on his watch again. It read back a phosphorous blue colour. He tapped it twice to get it to change, and when it did not he started to laugh even harder. He stood up out of the veil of trees and spread his arms wide in good humour, casting them skyward and feeling the warm glow upon his skin.

"Home," he said, with peace and joy. Tallis was back on Earth.

JD Ryot is the reclusive creator of the *Slipstreamers* series from Engen Books. JD is an avid fan of young adult literature and adventure serials. When asked if they had come to this world through a portal themselves, JD Ryot refused to answer. No record of their birth has ever been found... on this world.

Shannon K Green has been recognized in both the genre community and the contemporary literary community for his pursuits. In the past, he has been shortlisted for the 1996 Arts and Letters Award, and later won the 2015 Audience Choice Steampunk Newfoundland Showcase.

Green's short fiction has appeared in the *From the Rock* series, *The Hamthology*, and *Jibbernocky*.

Carolyn R. Parsons is a full-time writer residing in Lewisporte, NL. She has contributed to *The Central Voice*, the Saltire network of papers, and *Downhome Magazine*. Her books include a poetry collection, two novels and a collection of short stories. Her 2017 novel, Charley through Canada, attained bestseller status on Amazon.

Paul Carberry is a huge proponent of the horror genre and its place in literature. He has two children, daughter Dana and son Rick, with his wife Leah.

Paul has published four novels with Engen Books: the three book *Zombies on the Rock* series, and, *Carcharodon*, both of which are international bestsellers.

He has also had numerous short stories featured in publication in anthologies such as *From the Rock* and *Terror Nova*, including The Light of Cabot Tower, Into the Forest, and Halloween Mummers.